Z2134
Z2134
Book 1

SEAN PLATT
DAVID W. WRIGHT

Copyright © 2022 by Sterling & Stone

All rights reserved.

No part of this book may be reproduced in any form or by any electronic or mechanical means, including information storage and retrieval systems, without written permission from the author, except for the use of brief quotations in a book review.

The authors greatly appreciate you taking the time to read our work. Please consider leaving a review wherever you bought the book, or telling your friends about it, to help us spread the word.

Thank you for supporting our work.

To YOU, the reader.
Thank you for your support.
Thank you for the wonderful emails.
Thank you for the thoughtful reviews.
Thank you for reading and loving our stories.

Z2134

ONE

Jonah Lovecraft

OUTSIDE THE WALLS — the Barrens

JONAH LOVECRAFT FOCUSED through the rifle scope, staring at the zombies swarming around the tunnel's entrance. He had one bullet, with four undead blocking his only way forward.

"Fuck," he whispered to himself.

The Darwin Games announcer, Kirk Kirkman, sounded practically orgasmic from the speakers in the floating orb behind Jonah.

"Wow, Jonah's really in a tight spot here. Should he take his chances with just one bullet and a machete, and make the mile-long trek back to the last exit? Tell us what you're thinking as the Darwin Games continue, with just two players left! Jonah versus Bear!"

Jonah turned, glaring into the orb's main camera as he whispered, "*Keep it down. Are you trying to get me killed?*"

He was aching, tired, and starving, not in the mood to play dancing monkey for the asshole on the other side of the camera nor the millions watching the Darwin Games from home. Jonah was still a half-day from the Mesa and the Final Battle.

Whoever reached the Mesa first got dibs on the best equipment from the Bounty to use in the death match. The first player to make it to the Bounty usually won. Going head-to-head against Bear meant Jonah *had* to get there first. He needed every ounce of help he could get.

Bear was more than four hundred pounds and seven feet; an absolute beast, pouring a countless number of his life's hours into working the City 6 Quarry for most of his forty years breathing. He'd been imprisoned for robbery, stealing a can of soup, no less, to feed his wife and child when their rations ran dry earlier than they'd scheduled. Jonah hadn't been a City Watch officer when Bear was jailed, but Bear knew of his former occupation. He had a score to settle, and even if that score wasn't with Jonah personally, he'd serve as a fine proxy for the hardline authority that had wrongly punished him.

When this edition of the Games first started, there had been twelve contestants — two prisoners from each city — let loose into the wild, and Bear made an immediate run for Jonah. Fortunately, Jonah managed to slip away when someone else decided to take a whack at Bear. It would've been a decent strategy — hitting the strongest guy first — if it had worked.

But it hadn't.

Thankfully, though, it did slow Bear down long enough for Jonah to successfully make it into the woods, then over to one of the weapons caches. There, he managed to claim a machete before acquiring the rifle he earned by felling a pair of contestants who had wisely teamed together, then foolishly surrendered their guard long enough for Jonah to strike.

Z2134

Jonah had to reach the far side of the tunnel, then make his way to the spot of the Final Battle before Bear, if he wanted a chance to win and start his life over in City 7.

There were two boxes waiting at the Mesa. One was called the Bounty, which was a winner's box, with winner's weapons inside. The Bounty varied from game to game. Sometimes the TV network would stock it with something useful, like a bat, an axe, or even a pistol with a handful of rounds. But the other box was called the Joker's Box, left for whoever made it to the Mesa last, usually containing something far less effective — a brick, a piece of wood, or on one occasion, a bag of children's toys. It was the game's way of adding what Kirkman called "the wow factor" to the show — a moment that would shock viewers and get discussed in City plazas.

Jonah needed all the help he could get if he was going against Bear. Reaching the Bounty was non-negotiable.

He stared into the scope again, weighing his options as the orb hummed and hovered behind him, turning simple focus into heavy labor. Though Kirkman had momentarily shut up, or maybe muted himself so his inane chatter was broadcast only to the audience at home, Jonah could still hear the orb buzzing like a swarm of bees behind him, his awareness of it enough to shatter his concentration.

The orbs, which served as floating camera drones beyond the Wall, usually kept a decent distance behind or above their targeted players. But if the game was on the line, the orbs always hovered closer. And the game was definitely on the line now.

If Jonah died, then Bear, who he now figured *had* to be the last person left, would automatically win. Of course, most of the people at home were rooting for Jonah to make it to the Final Battle. It would be anticlimactic if he died now, and deny the audience the spectacle of a bloody duel.

The networks were no doubt pitching this duel as Bear against the very law that had imprisoned him and destroyed his family, despite the network being run by the City, which *was* the law of the land. Of course, such subtleties were lost on the common viewer, who only sought relief from the long days, not critical analysis.

Jonah tried to focus again as the orb hovered closer, its static purr lifting his hair in the breeze. He turned back, still glaring. The orb zipped several feet back, giving him additional space. It wasn't enough.

Jonah wanted to bash the fucking thing to pieces but knew better.

Sam Wallings had almost won the Darwin Games two years before, but had smashed an orb a half hour from reaching the Mesa. He was a half-day from the Bounty before his opponent and was stronger in every way. No one doubted he would win. But after smashing the orb, Wallings was found by a hunter orb four minutes later and violently exterminated, to many cheers and even more devastated bets.

Jonah would have to tolerate the goddamn orb.

He inched closer, deciding to take his chances by eliminating the closest zombies.

Erupting through the relative silence, Jonah heard an explosion of noise from behind — something galloping toward him.

Before he could register what it might be, the assault slammed him sideways and sent him down hard. Jonah's rifle flew from his hand and skidded across the ground.

Unfortunately, the orb had swung from danger just in time, clearing the area unscathed.

Jonah, on his hands and knees, looked up, hoping like

hell the zombies hadn't noticed him at the sound of charging deer. If they had, they no longer cared, every one of them too distracted by the deer barreling toward them.

Jonah grabbed his rifle and aimed, then waited.

The deer stopped short when it spotted the zombies. He stared through the scope as one of the zombies leaped at the deer, savagely grabbing it around the neck, then sinking its teeth past the fur and into the deer's flesh, dragging it to the ground.

A second zombie joined the feast, and hungry growls drowned the deer's dying cries. Grunts from the zombies echoed off the tunnel walls, a backbeat to the melody of ripping flesh below.

The zombies were fast and vicious, and they worked together — something Jonah had not yet seen in his thirteen days outside the Wall.

Jonah started moving as fast as he could toward them — toward the exit — without surrendering stealth, wearing the Wall's shadows for cover, and hoping to pass the zombies while they were distracted with their kill. Zombies, in Jonah's limited experience, rarely left one meal in pursuit of another.

They were preoccupied, but not for long. If one of the zombies finished, or was pushed from the pack for being too greedy and infringing on the feast of another, it might very well turn its hungry eyes to Jonah.

He was twenty yards away from them when he finally got a better look at the small pack of walking corpses.

Careful, careful. Keep your eyes on them. Be ready to fire and then grab the machete. Whatever you do, don't trip, stumble on a rock, or make so much as a decibel of noise.

Jonah's heart pounded so loudly he was certain the zombies would hear him. The thumping in his chest felt as deafening to him as the zombies' fevered grunts and the sound of ripping flesh, which grew louder as he drew closer.

He was five yards away from the zombies and another ten from the tunnel's exit when the sounds, wet like soaking gravel, slapped him hard and turned his stomach.

Do NOT puke here. They will hear and kill you.

Jonah tried to concentrate on the sound of the orb, still humming relatively quietly behind him, allowing the purring drone to squelch the horrible sounds of tearing, pulling, and crunching. For once he was thankful to have the orb so close, though he hoped the humming wasn't loud enough to invite the zombies' gaze. He saw their fists filled with guts and meat, and mouths painted with the sauce of their kill, and figured it wasn't.

The zombies had devoured about sixty percent of the deer so far as Jonah could see, and were now starting to push at one another. Fighting over food wasn't unusual. Soon, things would get ugly, with one of the zombies pulling at a leg or perhaps the head, trying to either drag the whole corpse away or tear off a piece for itself, plunging the rest of them into a battle. At least that's what happened the many times Jonah had seen the zombies fighting over humans, both on the show and, more horrifyingly, in person.

He carefully stepped past the zombies. He had just ten yards to go until he finally reached daylight, where he could start running, laying space between himself and the undead.

Jonah inched forward, not daring to turn back, using his ears as his only warning, accepting on faith that they couldn't see him at all.

Just keep walking.

Jonah was just ten yards from the exit. Ten yards from safety. Just ten yards.

"Looks like he made it, folks," Kirkman's voice suddenly crackled behind him.

Jonah's heart fell to his feet and he froze in his tracks, forcing himself to look back over his shoulder. Several of the zombies glanced up from their waning feast, then screamed in unison, leaping from the deer's torn carcass and charging toward him.

"Fuck!" Jonah raised his rifle and fired, hitting one of the four zombies in the chest and sending it to the ground.

The zombie cried out, writhing and slapping his arms against the ground, but even a bullet in the heart was only temporary. Anything less than a head shot only slowed the fuckers down.

Jonah was down to just his machete.

A machete against three zombies racing toward him — one female, and two males, one of which looked like a zombified version of Bear. Fortunately, the largest of the zombies was moving slower than the other two.

Jonah turned and ran to the exit, reaching daylight, then scanning for anything he could use to set distance between himself and the pack — a waterfall he could leap from, a tree he could get to and climb, a hole where he could bury himself and hide. *Anything.*

But he saw only snowy flatlands all around him, and the monsters were far too fast to elude in the snow.

Fuck!

Jonah spun around, grabbing his machete from the scabbard on his back. He gripped it tightly, dug his heels in the ground, and positioned himself to take on the first zombie, now only inches away.

If Jonah had pulled that same machete on a gang of living people, they would slow down, assess the situation, then determine the best means of attack. But the zombies were corpses, with minimal brain function, and knew no fear. Two of the running dead ran straight for him, ignorant of the danger of his blade.

Jonah yelled, as if his sudden scream might scare them, then swung at the closest, sending a fat chunk from his rotting face sailing from his head with a wide arc of thick blackish blood in the wake of the machete's swing.

The zombie staggered back, howling as it stumbled. Jonah wanted to finish it off while it was still swaying and unsteady, but the female was still racing toward him, hands outstretched.

Jonah leaped out of the way just in time as the zombie ran by and then fell to the ground. He spun around, raised the machete high, and swung down just as the creature was about to stand, bashing in the back of its skull with a sickening crunch.

As the zombie fell forward, Jonah's machete went with it, lodging inside its skull. The handle slipped from his grip just as a fat fuck of walking death came running at him faster than what should even be possible. Jonah looked up just in time to see the ruined man racing toward him like a train off its track.

Jonah ditched the machete to dodge the attack, but …

He didn't quite make it.

The fat zombie's fist caught Jonah on the side of the head, sending him to the ground in an explosion of pain.

Shit!

So far he had managed to kill just one of the zombies. As the largest of them was attacking, Jonah's machete was still jutting from the collapsed body of the female zombie.

"Uh-oh, looks like Jonah might be making his last stand!" Kirkman's voice said through the orb, sprinkling salt into the survivor's festering wound.

Jonah stood, his head pounding where the fat bastard

zombie had hit him, and looked around. He failed to see the big zombie coming back at him until it was too late.

The zombie grabbed him from behind. If the fat fuck pulled him into a hug, Jonah knew it would be seconds before its teeth were in his neck.

Jonah kicked his foot back hard into the zombie's left knee, hard enough to make it scream on its way to the ground. Pain wouldn't keep a zombie down, but they sure as hell couldn't walk without working knees.

However, zombies' tissue could not only self-repair, but even strengthen the muscles, despite their atrophied appearance. So Jonah wouldn't have long to end the undead fucker before its knee healed.

"Whoa! I did not see that coming!" Kirkman radiated enthusiasm.

Jonah ran back toward the fallen female zombie to retrieve his machete. The other zombie, the one with the freshly sliced face, stood between Jonah and the female, while the fat one groaned from behind, struggling to crawl forward.

The orb floated overhead. "What's he gonna go? Can he get to the machete in time?"

There were thirty feet between him and the standing zombie. Jonah and the zombie then ran straight at each other. The zombie's mouth opened with a scream, and Jonah wondered if they were feeling a similar rage. Maybe the creature's brain had somehow healed as well.

Seconds from impact, he pivoted left, causing the zombie to dive forward at him and miss. As it fell to the ground, Jonah went right, then slid and rolled to a stop beside the female zombie.

He grabbed the handle of his machete and yanked, but it refused to budge.

The fallen zombie shot up from the ground so fast it

was like he had never fallen, then started racing toward Jonah again.

He stood, put his boot on the female zombie's head, pressed down, and began working the blade back and forth as if drawing a sword from stone. He looked up, terrified, knowing he had mere seconds before the zombie would be on top of him.

With one final yank, the blade slipped free from the monster's skull, but the momentum from Jonah's tugging sent him flying back.

He fell to the ground, hard, while somehow managing to keep hold of the blade as the zombie lunged on top of him.

Jonah jammed the blade through the zombie's chest, then rolled over on top of it, straddling the zombie as it screamed like a banshee, wide white eyes frantically spinning around in their charred, hollow sockets, and rotting teeth chattering as putrid breath assaulted Jonah's senses.

He pulled the blade up, then out, before bringing it down between the zombie's eyes.

Jonah grabbed the machete and walked over to where the fat bastard was crawling across the snow, groaning, leaving trails of black in its wake.

The creature flung its arms wildly, trying to reach Jonah. He gave the zombie's hands a wide berth, then circled behind it, driving his wide blade through its brittle skull.

Jonah wiped his mouth and looked down at the bodies, disgusted, then turned his attention to the blackened blood caking his blade. He slid the length of his machete along the filthy tattered rags worn by the fat zombie, wiping blood from metal.

Jonah looked back toward the tunnel where he had left the first zombie — the one he'd shot — wondering if he should go back and finish it off or count his lucky stars and get the fuck out of Dodge before more showed up.

He decided to leave, but Jonah hadn't traveled more than twenty feet before the first zombie appeared. It was running toward him, not remotely slowed by the gunshot, despite a gaping hole in its chest, big enough to see through.

Jonah panicked, not sure how to take on the runner. He readied his blade. Then, as the zombie roared toward him, he swung at its arms, missing by inches.

But the zombie didn't miss, knocking Jonah to the ground so hard that it cleared the breath from his body.

The zombie straddled Jonah and hit the machete clear from his clutched palm. The weapon slid five feet across the snow, until it was *no way in hell* far away.

Jonah bucked against the ground, trying to throw the monster from his pinned body, but the zombie grabbed both of his arms, forcing them to the ground with an impossible strength.

The rampaging monster kept Jonah's hands pinned to either side of his face; its clawed fingers dug into his flesh, though not yet drawing blood.

The zombie leaned forward, its sick white eyes swirling around in their sockets. Jonah wasn't sure how the undead were able to see with eyes that shone with nothing but white, but the zombie *seemed* to be staring right at him. If he didn't know better, Jonah would think the zombie was savoring its seemingly obvious victory instead of following its instincts to chomp down and tear his flesh like skin from a chicken.

The orb floated above them both, hovering just inches over the zombie's head.

"Well, folks, it looks like this might be the end for

Jonah. He gave a valiant fight, but this wife-murderer and father of two couldn't escape Darwinian justice."

Rage pumped through Jonah as he slipped one hand free and grabbed the zombie by its neck, trying to choke it, or at least keep the writhing creature from getting any closer to his own neck.

They struggled in a war of inches as the orb floated in long, slow circles around them, announcing every action, subtle or not, milking the moment for every possible drop of drama.

"Do you have any last words, Jonah?" Kirkman's face beamed back from the orb's monitor, three inches above the zombie's menacing, chattering, rotting face.

The zombie's teeth were just centimeters from Jonah's face, as his arm — the only thing holding death at bay — started shaking, unable to keep up with the pressure.

Pain splintered through Jonah's body, starting at his arm. He had only moments before his cramped muscles betrayed the rest of him.

He thought of Anastasia and Adam, wondering if they were watching him die.

He hoped to God not.

He stared into the screen, wondering if their eyes were on him from their home in Chimney Rock, on the safer side of the Wall.

"Any last words to your precious children, Anastasia and Adam?" Kirkman asked, as though the announcer was reading his mind. Though his voice was soft and sympathetic, it crawled beneath Jonah's skin, worming its way closer toward his angry heart, and dropping a lit match on the rage he'd been holding in check.

Jonah surrendered his grip on the zombie's neck, then let the monster fall forward, its mouth wide open, ready to chomp down. Before it could make contact, Jonah sent his head slamming into the zombie's nose, blinding the rabid undead with a sharp shock of sudden but momentary pain.

In that split second, the zombie released its grip and Jonah seized his moment, reaching up with both arms, leaving his face, neck, and chest entirely exposed, but hoping, and perhaps even praying, that he'd properly gauged the orb's distance.

Jonah's hands seized its cold, glassy surface, then brought it down hard onto the zombie's skull.

The creature screamed.

Kirkman yelled, "What the hell?" as the orb whirred, hummed, and beeped, trying to find its bearings and free itself from Jonah's grasp.

He could feel the humming and a slight burning in his arms, but Jonah held on.

He stood, walked over to the zombie, now struggling to stand, and smashed the orb onto its head again.

"Die!" he screamed, as the orb split the monster's skull.

"FUCKING!" he bellowed with a second blow.

"DIE!" With the final bash, Jonah threw the orb at the zombie's crumbling face.

Its screen was cracked and flickering, the humming now only a sputter.

Jonah could see Kirkman screaming, but the speakers were silent, so he could only guess at what the announcer was saying — probably a warning about not destroying the camera orb.

Jonah reached down, retrieved the orb, then raised it to his face, swallowing the rising tide of venom.

"How's that for WOW factor?" Jonah asked the camera, before throwing the orb as hard and as far as he could back into the cave.

Then he headed for the woods.

TWO

Anastasia Lovecraft

Inside the Walls of City 6

ANASTASIA STARED at the largest of the more than twenty TVs that lined the Social, watching her father, Jonah, square off against the zombies.

She cringed when he went down and the zombie swiped his machete away. Ana thought that was it — her father was dead. But suddenly, he looked up and into the orb's camera, grabbed it, and continued to bash it into the zombie's skull until he finally stood, victorious.

The bar erupted into a nearly universal applause, but Ana stayed silent, burying herself in the long brown hair that hid her emerald eyes.

She glared at the TV.

"I'm sorry," said Michael.

Her best friend half-smiled from across the table, then set his warm hand on top of hers and gently squeezed. His smile was sympathetic, sewn on his mouth with a compassion no one else in the bar possessed.

As if to punctuate her thought, a group of guys at the bar traded a thundering round of high-fives.

"Jo-nah! Jo-nah!" they chanted, their cheers drifting through the bar's smoky fog.

"Why did I let you talk me into coming here?" she whispered to Michael. "You know I hate this place."

"I'm sorry." He looked down. "You said you couldn't bear to watch it at Chimney Rock. I thought this was better."

Chimney Rock was what they, and most of the younger people, called the orphanage where Ana had been placed. It was one of City 6's three State-run orphanages, and while they knew the place as Chimney Rock, its official title was the much less pleasant Home for Wayward Youths and Miscreants.

The Rock was a sprawling complex in the beating heart of the City, its outside as sooty and black as the spirit festering inside. The Rock was where they sent the children of State prisoners, and where Ana and her 14-year-old brother, Adam, had been living for the last two months, ever since their father destroyed everything.

Ana was assigned to stay at Chimney Rock until she turned eighteen — six long months away. Only then would she be allowed to claim custody of Adam, provided she earned her keep at the textile, where it was her job to sew buttons onto shirts, all day, six days a week, twelve hours a day, until her fingers were numb or throbbing. Usually both. As awful as the throbbing was, most times Ana preferred it to the numb sensation which tricked her into thinking her fingers had disappeared.

Where she'd go after Chimney Rock was anybody's guess.

Most likely, she'd have no choice but to move to the Dark Quarter, the nearly lawless ghetto of City 6. In some ways, she wondered if Adam would be better off staying on at the orphanage. Sure, he'd be miserable, but at least he'd be safe, something she couldn't guarantee in the Dark Quarter.

A day never passed when Ana didn't wish she'd tested well for any other aptitude back when she was fifteen and chose to test for sewing, but only because her friend Ginny Thompson thought it would be fun working together. Ironically, Ginny failed the test and wound up working the fields. How farming — being out in the open all day long — was what you got when you failed, and being trapped inside a hot factory through nearly every hour of sunlight was what you got when you passed ... it seemed a cruel joke to Ana.

She still remembered her mom congratulating her when she was first awarded her placement at the textile factory — as if she'd made a tremendous achievement and would thus be rewarded with meaningful work. It was easy enough for her mom, who had been gifted at planning and therefore landed a comfortable desk job with the City, as did her dad, who had worked all the way to major at City Watch before the events that upended their lives.

The chants of "Jo-nah!" finally died away, save for one lone screamer, a drunken, long-haired 18-year-old she'd known all too well. Liam Harrow was tipping back his glass and going on long past everyone else. He turned to Ana mid-swig, then turned his eyes back to the screen.

She kept watching him, a mix of annoyance and anger stewing inside her gut.

He turned to Ana.

"What?" he said, a slur of hostility thick in his voice. "Think you'd be happy your daddy made it to the Final Battle."

"Do I *look* happy?" Ana shot back. "Don't worry. He won't last five seconds against Bear."

"Some way to talk about your father," Liam said, finishing his beer. He climbed from his stool, breaking rank with his trio of drinking buddies, each of them ranging between ten and fifteen years older than him, and looking every bit as rough around the edges. Probably Underground scum.

One of them, a red-haired, green-eyed man with a thick beard, slapped a hand on Liam's shoulder and said, "Leave her be. Let's watch the recaps."

He shook his buddy's hand away, then glanced back as if to say, *Don't fuck with me.*

Liam was younger than the others, but also in significantly better shape. Fighting shape, though Ana had little doubt he'd be wearing a permanent ale gut by the time he was twenty-five — if he lived that long, or didn't wind up in prison. Or, even more likely, outside the Wall.

Michael started to stand as Liam approached their table.

Ana put her hand over his, then shook her head. "No. I'll handle this." She held his stare and made him silently agree.

It wouldn't do to have Michael playing hero.

He was a gentleman — sweet, good-looking in a nice guy sorta way, and in excellent shape, but not a fighter. Liam, especially drunk, could hurt him badly. If Ana were to lose Michael, she would be both friendless and motherless.

"Someone oughta teach you to respect your elders." Liam sauntered to their table, wearing a wide grin, as though just finishing a hysterical joke, with a punchline tailored for one.

"You're only a year older than me, hardly an elder," Ana said, half-laughing, and only on the outside.

"I'm talking about Jonah." Liam looked down at Ana, ignoring Michael entirely. "Your father was a good man."

"Yeah, I suppose … if you like men who murder their wives." Ana glanced at her hands, forcing herself to sip her sugar water rather than engage him any further. She had plenty to say about her father, but none of it was any of Liam's business.

"You still buying that bullshit about how he killed your mom?" Liam shook his head. "Come on, Ana, you know better than that. He was fucking set up."

"Whatever." Ana was tempted to say the only bullshit here was the stuff he was peddling. Ana had been there. She'd seen Jonah kill her mother.

It was, after all, her testimony that had sent him away. Ana was still considered a child, so that detail of the famous case had been kept from the News Agency and off the public reels, though she had assumed word had been whispered anyway. But maybe not, if Liam didn't know.

He laughed, a drunken, almost sick-sounding cackle, which quickly fell into a dry-heave, like he was trying to think of something more to say, maybe something clever, but couldn't draw even a single drop from the well. He raised a fist to his mouth, bit it, then turned from their table and stormed away.

Ana watched as he marched off, surprised when he suddenly spun back toward her and shouted, "You know, you really *are* a brat!"

Ana's mouth dropped open, shocked that Liam had called her a "brat," of all things. And the way he said it suggested it wasn't something that had just come to him — it was a long-held belief that he'd thought a million times before that moment. She wasn't sure which surprised her more — that Liam thought she was a brat, or that he'd thought about her at all. It wasn't as if their paths crossed all that often. Liam hadn't gone to school with her since he was placed in the orphanage almost a decade ago after his father killed himself. And they rarely saw each other outside of the occasional run-in at the market or City Park, where she used to hang out before starting work on her seventeenth birthday.

"I am not!" she snapped back, feeling her face redden as her fists curled into balls beneath the table.

"Oh yes you are!" Liam said, cackling like before, now louder. "Your father had nothing but the best things to say about you, and you have the gall to sit here, sipping on your sugar water while wishing him dead? *Dead?* You aren't just a brat, Ana, you're an icy-hearted bitch."

She was too shocked to punch the bastard right in his smug mouth like she wanted.

But Michael leapt from the table and to Ana's defense. "She said to leave her alone!"

"Sit down, *Michelle*," Liam snapped, moving surprisingly fast, shoving him hard toward his seat.

The nudge was just enough to send Michael's ass banging against the booth, where he only stayed for a moment. Then Michael lunged from his sprawl, swinging before he was standing.

Even drunk, Liam deftly stepped aside as Michael shot past him and fell awkwardly to the floor.

Scattered laughter rippled through the bar.

Ana fumed, then stood and yelled, "Stop it!"

Liam, whose back was to Ana as he waited for Michael's next move, turned to her, eyes wide, surprised by the sudden outburst.

Their eyes met — his were icy blue but blushed with spirits — locked in the realization that everyone in the bar was staring at them, and that trouble was a coiled snake, ready to strike.

Liam's friends were watching, but they weren't hooting or hollering, like most of the bar patrons. They seemed concerned for their friend, and possibly worried about what he might do next. They approached Michael as he stood, hands out, to show they didn't mean to hurt him and wanted to soothe the situation before it escalated further.

"Here, let me help," said the man with the light-red beard, extending a hand to Michael to help him off the floor.

Liam took a step toward Ana, blinking as his cheeks twitched. "You really think he did it, don't you?"

In that moment, for the first time since Ana had seen her father standing over her mother's dead body, a seed of doubt was sprouting.

It made no sense, but hell if it wasn't germinating anyway. Maybe it was the conviction in Liam's eyes. *How can he be so certain of his innocence?* She wasn't sure how he knew her dad, though she had her suspicions, since her father was a rumored member of the Underground.

What does Liam know that I don't?

Michael yelled something at Liam's friends, shaking off their assistance. He took a few steps toward the bar, grabbed a bottle from the counter, then raced toward Liam, bottle raised, ready to attack from behind.

Ana's eyes widened before her mouth could either warn Liam or stop Michael.

But Liam was fluent in danger. He spun around just as Michael swung the bottle and connected with Liam's forehead. Glass shattered. Liam screamed as they both stumbled forward and fell to the floor.

Ana jumped back, working to determine the best means of breaking up the fight.

Two seconds later, City Watch guards burst into the bar — a pack of six, dressed in black, heavily armed, faces concealed by impenetrable black enclosed helmets.

"Break it up," one of the men ordered through his helmet's muffled speakers, masking the Watcher's voice while adding several layers of menace.

Michael and Liam both looked up, surprised, then quickly untangled their fight.

The Watchers responded as if both were still a threat.

A pair of Watchers thrust out their safety sticks, connecting with Michael and Liam, a fierce electrical current sending them into writhing spasms, screaming on the floor.

As Michael and Liam twitched, incapacitated, on the floor, the Watchers began swinging their sticks as clubs, and bashing the fallen men repeatedly.

Ana started toward them, as if she might somehow talk sense into the Watchers, but someone grabbed her by the elbow. She turned, surprised. A Black man in his mid-fifties with graying hair and a scruffy salt-and-pepper beard was wearing the same serious look her father often wore — an expression that begged her to listen rather than run.

"Don't," was all he said, pulling her toward the back of the bar, away from the cluster of Watchers surrounding Michael and Liam.

"But—"

"If you get involved, it'll be way worse. Just let 'em get their steam out, do what they're gonna do, and leave."

"They're hurting them," Ana said, defending not just Michael — who didn't deserve to be beaten for helping her — but also, to her surprise, Liam, even though he'd started the fight.

"Yes, but they'll kill you, Anastasia."

How does he know my name?

She looked closer at the man. He was dressed just like anyone else in the bar, a working man's unofficial uniform: plain blue jeans and a button-down, long-sleeve gray shirt. Nothing fancy or which stood out enough to impress the few women mingling in the bar.

Yet he seemed strangely familiar.

"Trust me," he said.

"Let go of me!" someone shouted.

Ana couldn't tell if it was Liam or Michael since it was slightly higher-pitched than either guy's normal tone, but it yanked her attention back to the Watchers as they slapped a pair of black cuffs on Michael and Liam, roughly lifted both men to their feet, and marched them out the front doors.

Ana turned back to the man.

"Don't worry. They'll book them as drunks and let 'em out in the morning." He shook his head. "Unless one of them does something dumb. I'm sure Liam won't do anything too stupid. He's been through the system a few times and knows how, and who, to charm when he needs to. How about your guy?"

So he knows Liam. I'll bet he's one of the Underground. Figures.

Ana screamed, this man now the new target of her anger. "I dunno, but he didn't deserve this! He was standing up for me against that drunk jerk!"

The man opened both hands, waving them downward. "Keep it down, will ya?"

His eyes flitted to the bar. Ana followed his gaze. A pair of Watchers were still in the bar, questioning patrons. One of the officers stood by the doors, turning away two men as they tried to leave.

"They're gonna question all of us," said the man, clearly frustrated. "I suggest you stick to what happened and try to stay calm. Don't mention your father unless they mention him first. Of course, once they get your name from your chip, they'll know who you are and link you to Jonah. So, whatever you do, don't lie. They've got scanners in their helmets to see if you're telling the truth." He cleared his throat as though it added a layer of importance to his words. "You have to tell them the truth."

"Why?" she asked.

"Just do what I say. Go sit and wait for them to come to you. I'll catch up with you, soon as I can." The man turned, walked to the back of the bar, then disappeared into the men's room.

Ana looked around, noticing one of the men at the bar talking to a Watcher and pointing at her.

She returned to her table and sat, sipping her sugar water and dreading her looming interrogation.

On the wall, a ubiquitous City Watch poster, just like those that lined the city streets, the factories, and shops, asked an omnipresent question.

Do you REALLY know your neighbor? Watch. Listen. Report.

"WHAT HAPPENED?" the Watcher asked from behind his mask, his voice sounding more robotic than human.

Ana spoke to the guard, thinking of the man whose name she didn't know and the advice she couldn't ignore: *tell the truth.*

Though Ana couldn't shake the feeling that everything she said was being monitored for honesty and would probably be fed to someone in a room somewhere, or maybe recorded and added to her existing data log, to somehow, in some unknown way, be used against her someday, she did tell the truth. Ana remembered taking a tour of the City Watch Tower as a child and seeing room after room filled with computers and monitors, with Watchers observing camera feeds from the streets, from the woods, from the sky orbs, and even from within people's homes. No doubt there were also screens and maybe even separate rooms devoted to watching the feeds from the Watchers' helmets.

"Did Liam say why he thinks your father is innocent?" the Watcher asked.

Ana was frozen under the question's weight, wondering if telling the truth would lead to trouble for Liam. If he were part of the Underground, which she only suspected but didn't *know*, he could be held and tried as a traitor. She had to be careful not to get him into more trouble than his mouth had already made for himself.

"Hell if I know," she said, allowing her anger to surface just enough to shift the conversation. "He was drunk. He's always been a drunk since he could buy alcohol. He's always antagonizing me. I'd say he's trying to get in my pants, but again, you'd have to ask *him* why he's such an asshole."

She'd hoped to elicit a laugh from behind the helmet's dark glass, but nothing but silence surfaced from behind the keeper's visor.

"Okay," he said, finally standing. "Thank you for your time. We'll be in touch if we have any further questions. You're at Chimney Rock?"

"Except when I'm working at the shirt factory, six in the morning to six in the evening, all days but Sunday."

"Okay, then." The Watcher turned from the table and walked away, leaving her alone with a bottomless sigh.

Ana hoped nobody would smell her deception and

return to the table. Who would care for Adam if she went to jail? She kept sipping her sugar water until the last of the Watchers finally left and the racing pulse in her neck seemed to calm.

The Social returned to normal, with people drinking to forget, to celebrate, and a few, she suspected, just to get through the day so they could wake up tomorrow, start over, and pretend their way through the same shit again.

Though she was of drinking age, Ana had never touched alcohol. But as she sat alone at the table, wondering whether Michael was okay and worrying that she might have gotten Liam into worse trouble, she started to see its appeal.

She looked at Michael's half-full drink — red, like her sugar water, but alcoholic. She forgot what he'd called it when he ordered — a Crimson Bomb, she thought. She looked around the bar, still feeling every eye on her, although not a single gaze appeared to be pointed her way. Most of the people were watching the replay of Darwin Games highlights before the network returned to a live stream.

She reached across the table, grabbed the glass, then lifted Michael's drink to her lips, resting it just under her nose and wincing at the strong blend of fruity and pungent.

How do people drink this stuff?

She looked through the glass, marveling at the deep red color, much deeper than her own drink, which was almost pink, diluted by the slivers of melting ice. Michael's drink looked almost like blood. She dared a sip, then nearly spit it back into the cup. If Ana was alone she would have, but the onlookers would laugh, so she swallowed the bitter liquid, then set the glass back on the table and pushed it to the other side.

Wow! That tastes like cat piss!

Not that she'd ever tasted cat piss.

"You have to swallow faster," said a voice from behind her.

She turned to see the old Black man again, motioning toward the chair.

"May I?" he asked.

"Sure." Ana nodded, feigning indifference, which she figured was better than seeming too eager, or too easy a mark. That was one of the lessons her father taught her long ago, back before whatever turned him into a monster had done its dark work.

"You have to watch out for opportunists," her father had said. "They're always around, and always have an angle. Disarm them by never showing interest in their pitch."

"My name is Duncan. I'd shake your hand, but I prefer not to draw any glances to the fact that we're just meeting." The man winked, but there was nothing untoward in it.

She folded her arms across her chest. "Wanna tell me how you know my name?"

"I knew Jonah."

Ana resisted the urge to storm out of the Social that second. "So, what, does that mean you're with the Underground?"

"Well, we don't go around calling it that, especially in mixed company." His eyes again flitted around the bar. "But, yes. And let me tell you, Anastasia, you don't want any more attention from City Watch. What did you tell them?"

"The truth, like you said."

"What did they ask?"

She told him.

Duncan nodded.

"So," she asked, "did I get Liam in trouble?"

"Probably no more than he usually gets himself in. That boy is too reckless."

"No shit," Ana said.

Duncan burst out laughing, surprised by either Ana's candor or choice of words. "You're a lot like him, you know."

"Like Liam?"

"Well, him too. But no, I meant your father."

She ignored the compliment, assuming it was one. "So, how did you know him? My dad. Was he with you all?"

"Yes. But we met when we were both on City Watch."

"And what, you think he's some sorta hero or something?" She tried to keep from rolling her eyes.

"I don't think he did what you think he did, if that's what you're asking."

"I saw him do it," Ana said, shifting uncomfortably in her seat. This was the first time she'd told anyone other than Michael, Adam, or the law what she'd seen. "Though I do love how everyone thinks they know better than me."

"You've gotta understand: people looked up to your father, and most who know him can't believe he would ever kill your mother." Duncan shook his head. "He wasn't that kind of man. He loved her. He loved you, and your brother."

Ana looked down because she couldn't keep looking into Duncan's eyes without wanting to cry. "You think *I* wanna see him that way? He was my *dad*. He was the world to me. But I was there, and I saw what he did. And I see it every time I close my eyes. And anyone who claims that he's innocent is calling me a damned liar."

Duncan smiled, a hint of sympathy like a shadow in his eyes, as if he were talking to someone too stupid to see the simple truth of what he was saying.

Ana grabbed the Crimson Bomb and took a long gulp, swallowing without tasting, then slammed her empty glass on the tabletop louder than intended. The alcohol was awful, but she hoped the burn in her throat would numb the pounding in her head.

She stood to leave, turned away from him.

"You're not a liar, but you *are* lying."

"What?" Her voice rose in pitch as she turned her glare on him, realizing in that moment that she didn't care what Duncan had to say. "Just leave me alone."

Then she stomped toward the exit before Duncan could issue another word.

Ana pushed through the doors and stepped into the bustling, frigid City street, crowded with walkers and carts and the omnipresent City Watch orbs; floating, observing, forever monitoring the streets for any sign of dissent or crime.

Somewhere above the towering buildings on either side of the wide street, the pale moon was waking from its slumber, concealed beneath thick smog. Ana stared enviously at the lit windows along the upper floors of the apartments across the street, wondering if she'd ever see the inside of something so nice.

Of course not. Girls of my station can only dream ... or marry into that kind of life.

The City's upper floors were reserved for the powerful and the wealthy, never the commoners. And now that she was the daughter of a convict, no man of wealth, power, or even a decent reputation would ever be seen with a girl such as her. She was surprised that Michael still spoke to her, though Ana suspected he harbored a crush and was too shy to admit it.

When her father was arrested, her friends suddenly distanced themselves as if her condition were contagious.

All but Michael had left her side. Ana couldn't risk her last remaining friendship by introducing romance into the equation.

She was so caught up in staring above and thinking about Michael that Ana never saw the crash coming until they were both spilling toward the ground in opposite directions. She was startled, but even more surprised by the realization that her collision was with one of the older men from the bar — the one with the light-red beard who had been standing beside Liam and had offered Michael a helping hand up.

Red Beard helped Ana to her feet. She accepted, a cool confusion through her body as she felt him slip something that felt like folded paper — *maybe a message?* — inside her hand before closing her fist around it.

"*Wait until you're out of sight,*" he whispered, before falling a step back, clearing his throat, tipping his head, and in a louder voice saying, "Sorry, miss, all my fault. I should really watch where I'm going."

"Oh ... okay," Ana said, slowly shaking her head, confused, wondering what he'd slipped into her hand, but also hyperaware of the orb humming twenty feet above, watching, likely recording their every move and word.

She tucked the folded paper into her pocket and briskly walked away, eager to find a spot far away from the prying eyes of City Watch to read her message.

THREE

Anastasia Lovecraft

Ana raced home, though she could never, and would never, consider Chimney Rock her *home*.

Her home — the one she grew up in, an apartment on a middle floor just uptown — was seized by the City after her father's guilty verdict. She'd been staying with her little brother, Adam, thinking that she'd be allowed to raise him until they were both of age. She was close enough to eighteen that Ana believed she'd be permitted to stay, or at least be given the chance to find a cheaper place.

The City Court decided otherwise. Punish the children for the sins of the father.

She and Adam were shipped to the orphanage, where they would stay until she was eighteen, at which point she could petition for custody, provided she was able to care for her brother in full. If not, Adam would stay at the orphanage until he was eighteen, unless he joined City Watch, which he could do a minute after his fifteenth birthday.

For a kid like Adam, on the painfully shy side, with a

slight learning disability, a City Watch career was a long shot, and a painful life of misery a near certainty.

Watchers had come into their house the day after the trial and said it was time to go.

Just like that, the Watchers had started stripping stuff from their house, starting with their paintings — the ones Ana's mom made when Ana was little. City Watch had torn the paintings from their hooks and carried them into the hallway, handing them to a waiting line of police, who moved them to the elevator.

"What are you doing?" Ana had cried. "Those are ours!"

The Watcher closest to her had explained that they could each take two personal items. Everything else belonged to the City and would be auctioned to pay for the trial and their care at the orphanage — strangers bidding on her family's possessions.

Though Ana would have loved to keep something from her mother, or one of her few childhood toys, she took nothing. She hadn't been sure what the orphanage would be like, but if it was as bad as the kids in school whispered it was, she'd wanted no weakness to enter the walls alongside her. Something of value for Ana was a bullseye for someone else.

Ana would never give anyone that sort of power over her.

Adam was different, though. A sensitive kid even before their lives went to hell, he would need reminders of his past to carry him through.

It was hardest on Adam when they'd taken his books — relics from Before, which his father had collected and read to them both, but which Adam had taken a deeper interest in. Books were the only thing Adam had ever taken an interest in. He'd spent hours lost in the old stories, so their father had spent even more time, money, and general attention building their collection to give Adam something of his own.

As City Watch invaded their reservoir of treasured words, Adam tangled himself in tears, scuffing his knees as his heart broke against the floor, begging the two Watchers in the tiny library to please let him keep some of his books.

"I have nothing," he'd sobbed. "My mom is dead and my dad is in prison. Please."

"No way, kid," said one of the Watchers with a shake of his dark helmet. "These will fetch decent credits at auction."

Adam had cried out, grabbed the box from one of the Watchers, then turned to run away, though clearly with nowhere to go or thought behind his actions.

The Watcher had reached for his stick, as Ana screamed, "No!"

She'd thrust herself between the two Watchers and Adam, who was clutching his box of books and crying.

"He didn't mean anything, officer," she'd said, staring into herself reflected in the man's black glass mask. "He's been through a lot, and this is all he has. *Please* don't hurt him."

She'd wanted to cry but stayed strong for Adam as both Watchers stayed silent.

"Please, just give them the box," she'd begged him. "I promise, I'll get you more books the second I'm able."

She'd thought Adam would cry or argue, or point out that she couldn't possibly afford to ever buy books. But his eyes met hers and she could tell that he was afraid of the Watchers. Once they'd pulled out their sticks, they could have done whatever they wanted.

Adam had handed the box to Ana so slowly that she

thought he might change his mind, and then she handed it to the nearest of the two Watchers.

The Watchers had continued to say nothing, just stood there with their faces invisible behind the black glass. Ana had been certain Adam had pushed things too far — the Watchers would be forced to respond by making an example of him. Rarely did Watchers allow a citizen to challenge their authority.

She'd looked into the Watcher's mask, her eyes pleading. "*Please*. He didn't mean anything. He's harmless, I swear."

The keeper had looked down into the box of books, reached in with his black gloved hand, pulled out two, then handed them to Adam and left without a word.

Thinking of the moment, and the anonymous Watcher's kindness, always made her want to cry. That had been the last day they lived in a place someone could rightly call a *home*.

Chimney Rock was one of the largest buildings in the City, and maybe the ugliest. Thirty stories of dark brick exterior, iron bars on every window, and a large set of black iron double doors that seemed to weigh a thousand pounds each served as the mouth into Child Hell. But it was the spiraling chimney twisting high into the smoggy murk that gave the orphanage its nickname.

If the outside of the orphanage was the stuff of nightmares, inside was worse.

Someone had decided the halls should be painted black, since according to the State, other colors seemed to inspire "ill tempers." And as if black didn't lend to the darkness enough, lighting in the hallways was often neglected, left in a state of perpetual flickering.

The bottom five floors were devoted to classrooms — orphans were taught in separate schools from the other children. Though what Chimney Rock called school was in reality a mockery of education. It taught basic skills to be a better worker, and little to no critical thinking.

A dumb populace was easier to control, and made for better employees.

The sixth floor housed the kitchen and dining hall. The remaining floors were divided between boys and girls, grouped by sex and age. Instead of bedrooms there were wide-open areas lined with two rows of beds, twenty on either side of the room, with each child given a trunk and a lock for the foot of his or her bed — the small box meant to harbor all of their earthly possessions.

Ana rarely saw Adam any more, except at dinner — when she returned from work in time — and occasionally on Sunday, when their schedule was mostly free. This wasn't a kindness to the children so much as for the adults wanting a day away from the orphanage. While the schoolmaster and a few of the counselors lived on the upper floors, most of the staff was away on Sunday, doing whatever adults did when they didn't have to work.

Ana pushed through the heavy iron doors, eager to get upstairs and alone, so she could read her note.

She went to the main desk to sign in. As she waved her wrist, and the chip inside it, across the black square glass in the large reception desk, she was greeted by Merta, a large, unfriendly woman who seemed right at home in the long, black, shapeless dresses the staff were required to wear.

Tonight, the woman greeted her with a rare smile. Maybe a child had fallen into an oven or something. "Congratulations, your father really pulled off a stunner!"

"Yeah," Ana said, trying to be friendly and avoid explaining how she'd wished the Darwin Games were over already, and whether that meant her father dying or winning, she couldn't care less. She just wanted to stop seeing his face on TV every damned day. Then she smiled, suddenly meaning it after thinking about how Michael said her smiles seemed like she was trying to keep her gas in.

"To Jonah!" Merta said, raising her fist — one of the more annoying ways fans of the show celebrated their favorite contestants.

"To Jonah," Ana repeated, playing along and raising her fist halfheartedly.

Ana smiled again, then left the main desk, went to the elevators, and pushed the up-arrow button. From behind, Merta said, "They're out of order again."

Ana closed her eyes.

Of course.

Ana began the long trek up to the 25th floor, eager to reach the restroom on her level, the only place where she could find enough privacy to read the note. She ascended the stairs, wondering how her brother was doing.

He'd made friends with a group of boys a bit older than him, and she was happy to hear it. She also knew that Adam was too trusting and could be easily taken advantage of. She planned to meet the boys on Sunday and check them out for herself. She hoped they'd be as nice as Adam insisted they were, and hated the thought of someone having fun at her brother's expense, like what used to happen back home and in regular school all too often — kids making fun of the daft kid because they figured he didn't get it.

Adam wasn't daft, though. He was damned smart. Just quiet, and had some trouble communicating with others in a normal way. That didn't make him stupid.

If Ana found out these kids were messing with him, they'd have hell to pay — even if it meant her getting thrown into the Rock's basement for a spell.

Ana pushed open the door on the 25th floor and

passed two girls chatting in the hall, ignoring their cries of "To Jonah!" along with their fist salutes, and headed straight for the restroom and a private stall.

Ana went to the farthest stall, sat to pee, then slid the note from her pants pocket and carefully opened the note.

It read:

874 STONE STREET *Church*
Sunday
Come alone
And don't let the Watchers see you.

SHE KNEW THE ADDRESS. It belonged to the small church with the slightly crooked sign, across the street from her old apartment.

FOUR

Jonah Lovecraft

The Barrens — the next morning

JONAH FELT like his heart would burst. Then it did.

He stopped, clutching at his burning chest. Once he realized nothing had erupted, and that it only felt as if he were going to die, he pushed himself to run faster.

It had been a while since Jonah had heard any zombies, and even longer since he had felt them. After another twenty minutes, he stopped again, just long enough to catch his breath, sucking fresh, cold air into his lungs like the last swallow in a canteen.

After catching his breath, Jonah looked behind him, scanned the snow-capped tree line for zombies, then turned back and started walking quickly toward the Final Area.

He passed a lake, walked the long way around the same wooden shack that had been used as a makeshift hospital, a camping ground, and a last stand more times than he could count, or at least remember, in the more than thirty-six years since he first started watching the Darwin Games.

Jonah didn't go inside the shack, but as he passed, he smelled something inside that made him want to vomit.

Past the shack, Jonah reached the large black wall surrounding a clearing — two empty acres in the middle of the forest.

He wondered how much longer he could continue breathing. His heart was still beating like a jackhammer and threatening eruption. His lungs were a bucket of magma. His throat was dry and raw, and his eyes tired and scratchy, but he couldn't risk letting his guard drop now, of all times.

This was the staging area of the Final Battle.

Jonah found the gateway into the clearing and then swallowed as he looked up to the Mesa, a fifty-foot giant rock structure fitted with a raised metal platform surrounded by a large steel cage, and saw the goliath had beaten him there.

Bear looked down at Jonah, waiting.

Bear was too far up for Jonah to see his smile, but he was no less certain that the giant was wearing one. For a man Bear's size, who crushed skulls like fruit in his palm, he wielded a surprising amount of mirth. Jonah had caught the screen captures from the orbs on the replays each night. He wouldn't have been surprised if Bear was the first survivor in history to get his own spinoff show — if he beat Jonah.

Three days before, Bear had survived a midnight zombie attack by wrapping his arm around a monster's neck, squeezing it tight enough so that the zombie couldn't bite him.

Bear had been sleeping soundly when the first zombie made it into his camp, so he wasn't able to grab a weapon before the first zombie was on him. Bear used the zombie's body as his only weapon until he tore an arm from another charging zombie, then used that as a bat to fend off the approaching swarm long enough to get his store of weapons, starting with a gun that he fired to empty before switching to an axe that left a littered heap of zombies in piles across his campsite.

After just two hours' sleep, Bear had figured it was time to hit the trail again, so he crept through the dark, axe in hand.

That axe was still in his hand, three days later, as he stood like a king atop the Mesa.

The Darwin Games started at the Halo and ended at the Mesa. Sometimes no one made it. Most often, and fittingly for an audience surveyed to greatly prefer a one-on-one showdown, there were two survivors. Occasionally, there were three. Once, seven fought to a bloody death at the top.

There were only two ways to leave the Mesa: dead or by way of the winner's trip to City 7.

Bear watched Jonah, waiting, presumably smiling, holding the same axe he had sent through the bodies of who-knew-how-many humans and zombies alike. He slapped the flat side of the blade into his left palm, and yelled something that sounded like a war cry.

Jonah imagined all the people glued to their screens, watching and cheering for the big man to kill the Watcher. That war cry would be played forever in specials and repeats and clips if Jonah died here.

The first to the Mesa claimed the Bounty — a foot locker-sized box that harbored everything from medicine to food to fresh weapons. Jonah had no idea what other weapons were in the Bounty, but Bear clearly preferred his battle-tested axe. He was fully garbed in a full suit of thick leather-padded armor, loosely covering his massive body. Jonah wondered if there was a second, smaller suit inside the Bounty tailored for him, if only he'd been fast enough to reach it. Or if they knew Bear would reach the Bounty before him in enough time to only make one.

With the Bounty box locked, Jonah was forced to the Joker's Box to see what awaited him. He opened it, hoping for something more than the machete in his hand, though he'd gotten proficient at using it and preferred the wide blade over most other melee weapons.

But instead of better armament or anything to protect himself, Jonah was gifted with a photograph of his family, taken just after Adam was born.

He looked at the memory and felt the sting of tears wanting to break him down.

No time for this. Not now.

They're messing with your mind.

He left the photograph in the box and slammed the lid, hearing it lock a moment after.

Jonah held Bear's eyes for a minute before breaking his gaze and stepping onto the first step in the long and winding staircase wrapping the rock to the top of the Mesa.

A pair of hunter orbs hovered above the stage, making long and lazy circles over the Mesa as Bear wiped the back of his hand across his beard, then turned to spit on the ground, twisting his grin into a growl.

Jonah began to climb the ramp toward the cage and certain death for one of them. Once on the Mesa and inside the cage, the gate would lock behind him. Jonah couldn't flee. The orbs were there to make sure no one did, even if they managed to force the gate open. Anyone watching the Games long enough had seen the hunter orbs reducing a person to ashes in just seconds.

It had only happened a few times in four decades, but always drew the loudest cheers when a coward was obliterated for trying to escape. Viewers felt robbed when a contestant tried to avoid a fight, and nothing appeased a burgled viewer better than an orb's powerful blast disintegrating a person.

He paused at the door into the cage, either at the end of his life or taking his final steps into the rest of it.

Zombies no longer mattered.

Not today, and probably never again.

He looked over at Bear, who was relaxed and waiting, indeed smiling as if Jonah wasn't any threat, even with a machete curled tightly in his palm.

Jonah looked at the cage entrance once last time, then stepped inside, blinking twice as the gate swung shut behind him and a metal rod slid shut, locking him in.

Bear stopped slapping the axe into his palm and started swinging it in the air instead, tossing it from his left hand, then back to his right, like a hot potato.

Jonah circled the man beast, ready to die but not willing to fall just yet, keeping far enough away from Bear that the giant would have to throw his axe to hit him. Jonah was quick enough to duck, but in rough enough shape to miscalculate and make a fatal error.

"It's over for you now, Mr. Watcher Man!" Bear laughed, then shook the axe above his head and brought it down hard against the Mesa's metal surface to show Jonah he could hold the rattle in his arms.

Jonah continued to circle.

Bear laughed louder. "Watch, listen, and report this!"

Then he swung his axe in a wide arc, probably intending to scare rather than hit Jonah. But what really scared him was that laugh. There was something horrible and knowing in it.

Bear paused, looking down.

Jonah followed the giant's gaze to the left and over the Mesa's lip. Fifty feet down, on the ground, were nearly a dozen zombies, moaning their banshee cries as they ambled into the clearing, quickly crossing the empty land to the base of the Mesa. Jonah wondered if the zombies had found the entrance he'd used, or if the network opened up other doors along the wall surrounding the clearing.

No time to look. He had to keep his eyes on Bear and his mighty axe.

Death was a matter of preference: the killer without mercy before him or the walking dead below. The cage had never opened during a final battle before, and he hoped the network wasn't introducing a new wrinkle to add to the Wow Factor — *a cage battle plus zombies!*

But as the zombies ascended the same stairs he'd just crested, Jonah was almost certain that something unspeakable was about to happen.

Once the zombies reached the Mesa, they'd be able to walk around the lip of the cage, and likely reach inside, which limited how much room each man would have to move around. One step too far, and the zombies might reach in and get them.

Jonah imagined the audience back home and how much they must be cheering through the streets. He hated that Adam and Ana were probably watching from wherever they were, that they had to witness people cheering for their father's death.

The Final Battles were almost impossible for civilians to avoid; even four-year-olds knew when it was Finishing Day. The biggest day for the State-run television, always on a Sunday so everyone could watch, and a huge boon to the gambling industry — both legal and otherwise.

Death was life, and entertainment for the masses.

But this was his life, and his death — and knowing his children would probably see him torn to tatters, either by zombies or man beast, was something he couldn't accept. Worse was the realization that they might be rooting, along with many others, for him to receive Darwinian Justice.

Jonah wasn't guilty.

The City was guilty. From the esteemed "one true leader" Jack Geralt to the leaders of the Inner Circle, to the Directors to the Watchers — everyone who had played in the charade was guilty.

And in that sense, Jonah, who was an unwitting part of the machine for so long, *was guilty*.

He hadn't murdered his wife, but nobody would ever know of his innocence if he didn't make it out of the Darwin Games alive.

He screamed, then charged at Bear.

Bear was expecting the rush and didn't care. He stepped aside, surprisingly quick, and avoided Jonah's blade while managing to wrench the machete from his hand.

Jonah stumbled forward.

Bear threw the machete through the bars, where it fell fifty feet to the snow-covered field below.

Jonah fell to the metal floor, and Bear laughed as if it were the first joke at the end of the world.

Bear threw his arms into the air as four orbs circled outside the cage, above and around them. He hurled his axe into the corner, then threw his arms up again, waiting through the applause he couldn't hear but probably felt in the cells of every overdeveloped muscle.

He ran at Jonah, grabbed him roughly by the collar, lifted him overhead as though he weighed nothing, then smashed him onto the floor.

Pain ripped through Jonah's back and skull, tightening his entire body as he stared up helplessly.

Bear raised his arms in the air again, screaming in victory, as if he were a real bear, waiting through the orbs' whirring whispers of broadcast glory.

Jonah was going to die.

It shouldn't end this way, it wasn't fair.

A year ago, everything was different.

A year ago, Jonah didn't know, and ignorance made everything perfect.

But that was before Jonah knew that life was a lie, and that everything he'd ever suspected actually was, and that the sour truth might spread farther than the Walls of City 6.

Molly was everything to him. Ana and Adam knew it because Jonah had given them a lifetime of proof. Ultimately, truth held no court in a world built on lies.

Not when the "truth" could be created wholesale from false memories.

Neither of his children believed in his innocence, and his daughter had testified against him, sending him first to jail, and then outside the City walls where he fought the dead to keep breathing. She was probably watching and wishing him eaten.

Jonah looked up at the orbs, then back at Bear.

This is it.

The City's setup was finally finished.

Jonah was arrested, convicted, and expelled from a safe life behind the Wall.

Maybe the State and City were finished with him, but *he* wasn't done with them.

Jonah held his own roar, swallowing a swirling tornado inside him through the extra half second of silence that might be all he needed to win life from death at the Bear's bloody hands.

Jonah stood, surprising the giant.

Bear swung and Jonah dove, landing at the man beast's ankles, thrusting forward with every one of his 198 pounds.

He sent Bear to the ground with a scream.

Jonah wanted to turn and finish him off, but he had no blade or anything else, and the axe was too far with Bear already rising back to his feet.

Jonah was standing again, adrenaline overriding the pain, but just barely.

Bear roared like the beast he was, and the rage in his bellow managed to do what Jonah's machete couldn't — strike fear, or at least curiosity, into the surrounding zombies.

The moaning grew louder as their heads spun slowly and wildly around. Their stride never slowed as they ascended the stairs on their way to the cage.

If the zombies somehow got inside the gate, Jonah was finished. Even winning against Bear would only prolong his death. Producers never interfered. And no way could he fight off a horde with only his hands.

But Jonah wasn't going to die.

He would kill Bear and earn his way into City 7, so the plans he'd been making since seconds after his arrest could finally get started.

Bear finished his roar, then raged at Jonah, catching him before he could get away, then raising and throwing him to the ground again, like a rag doll.

Jonah crumpled as the pain won out against the adrenaline. And like a rag doll, he felt like he might fall apart any second.

There was a cold rush of something, maybe internal bleeding, in his left shoulder.

He gasped for breath and choked up blood, but his heart was still beating.

He spit a giant gob of bloody snot from his mouth. It landed on the Mesa floor a foot from Bear's blood-crusted boot.

Bear grunted, then turned black eyes from Jonah to the closed gate door as the zombies reached the cage and pressed against the door.

Jonah wondered how long the gate would hold, with the inevitable thousands of pounds pushing their dead weight against it. Bear turned to the cage, screaming at the zombies on the other side, either trying to intimidate them, or perhaps rile them up and encourage them to push the cage door open.

Bear turned around, not looking altogether surprised to see that Jonah had made his way across the cage to retrieve Bear's carelessly thrown axe.

Jonah held the weapon with both hands, muscles straining from the weight and bulging from his tired biceps.

Bear laughed. "You better hope you swing true, little man. 'Cause if you miss, I'm gonna get it. And I promise: *I* won't miss."

They stared at one another, each of them snarling. Jonah didn't have the strength to charge. He barely had the strength to stand without dropping the axe.

And Bear knew it.

Both men were bleeding — and the zombies were pressing harder against the cage door, crowding the bars closest to the door, rotten arms reaching in, swinging wildly, spurred by a hunger for flesh.

Jonah stared through the layers of certain death.

Z2134

Compared to the zombies behind the bars, being torn to bitter memory by Bear would be a blessing.

Jonah had two children and a City to save, if not a world.

His time was now.

Jonah ran toward Bear, then swung his gait wide at the last minute, rounded past the startled behemoth as he charged toward the cage door. Jonah swung the axe, severing several ruined hands and covering himself with a gallon of blood, but he struck his target — the metal bar holding the gate closed.

The lock broke and fell to the ground with a clank.

The cage exploded open, the door slamming Jonah back against the wall of iron bars, as a dozen zombies rushed in. They raced past Jonah, secured by the door, which trapped him against the wall of iron bars, and toward Bear, who was racing to the far corner of the cage while screaming.

Fortunately, the zombies who had been on the left side of the door weren't still there, or Jonah would have been trapped and they would have torn him apart. They'd raced inside with the other monsters, leaving the ramp to the cage clear.

Jonah swung the cage door back open, and grabbed the axe, which had fallen from his hands when the door exploded open. Heading through the open door, he looked back to see that none of the zombies were paying any attention to him. They were all in the corner — surrounding Bear, who was pushing and fighting them as best he could.

Jonah wasn't waiting to see who would win the battle.

He descended the ramp, sneaking one last look back.

Bear yelled as if three men were dying inside him, then fell to his knees as a river of blood gushed from beneath him. The zombies in the cage piled atop him like flies to a dying cow's asshole.

Then came the sound of ripping, and Bear's screams were choked in gurgling blood.

Jonah looked down the stairs to see that he wasn't alone.

A female zombie, late to the party, was headed straight toward him.

Her white eyes locked on him as her mouth yawned opened and teeth began to chomp in anticipation of a feast.

He gripped the axe tight and headed toward her, cautious not to fall over the edge of the stairs and take a plunge that would kill him right after he won The Game.

As they drew closer, Jonah realized that if he swung the axe and missed, his momentum, and the cool wind, could send him right off the edge.

The zombie was closing in — twenty feet, and then ten.

Jonah readied the axe, and as the dead woman closed the gap between them, she shrieked.

But he didn't swing the axe. Instead, he shoved the blade right at her chest, thrusting it forward to knock her off the stairs.

Her arms reached out for his as the axe struck and Jonah was forced to let go.

The zombie stumbled back, slipped, then sailed off the edge, screeching all the way down.

Jonah wanted to run down the stairs in search of somewhere safe to wait until someone showed to declare him a winner. But more zombies had gathered below, starting to ascend.

"Shit!"

He turned around and headed back up the ramp to the Mesa.

The zombies were feasting on Bear's ample corpse, but they wouldn't be distracted for long.

He couldn't go in the cage, or lock it.

He'd have to climb it and get on top. But to do that, he'd have to circle halfway around the ledge and hope to God that the zombies didn't see him before he could flee their reach.

He glanced down to see at least six zombies heading up the stairs. They weren't running, but it would be less than a couple of minutes before they reached him.

He began making his way around the lip of the Mesa platform, which extended just two feet around the cage in every direction.

The only crossbar within reach was around the corner, about thirty feet away.

He forced himself to move faster, gripping the bars tight as he navigated the outside of the cage. Just as Jonah rounded the corner, one of the zombies was pushed from the pack feasting on Bear.

It looked up and saw him standing on the other side of the bars — fresh food!

It shrieked, drawing the attention of the others.

"Fuck!" Jonah screamed, as he was still ten feet away from the crossbars and would have to pull himself up once there.

He raced, heart pounding against his chest as he finally reached the crossbar, just as a zombie's face and wide-open rotting mouth greeted him with a scream — inches away and wildly reaching for Jonah.

His foot slipped and he fell, slamming his knee, as his hand slipped down the bar, and sent the bulk of his body over the ledge.

He barely held onto the bar as the rest of his body slipped down, coming to a sudden wrenching stop as his left shoulder exploded in pain.

But he held on, the rest of his body dangling off the Mesa platform.

His relief was short-lived — the zombie clawed at his hand.

Jonah raised his right hand, grabbed the edge of the Mesa, then let his left hand release the bar and fall to the lip of the platform, where he held on for dear life by the tips of his fingers.

Six zombies gathered, shoving themselves at the bars just above, moaning, screeching, and reaching through the bars, swiping at him.

Jonah moved his hands repeatedly to avoid their swings as his fingers felt like they might fall off at any second.

He looked down. The ground beneath him was soft with snow, but the snow wasn't that deep. And there were more zombies gathering beneath him.

He had nowhere to go.

Just when Jonah figured the drop's instant death might be better than getting grabbed and yanked into the cage, a pair of orbs flew into sight and hovered above him, displaying a screen filled with people in the studio audience at City 1, cheering.

"This might be the best finish on record, ladies and gentleman!" Kirkman proclaimed from the orb's speakers. "WOW! We'll be talking about this Darwin Final between Jonah Lovecraft and Dimitri "Bear" Aronofsky for years!"

One of the zombie's hands grabbed ahold of Jonah's right hand, and he tugged it back, nearly losing his grip with his left hand in the process.

"Get me outta here!" Jonah cried out.

A harness threaded itself around his chest, then a tightening pressure as he was slowly pulled toward a silent hovercopter above.

Kirkman continued from both orbs on either side of Jonah as he floated up and away from the cage, looking down at the screaming zombies and Bear's fleshy, bloody remains.

"Any last words for the final few seconds of the Finish, Jonah?"

The orb went silent, waiting.

Jonah was too tired to say a word and had nothing to say even if he weren't exhausted. He shook his head, trying to keep from passing out.

"Oh no," Kirkman chimed. "Looks like Jonah needs a nap!"

The screen suddenly brightened and showed Jonah's face in a live-action shot. The word *WINNER* was written in bold blue beneath him.

"Jonah Lovecraft is our newest Darwin Games winner!" Kirkman shouted. "He will now be cleaned up and rubbed down, and will get a reminder of what it means to be a man as he's prepared by the Darwin Games producers for his first-class trip to the rest of his life in SUNNY City 7!"

The screen suddenly lit with vibrant images of City 7, showing Jonah the same sight the crowds were seeing — in every bar, public square, dark alley, and private home in all the Cities.

Kirkman then repeated the mantra spoken before the end of every broadcast: "All hail the one true leader, Geralt."

The audience said, "All hail!" and erupted into a round of applause. Jonah was sure some of the applause was for Geralt, but he also knew at least some of the people — those who sought change in the system — were secretly applauding his win.

Jonah stared at the screen. Hope swelled in his chest, intense enough to make him cry. Like every second of footage he had seen since he could remember, City 7 was gorgeous, so clean that it shimmered, especially when compared to City 6's all-too-lived-in streets and alleyways. No smog polluted the pristine blue skies.

The pixels of City 7 were every one of them paradise: people either relaxing, or stuffing their faces with heaping plates of piled pasta and lean meats — the opposite of the packaged synthetics found behind the Walls of City 6. There were tall glasses filled with richly colored wine and spirits, and beaches swarming with beautiful men and women wearing only their smiles.

Jonah's body was lifted into the hovercopter.

Kirkman's voice invaded its interior as the orb hovered an inch from his face and he asked if the first thing Jonah wanted to do in City 7 was take a nap.

Jonah opened his mouth to answer, then passed out instead.

FIVE

Anastasia Lovecraft

INSIDE THE WALLS OF CITY 6 — Sunday

IT TOOK Ana a day's worth of courage to finally visit the church. Then she spent the service sitting alone, wishing she hadn't been so stupid.

It wasn't easy getting to the church, since Ana didn't want Adam to know she wasn't around. She got Michael to look after him while she was away, which made her feel bad since he'd already spent the morning in jail defending her name.

Michael pulled Adam from Chimney Rock with a day pass. He was one of two authorized white-card friends who could sign her little brother out for a four-hour interval, twice per month. This particular day pass bought Adam a half-day in the Arcade — his favorite place in the world. Michael loved the Arcade, too. Of course, everyone did.

The Arcade was filled with every game, movie, and digital book in the City's library. A digital paradise. Beyond the countless games and miscellaneous media, there were long aisles of simulators, though unlike everything else in the Arcade, simulator time needed to be booked. It was the most popular part of the Arcade by far, so walk-ins were never available.

The Arcade offered everything from foods you could never eat otherwise to lovers real life would never allow you to taste. Adam hadn't visited any of the adult delicacies, but Michael had, even though he wouldn't while at the Arcade with Adam, and it had taken him a forever and a half to admit the truth to Ana the first time he did.

She imagined Michael at the Arcade with Adam, standing in line for the virtual coasters, eating fry bread dusted with sweetener, and maybe catching a movie — probably *Interior Solace*, the story of the Third Plague and Jonathan Clark's midnight ride into the forests just outside City 2.

Interior Solace was one of Michael's favorites, and Ana hoped he could share it with Adam, who had never seen the film before. Michael was good to her, the best. No one else in her life would have ever risen to defend her like that, or gone to jail for the honor.

Michael had, and without flinching.

Ana's mind flashed to Liam, and she couldn't help but wonder if he'd made it out of jail. She hadn't seen him since the incident at the Social, not that she ran in the same circles as he did. But Ana was worried and couldn't help but feel responsible for his whereabouts, even though Liam had started the incident.

Ana had asked Michael if he knew what happened, but he wouldn't even look at her when he answered that he didn't know, or particularly care, what happened to the "jerk."

Ana turned her attention back to the pulpit. The pastor

was the same man — Duncan — she had met at the Social.

Sitting in a pew with her hands folded in her lap, looking up at the pulpit like everyone around her, Ana felt like a fraud among so many holy people. She wasn't a believer, and the words flowing from Duncan's mouth didn't sound all that different from the fairy tales her parents had recited to her as a child.

Ana wondered why Red Beard had given her the message to come here. Had he been offering her a place of worship, or did Duncan want to see her? She assumed the latter, given their conversation at the Social. Perhaps Duncan was going to offer "proof" that she was a "liar," and that her dad hadn't done what she had clearly seen him do.

There was a small girl sitting one row up and to Ana's left, tiny really, and adorable enough to crease Ana's unhappy face with a smile. Most of the children living in the lower floor apartments of the City looked malnourished. Their clothes were often threadbare and dirty, no different from their spirits.

This girl seemed different — scrubbed rosy, her body clean and almost glowing. Her clothes were thin but well-mended, neatly pressed despite their wear. Her short blonde hair was trimmed in a severe line just under her chin. She stared up at the pastor, lightly swinging her legs, fingers braided and resting in her lap, wearing a smile that seemed so big and *happy*.

Ana couldn't ever remember a time being filled with that much joy.

The girl hung on the pastor's every word, singing every song while swinging her feet beneath the pew. Duncan finished speaking, then went to the front of the room, standing beside the exit to shake hands and speak with people as they left.

Ana stayed in her seat, waiting behind the girl, who was also still seated, waiting to see where her parents were. But nobody came for the child.

She just sat there, smiling, watching the pastor.

Ana moved closer and leaned toward the girl. "Are you here alone?"

The girl turned to her. "Yes, Mommy and Daddy let me come to church whenever I want. They said it's better than being at home and watching the Games."

Ana swallowed, still confused about whether she should be celebrating or mourning her father's win this morning, which she had seen just as she was leaving for church.

"I haven't seen you before," the girl said, looking sideways at Ana. "Is this your first time?"

Ana nodded.

The girl smiled. "It's great to have you. Father Duncan says we can never have too many people in church." After a pause, barely long enough to draw a decent breath, she said, "My name's Iris, what's yours?"

She had "Ana" in her throat, then choked on it and said "Rebecca" instead.

"Nice to meet you, Rebecca."

"Nice to meet you, too, Iris."

She was about to ask Iris where she lived when a strong hand fell on her tightened shoulder. "Come with me," Duncan's soft, firm voice said from behind her. Ana turned and met his eyes, larger than what she remembered from the Social, and infinitely sadder. "I have something to show you."

Ana said nothing, just nodded, turned to Iris, and waved goodbye, then followed Duncan through the church, past the pulpit, then down some stairs and into the basement where a handful of kids and grownups were sharing food and discussion. A few of the adults looked at her as she entered, some nodding and others smiling.

Despite the goodbye, Iris followed them anyway, jumping from the second to the final step, then onto the basement floor a beat behind them, practically skipping across the room to the table on the far wall, where she grabbed a piece of bread with a layer of sweetener crusted across the top, then started nibbling on the end, like she probably did each week.

Ana gave Iris a one-fingered wave, her curled pointer bouncing up and down from across the room. Iris looked up, smiled with her crumb-coated mouth, then waved back at Ana with her entire hand.

"Have a seat," Duncan said, leading her to a far corner of the room, away from the others, to a pair of tattered fabric chairs.

Ana sat, trying to swallow her rising tide of panic while slowly breathing through an obvious new truth: the church, and everyone in the basement, were clearly members of the Underground.

Duncan slowly sat across from her, his knees popping as he sat with a sigh.

She couldn't hear what the other adults in the room were saying to one another, or be completely certain they were Underground Rebels, but the same father who had murdered her mother sharpened Ana's instincts as well.

This whole place felt wrong. She imagined Watchers bursting through the doors, arresting everyone here.

If that happened, she was done for. And Adam would have nobody to look after him.

She had to get out of there. But she also had to find out why she'd been summoned. "You're part of the Underground?" she said, half statement and half question.

"Yes, I am." Duncan nodded. "And so was your father."

Ana was about as surprised to hear her father participated in the Underground as she would have been to hear a City Watch broadcast announcing early curfew. "Why did you ask me to come here?"

Duncan smiled, slowly rubbing his hands across his knees. He looked like he was about to say one thing, but then drew in his breath and said another. "Before I start, Ana," he narrowed his eyes, "I want to thank you for coming here today. I know it wasn't easy, and that getting brought down into a basement by someone you don't trust, well, that's scary, and I admire you for swallowing your fear and listening to your gut long enough to get here and maybe listen. Your father would have been proud."

Duncan smiled.

Ana didn't want to admit it, not to Duncan, Michael, Adam, or anyone else, not even to herself, but Duncan was right. The layers of her last two months were horrible — every one — and walking up the church steps and following the address on a scrap of paper slipped to her in secret by someone who could be seen as an enemy of the State, it was all a bit much.

"I want to know the truth. What was my dad doing before … you know, before he got into trouble?"

"You deserve to know." Duncan nodded. "Would you like anything first? Sugar bread, or water?"

Ana shook her head, then Duncan started his story.

"Your dad came in here one day, slipped into a pew, and sat for a sermon — as if he'd been coming to church forever, even though he'd never been here before, and I'd not seen him other than as a wave across the street since I stopped working City Watch. Your daddy sat in the back pew, two behind where you were sitting behind Iris tonight.

He listened to the entire sermon, then, when it was over, he didn't want to leave. Instead he stayed put in his pew for several minutes until I finished shaking hands, then when I approached him, he asked if we could speak, said he wanted to clear his guilty conscience."

"Why?" Ana raised her eyebrows. "What did he do?"

"He said he couldn't stand the horrible things he'd been forced to do in the law's name. Your daddy said he wasn't sure if there was a God, but respected that I did, then said it seemed hard to swallow, seeing as how there was so much sickness in the world, on both sides of the Wall. If there was a God, Jonah didn't want Him thinking he enjoyed doing what he had to do, and wanted a pardon if possible, at least until he could figure out a way to stop doing it for good."

"And you gave him a way?"

"That I did." Duncan smiled, then gestured around the room. "These fine folks, and many more who aren't with us tonight, look to me. They trust I'll guide them right, make the correct decisions. I'm a man of faith, acting on my instincts and His guidance. I trusted your father the second I saw him, Anastasia, so I saw no reason to wait."

Ana leaned forward, starving for the rest. "Wait for what?"

"I told him we were part of the Underground, and I told him in less time than it takes me to get my water hot. And your daddy never gave us up. Not even when they tried to beat it out of his broken body."

Duncan paused, then tugged on his right ear and stroked the bottom of his chin, like he had a full beard instead of two days' worth of stubble, then he looked at Ana like he was about to tell her something she'd never forget.

"Your daddy, Anastasia, he was a good man who did

great things, things you don't know about yet and maybe never will." He shook his head without moving his eyes. "There are more City 6 citizens owing their lives to your old man than you can count, not that he was ever one for keeping score."

Duncan grinned, probably happy Ana wasn't arguing her old man's merit, then continued. "Not only did your father never out any of us, he acted as a sort of double agent, feeding the resistance information we couldn't get otherwise. Jonah," Duncan cleared his throat, "your daddy, kept the candle burning, making sure we stayed alive and that the movement kept moving."

Ana nodded, wanting to believe the man who had taught her to think and love, and to never cross a line once drawn, no matter how thick the mud at your ankles; the man who read her stories from books that no longer existed, and promised to never tell her a lie — even if it was the only thing that gave him breath, was the same man whose honor Duncan was protecting. If what Duncan was saying was true, then of course the State wanted him outside the Wall.

It didn't matter. Even if Duncan's version of her father was the same man who had raised her, that man *had* murdered her mother. Ana still saw him standing over her dead mother, every night and most times when she closed her eyes.

As an eyewitness, she had said almost nothing in the trial until she sat in the box and answered every question, true to her recollection, as the prosecution rattled them all off, each one a bullet tearing into her body and leaving shrapnel inside her for life.

"Why did he kill my mother?" Ana said, chewing her lip to not lose a tear.

"He didn't." Duncan shook his head, his eyes now

larger and somehow sadder. "I told you that. You didn't mean to tell a lie, Anastasia, but you did. Your brain lied to you. Not your fault, since I'd bet my Bible and every verse in it that the City implanted a false memory, or several, inside that noggin of yours." The pastor tapped the tip of his head as Ana collected her breath from the lie that had stolen it.

"No." She shook her head. "That's not possible. No one can do that."

Duncan smiled, though there was no humor in his lips. "Sorry, sweetie, but the City does that sorta shit all the time. Trust me."

Ana would have found it impossible to see herself skirting the edge of a laugh even a minute before, but something in the way Duncan said the word *shit* split her serious face into a small smile. She shook her head. "I don't understand."

"It's the chips they put inside us when we're born. There's two of 'em, at least two that we know of. I think there's three. The tracker and ID chip everyone knows about, but then there's a second one for sure. Some folks seem to know about it and some, maybe even most, don't. And almost all those who do have no idea what it's for."

"What does the second one do?"

"Sends a signal to your brain. That signal can modify your perception of reality, and thus, your behavior."

Ana's chest tightened, uneasiness turning her dizzy. She swallowed, then stood from the tattered chair, needing to leave, thank Duncan for his time, and get back to Adam.

Put the atrocity of the truths she had started to question out of her head. The weight of her new world was too heavy to hold. Ana collapsed back into the chair.

"That can't be true," she barely managed to whisper, shaking her head. "It would change everything."

Duncan pulled her hands into his. "It's true, Anastasia, and everything's been changed for a while."

There was a boom from a door in the hall behind them. Ana turned and saw Liam standing there.

"It's all true," he said. "Every fucking word."

Ana kept her eyes on Liam as he passed their chairs, then crossed to the far side of the room, where he bent to his knees and whispered something into Iris's ear. She laughed, then threw her arms around his shoulders.

He hugged her, tousled her hair, then stood, grabbed a piece of sweetened bread, and ambled back toward Ana and Duncan.

"What are you doing here?" Though Ana was reasonably certain she knew.

"Making a difference. Not that you care." Liam crouched beside her, then put his hand on the back of her chair. "Your dad was a good man. They set him up, and you helped make sure everything went according to plan."

"Why would they want to do that? Because they found out he was a double agent?"

Duncan and Liam opened their mouths in unison, but neither managed to say a word before the deafening bray from City Watch megaphones blared from upstairs and drifted down into the basement with an icy echo.

"No one move!" the voice repeated. "All parishioners must be cleared for Appraisal."

A few of the parishioners who had stayed to pray after the service and a few of the staff still upstairs began to scream as heavy boots thundered onto the hardwood floors above and echoed down through the basement.

Duncan leaped from his chair, a firm order out of his mouth. "Everyone stay put! We're only having coffee and cake, mingling with Jesus in the sunset of my sermon."

He grabbed Ana by one arm and Liam by the other,

then led them both toward a door on the far side of the basement.

The sound of chaos settled upstairs. In its place was a slowly collapsing quiet, like a cold blanket smothering hope up above.

How long before the Watchers come down here?

Duncan opened the door to a storage area, then shoved Liam and Ana inside with a whisper. "*Hide in the floor, and stay in there no matter what. Got it?*"

Ana and Liam nodded as they retreated into the dark room stacked with chairs, tables, and dusty boxes that looked as if they hadn't been touched in decades.

"What about you?" she said.

Duncan smiled. "I'll be fine. I still have a few friends on the force."

The door closed, and Ana turned to Liam, barely able to see him through the dim light spilling in through a small, grimy window leading out to the city streets. Too small to escape through.

He moved a short stack of boxes to the side, then lifted a thick floorboard beneath them. He turned from the crawl space to Ana, then gestured for her to come closer. She swallowed, then stepped nervously toward the lifted board as she heard Watchers storming the basement.

She stared into the crawl space; it would hold them both, but only barely.

"It's now or we're both dead," Liam hissed, offering his hand.

Ana took it, letting him help her down into the crawl space.

Liam slithered in, squirming behind her, fixing the floorboard into place as noises drew closer on the other side of the door.

A tiny, involuntary shriek fell from Ana.

Liam's sweaty hand slapped her shivering lips to make sure it didn't happen again. "Shhhhhh ..." he soothed. "They'll hear us."

They huddled in icy terror as the Watchers came downstairs and interrogated Duncan. Ana listened as they explained that Liam had escaped custody and was last seen entering the church.

"I know the boy," Duncan said. Ana imagined him shaking his head. "He's a poor lost soul, for sure. But I've certainly not seen him today."

As one Watcher questioned Duncan, Ana heard a second one approaching the storage room.

Liam's hand tightened on Ana's mouth.

The door to the storage room creaked open.

Light spilled into the darkness, giving them a splintered picture view up through the floor.

"Find anything?" said the Watcher beside Duncan.

The second Watcher was looking around the storage room, footsteps clopping on the floor above them as he scanned the darkness. He turned over his shoulder and called, "Not yet," then added, "Get the ID scans started. I'll be out in a minute."

The next three minutes rang with the scanners' light shrill as data chips were read and those still in the basement were cleared to leave, one by one.

"Everyone is free to go but you three," said the farthest Watcher.

Ana listened to footsteps on stairs. She wondered which three were held behind.

"No," said a woman. "We didn't do anything."

Then Duncan: "Please, let them go. I'll stay and answer any questions you have."

"Please, Mr. Watcher," Iris pleaded.

Oh God, they're holding the little girl! Why?

Z2134

Liam tightened his grip around Ana's mouth as the footsteps of the closest Watcher stopped right over the false floorboard.

Her heart stopped in her chest, waiting for the officer to recognize the difference in sound from one part of the floor to the other before ripping it open and flashing the light from his helmet down on them.

They were about to be arrested. She'd done nothing wrong, yet was now hiding under the floor with a known fugitive.

They would take her in for sure. Then what? With an even bigger *what* for Adam.

The silence was killing her as the Watcher stood in place for eternity.

He's toying with us. He must know we're here. Why else is he just standing in a dark room?

Then the Watcher left the storage room, the door still wide open behind him.

Ana vented a deep breath, and her heart seemed to start back toward its usual beat.

The Watcher joined his partner in the room for a moment and then went up the stairs.

Ana couldn't see anyone from her angle, but could hear every movement and word.

The first sound was the familiar hum of the shock stick charging. While the standard-issue weapons delivered a painful non-lethal surge on contact, they could also fire a deadly blast that tore through a target's body in an instant.

The Watcher's voice crackled through his helmet's speaker. "I'll ask you once. Where's Liam?" Then, after a moment's pause, "I'll know if you're lying."

"I don't know," Duncan said.

Apparently *Thou Shalt Not Lie* didn't apply to protecting your flock.

Without warning, the Watcher fired a blast of energy that thundered through the basement, followed by the intermingled screams of Duncan and Iris.

A thud as what was left of a body hit the floor.

Liam's grip on her mouth tightened as tears streamed down her face, a scream dying to rage from her lips.

"Why?" Duncan asked, his voice shredded by anguish.

The only voice Ana couldn't hear crying was the woman, whom the Watcher must have murdered. She shook as dread chilled her blood. She couldn't believe what was happening. And there was nothing she could do to stop it.

"Tell us," said the Watcher, with zero emotion in his robotic voice.

"I swear, I don't know," Duncan kept lying. "I've seen him, lots. He comes in here, but I haven't seen him today."

The second Watcher returned from upstairs. "We have three independent confirmations. The boy was down here before we arrived."

"Is that true?" the other Watcher asked.

"No, sir," Duncan replied.

"I'm going to ask you one more time. You lie and I shoot the child."

Iris screamed, then the sound of tiny footsteps raced across the floor above Ana.

Iris ran into the storage room, just above them, crying.

Ana pulled away from Liam, shoving his hands away, and reached up for the floorboard to get to the girl before the Watcher.

She looked up, seeing Iris looking down at the floor. She saw them hiding, knew they were there. She cried out something, but her wail was severed by the shock stick, still reverberating through the room.

Z2134

What little remained of Iris hit the floor with a sickening thud, blood raining through thin slits in the floor.

Ana screamed.

The Watcher stomped across the floor and ripped the false floorboard away, exposing her and Liam.

He grabbed Ana by a handful of hair and yanked her up while aiming his shock stick at Liam. "Up! Now!"

Ana screamed as she was dragged from the hole. She glanced down and instantly regretted it at the sight of Iris's body with a giant, charred hole eating through her back.

She stumbled as someone shoved her, snapping Ana's attention back to the men with weapons. A third Watcher stormed into the room and forced Liam out, gathering them into the area where everyone had been chatting and eating only moments ago.

"Hands up!" the first Watcher ordered.

Two aimed guns, while a third held his shock stick, poised to deliver pain or death.

Ana raised her shaking hands, unable to stop crying over the murder of this little girl.

"Easy, guys." Liam raised his hands slowly. "We can work this out. You want the Underground, and I'm not Underground. But I can take you there, and we won't even have to get in a van. We're close. *Real close.* The leader's here." He pointed at Duncan. "Right there."

Two of the three Watchers spun toward the preacher, weapons ready. The closest, and the one with the clearest shot, stayed trained on Liam.

"Okay, okay, you got me. I'll confess everything, but first, I need to get your word on something."

"What is it?" one of the Watchers asked Duncan.

"I need you to take off your helmets and look me in the eye, like men."

All three Watchers looked at him, their helmets still on.

"We're not taking our helmets off. Speak, now!"

But it was all a ploy, maybe even one Liam and Duncan had coordinated in advance, just in case of such a situation. Unwatched, Liam drew a pistol from behind his back — an antique from back before the Walling — and squeezed the trigger twice, both shots tearing through the black material that covered the Watchers' necks, sending them to the floor, writhing in pain.

Liam shoved his elbow into Ana, sending her flat on her ass before turning to fire a pair of shots at the third Watcher as Duncan grabbed one of their sticks and cracked the helmet, sending a current past the glass and into the helmet, causing the Watcher's body to burn as it shook.

Liam fired two more shots into the glass masks, killing the other Watchers as well.

Ana stumbled to her feet and raised her head to Liam, shocked.

Duncan was blinking slowly, without surprise. "Get out of here, NOW!"

Liam nodded, a silent confirmation, then pulled Ana's hand and dragged her past Duncan and up the stairs. Just as they hit the top, they heard footsteps thundering toward them — more Watchers.

Liam shoved Ana down the stairs as bullets split the door behind them.

Then he followed her, tumbling down to the cold basement floor as bullets blasted the stairwell above.

"What are we supposed to do now?" Ana cried out.

"Just wait." Liam held up a finger.

Ana wasn't sure whether he knew what would happen or simply had faith that *something* would.

Gunfire erupted upstairs, not as loud as the Watchers' weapons, but faster.

Liam laughed, "Fuck yeah!" and headed back upstairs, carefully, his gun out in front of him.

Red Beard was suddenly in the doorway, holding a strange-looking gun that Ana had never seen. It looked like a shortened rifle, and antique.

His eyes were all business.

"What's the score downstairs?" Red Beard asked.

"Three Watchers dead. But they killed Rose and Iris. Duncan's all alone downstairs now."

"Fuck." Red Beard looked down for only a moment, all he had for mourning. "Okay, three down up here, and Scout says there's two more Watchers on the way. You all have to split. I'll get Duncan out."

"Thank you," Liam said, and pulled Red Beard's fist toward his own in an embrace.

Then they split, and Liam led Ana through two doors in the back of the church to a long alley leading to the back of several small stores on one side and tall apartment buildings on the other.

Liam searched the sky for orbs. None were there — yet. But Ana knew if they waited around, it was only a matter of time before the sky was thick with the things.

"Come on!" Liam shoved Ana forward until they reached a manhole.

Liam bent and pulled the thick metal cover aside, and pointed down a rung of ladders in the wall, into darkness below.

"Ladies first."

"The sewers?"

"Unless you wanna take your chances on the streets," Liam said with a sarcastic grin.

She ignored his attitude, kneeled down, and climbed into the sewer.

He followed, pulling the cover over them and plunging the tunnel into darkness.

The sewer was dark and smelled of waste. A stream of filthy water ran over their shoes.

"Oh God," Ana gasped. "This is disgusting."

"It gets worse when it rains; goes right up to your chest. Just keep moving. Up ahead, there's a manhole that leads to a crash pad. You can shower and change. But then you have to get back to the orphanage before someone comes looking for you."

THE "CRASH PAD" was a row of tiny apartments hidden in the basement of another building. The rooms were cramped and the denizens shady-looking, but the place was a safe harbor nonetheless. And for that, she was grateful that the Underground had planned for such events.

Though the shower was cold and the bathroom small and dingy, there was plenty of soap, which helped to cleanse her stench.

As the water rushed over her, Ana couldn't rinse her memories of the dead girl.

Iris.

The Watchers had killed two people in cold blood.

They would have killed all of them if given a chance.

What the hell is going on?

And what does my father have to do with this?

ANA DRIED off and looked at the clothes Liam had left on the sink — plain black pants, white underwear two sizes too big, and an even blacker shirt. Plain enough to blend in with others, but different from what she owned. She hoped nobody at the Rock would notice.

Liam rapped on the door as she finished dressing. Then sharply, he said, "Come on."

She opened the bathroom door, surprised to see him angry and glaring. His eyes were red, as if he'd been crying.

"What's wrong?"

"You have to ask?" he said, his eyes wide.

She stared at him, and then it dawned on her. "What? You're blaming *me* for this?"

"You should never have come to the church!"

"Duncan asked me to! After you got arrested at the Social."

"Well, I wouldn't have gotten arrested if *you* had kept your mouth shut!"

"Me? *Me? You're* the one who started it. *You're* the one who had to go all macho and pick a fight with a girl."

Liam glared at her, like he wanted to say something else. Or maybe even wanted to hit her. His fists shook, and he looked down, closing his eyes. "She was just a kid. She died because of us."

Ana wanted to fight the accusation, but then let out a long sigh instead. "You're right. I'm so sorry."

"Sorry's not gonna bring her back. Now get out."

Ana wasn't sure if Liam was crying or throttling an angry scream. Either way, she heeded his advice and headed back toward the Rock, knowing that nothing in her life would ever be the same again.

SIX

Anastasia Lovecraft

INSIDE THE WALLS OF CITY 6

ANA WANDERED through the next few days in a fog. Concentration was impossible, though still easier than forgetting the church massacre and the million truths it unspooled into the haunted hallways of her now liquid reality.

The second day was a pale echo of the first, long and lingering, with Ana moving mechanically as the factory machines she handled at her job. Hours blurred with memories that felt as real to Ana as her first memory of ice cream — not the "taste" you could buy at the Arcade, but the real stuff she ate on her birthday. She thought of her mom painting, walks with her parents in the park, her first fight with her mom, and her first, and last, kiss with Bobby Long — the only boy she had allowed herself to like, until he turned out to be a big jerk.

These memories blurred with that of her father standing over her mother's slaughtered body.

They seemed no different. No less real. But if one was a lie, how could she know that all of them weren't? If the truth wasn't memory, then of course it was a lie.

If memory could be faked, then what else in her life was false?

Ana found no solace, no matter where she went. Every eye was on her, even when they weren't. She had no clue whom to trust, or worse, what to do. She was no longer confident of where the line stood between fact and fiction and had no idea where in her world was an open window to truth.

She wanted to go back to the church, or even the secret apartment, to see if Duncan, Red Beard, and Liam were okay. But she didn't dare go near any of them. Chances were excellent that all three men had gone wherever fugitives went while hiding. Or perhaps they'd already been arrested.

She watched the news on TV every morning and night, waiting to hear anything about the church incident. But there hadn't been a single word. *Nothing*. As if it had never even happened.

Another truth altered?

Something about that scared her more than if the news had run a story about a terrorist group being broken up but covered up the murders of the innocent.

They weren't whitewashing the story. They weren't reporting any of it.

She couldn't help but feel like that was an ominous sign that Watchers were still investigating, and they might come banging on her door at any moment to drag her off into some dark cell for interrogation.

If the Watchers had already gotten any of the men, Ana wondered how long it would be until Liam or Red

Beard went finking to tell the authorities exactly where they could find her. She didn't see Duncan giving her up. He'd stood his ground in the basement. But she didn't know Red Beard.

And Liam ... was pissed at her. She couldn't imagine him protecting the person he saw as a "brat."

If either of them gave her up, the Watchers would come for her next. Because now it wasn't about just finding members of the Underground. Now it was about burying the truth, and eliminating anyone who knew it.

If they could do it to her father, they could do it to her.

IF they had done it to her father.

Because, despite everything that happened, Ana couldn't ignore her memory's architecture. Too many of the ceilings and moldings and floors inside her mind were of her own design, making it difficult, and in weaker moments impossible, to truly believe that a lie could be holding the whole house up.

Just because a pastor — who might have been crazy and was definitely a criminal, at least according to the City — said it was all a sham implanted in her brain, and her father was innocent, didn't alone turn her memory into a lie.

She wished she could talk to Michael or Adam; either one might help her untangle the situation, but she couldn't be sure until she was certain that Duncan was either right or wrong. No point in muddying everyone else's reality while she still felt less than certain.

Though she and Michael both worked at the same factory, and on the same floor, Ana was stationed in D-Section and he was in F, so their work paths rarely intersected. Sometimes, on rare occasions, they were able to lunch together.

On the third day following the church incident, she had to clock out early to make sure she could take her break with Michael in the giant cafeteria and its too-bright lights overhead. She wouldn't tell him, of course, or he would worry that she'd get in trouble. But she had to see him. And talk to him. She had to say *something*.

Though *what* that something would be was still a mystery even as she sat down across from him at a table near the rear, far away from most of the other workers who so often huddled together as if they were required to conserve space in the cafeteria.

"What's gotten into you?" Michael scooped a spoonful of what the kitchen called oatmeal into his mouth. "I'm happy we got lunch together, but it won't be nearly as fun if you're gonna be all mopey. You're not still thinking about that Liam jerk, are you?"

Ana wrapped her lips around her spoon, hoping to trap the tears. She shook her head, nursing the spoon, then after a minute of breathing, when she felt strong enough to maybe speak, she popped it from her mouth, plopped her spoon into the bowl, and leaned forward and whispered, "*I think my dad might have been set up!*"

"What?" Michael dropped his spoon and peered at Ana, almost as though he were angry. "Who have you been talking to? And why have you been listening to their lies? You saw your father with your own eyes! How can *that* be a setup?"

She looked around, feeling watched, even if nobody seemed to be watching. "Keep your voice down. What if *they* can implant false memories in your brain?"

"They can't. That's impossible."

"Says who? There are already chips inside us for tracking and scanning, so the City can do that weird people inventory they do. Why couldn't they do other things?"

He said nothing, chewing on the thought like unfamiliar food. Then finally: "I guess it's *theoretically* possible, but still, doesn't seem all that likely. Besides, why would anyone want to mess with your memories or set up your dad? Sounds like a wacky Underground conspiracy." Michael scooped another spoonful of oatmeal into his mouth, narrowing his eyes at Ana as if to suggest she'd been talking to Liam.

"I don't know." Her voice dipped even lower. "I saw things."

"What things?" Michael narrowed his eyes, his expression shifting as he leaned closer. "I'm not sure I like where this is going."

Ana didn't know where to start, and that she wouldn't be able to finish even if she did. It was only minutes until Michael's lunch was over, and she was eating on stolen time.

"*Awful things*," she whispered through gritted teeth. "Just terrible." She shook her head. "I don't want to tell you here. Not now, and not with only a minute or two left." She brought the spoon to her lips again, but only for a second before lowering it back to the bowl and leaning all the way forward across the table. "After work, meet me at the Social, okay?"

Michael agreed, though he looked angry more than anything else, including concerned. They finished in silence, then took their trays to the counter, said goodbye, and returned to work.

Ana trudged through the workday, wishing she'd never brought anything up to Michael, at least not without being able to finish. Now he was probably worried sick about her. She hoped he wouldn't say anything to anyone.

She didn't think he'd betray her confidence, but she didn't know what he might do in his serious efforts to protect her — what damage he might inadvertently cause.

Like the bar.

And Iris and the lady in the church.

Ana shook the blame from her mind before it poisoned her.

As the day wore on, Ana found herself wanting to spill her guts to Adam, whether what Duncan said was true or not. She'd have to wait until after dinner to get him alone.

But what would she say then? Adam wanted to believe in their father's innocence so much, he would easily buy a City setup. But then he might blame Ana for testifying against their father and sending him to die outside the Wall.

Ana would have a better idea after speaking to Michael. He would be harder to convince than anyone she knew. That would give her the confidence to imitate her conversation with Adam.

She kept her nose down, counting minutes until the end of shift so she could finally ditch the factory and get to the Social. She'd try another Crimson Bomb, work up some courage, and then go home and tell Adam everything.

WHEN HER SCHEDULED workday ended at 6:14, Ana powered down her station, set her thumb on the scanner to clock out, then heard the voice of Section-D Supervisor, Trudy Giff, behind her.

"Sorry, Ms. Lovecraft, but you're going to be working overtime tonight since you left early for lunch this afternoon — twenty-two minutes early means forty-four minutes of overtime, due immediately."

She boiled with rage, though Trudy probably couldn't tell from behind Ana's fake smile and syrupy-sweet voice. "But I worked my entire shift. And I didn't take any extra minutes. I just left a few early, then came back and finished everything for the day. I'm even ahead with my work — I've already started on tomorrow's!"

It was true. Ana's sorrow made for a high level of efficiency.

Trudy shook her head. "I'm sorry, Ms. Lovecraft, but you took off mandatory work so you could eat with your friend without prior approval. That's never permitted. You've let me, yourself, and everyone else in D-Section down."

Trudy turned without another word and disappeared from the factory floor. Ana powered her machine back on and began to feed material through.

After her forty-four minutes of punishment were over, Ana returned her thumb to the scanner. It cleared her to go, then she stiffly rose from her seat, stretched her back, grabbed her bag, and headed for the door, hoping Michael wouldn't be even madder at her when she finally arrived at the Social than he seemed to be at lunch.

The elevators retired each evening at 7:00, so Ana went straight for the stairs, racing to the bottom floor — two steps at a time — spilling from the factory and out onto the City 6 streets only a few minutes later.

She would get to Michael, gain some perspective, go home to Chimney Rock for a good night's sleep, then wake up in the morning to tell her brother everything after breakfast. After that, she would figure her next move and maybe deal with the possibility that she had betrayed her father.

A reasonable plan, that would never happen.

Because two blocks from the Social, a rough, gloved hand fell onto her shoulder from behind as a synthesized voice filled her with dread.

"Anastasia Lovecraft. You're under arrest by authority of City Watch."

SEVEN

Anastasia Lovecraft

ANASTASIA FELT LIKE LUGGAGE.

Her arms were yanked behind her back, hands roughly cuffed, body tossed into a large, unlit cargo hold in the back of a black, windowless van. The van's door hummed with the same unsettling electric warble that buzzed around the Wall, or even the invisible "gate" surrounding Lookout Gardens, where citizens could stare outside the City, eating open-faced sandwiches while watching the grazing zombies.

The front of the van slid open, then closed, followed by a muffled *THWAP* behind the solid wall between cabin and cargo box. The engine purred a second later, and Ana pictured the giant tires of the raised van peeling from the City curb.

She kicked at the van walls and screamed, "Let me out!" and "Help!" but was answered only by silence as the vehicle gained speed.

The Watchers had come to get her, maybe even kill her.

Ana had seen what they could, and were willing, if not

eager, to do. She raced through the scenarios. Why had they come to get her, and what were they going to do now that she was in their custody? Had they discovered she was at the church and that she knew what the Watchers had done to several innocents — that they had killed a child for nothing?

If so, Ana was sure she was as good as next.

She struggled against her cuffs, the thin humming magnets biting deeper into her wrists as she yanked harder at her restraints, tugging with all her strength against them, not stopping until they felt like they might slice her hands clean off.

Ana wanted to scream or cry, but kept everything inside. Emotional control was her only shield, and she had no sword or shield to speak of. She had to stay strong, prepare for whatever would happen when the van stopped and the doors opened.

Maybe she could save herself if she was smart enough to see opportunity's arrival.

Ana closed her eyes, trying to calm her thoughts, and turned her mind to Adam — how sweet he was, and how she would still think that even if he weren't her brother.

When Adam was five, they used to lie outside together, under the stars, on the roof of their apartment building. There was one stretch when they didn't miss a single night for nearly a month. The clouds were always too thick and too dark, but there was a two-month period back then when much of the sky went clear for some reason. It looked like the atmosphere was improving, but then it got bad again and hadn't cleared since. Now, the only time Ana saw a sunny sky was while watching a City 7 promo.

Those nights when she and Adam stared at the stars together were magical. Every wish made then was a wish never forgotten, even if it could never come true. He'd spent much of the time asking her questions — the typical stuff kids ask a million times and a million different ways. It was easy to be annoyed by a younger siblings' endless questions, but Ana loved being a big sister and having Adam look up to her.

And back then, she'd had all the answers. Now, lying helpless in a van, she had none. If she were locked up, or worse, killed, Adam would be truly lost.

The pain formed a knot in her throat, and she wanted to cry.

But she had to be strong.

For Adam.

ANA WAS LEAVING the terrible scenarios behind and turning her mind to possible solutions when the van finally slowed, then stopped. The doors opened.

"Out!" one of two Watchers said in a crisp warble coming from the mask. Both Watchers aimed their sticks at Ana, as though a 98-pound girl was a serious threat.

They were in the underground parking of the City Watch Tower, packed with trucks, cars, and a cluster of motorcycles. Ana had never seen so many vehicles up close, or in one place. Most people didn't own, or even ride them. She'd only been in a vehicle three times before, back when her father was assigned to chauffeur some visiting official from another City and able to bring the vehicle home.

"Go!" The order was followed by a stick's jab at her back. Thankfully, they hadn't delivered a shock with the blow.

She wanted to turn and yell but was cuffed and alone.

Ana did as she was told, stepping through a sliding door and then into a long hall.

She crossed the hall, then was thrust into a room where she was surrounded by four Watchers, all of whom held her down and ripped the clothes from her body like the husk from an ear of corn.

She screamed, fighting with her feet, sure they were trying to rape her.

The pair of guards who had brought her in stood behind Ana while a new pair in front shoved her face to the floor, pulled her underwear past her ankles, then cast them without ceremony to the floor. Her head was shoved down, so she couldn't see as they spread her legs apart. Gloved fingers were suddenly invading her, inside and rooting around, searching for God knows what.

She screamed at the violation, kicked, and cried, but nothing would stop them.

They flipped her over, and she cried out, staring at her reflection in their helmets as they moved their hands from her middle to her mouth.

Ana gagged, nearly puked, until the four Watchers were finally satisfied that she had nothing to hide in her body.

"Get up!" one of them barked, then roughly shoved her into a small chamber where she was hosed with scalding water that made her scream, thinking she was being set on fire.

She was yanked from the shower, then thrust into another room and ordered to don a pair of bright orange coveralls before getting marched into a slightly nicer-looking suite where she was photographed and scanned for processing.

From there, Ana was led to a tiny cell, where she spent

the next twelve or so hours cold, wide awake, angry, and terrified.

Her cell was just long enough to hold a thin bed and wide enough to squeeze a toilet beside it. Fortunately, Ana wasn't claustrophobic, or she would have suffered insanity in minutes. Even so, the walls might as well have been closing in around her, like the clenched fist of her life squeezing her future to nothing.

Her cell didn't lock like the van door and wasn't like the cells she'd seen on TV and old movies, with the rows of thin metal bars. Her prison was made from a large, paneled alloy wall, with a thin and rather long rectangular window resting at the top. Her cell was small, but no smaller than the many others running along either side of a yawning hallway. Ana wasn't sure if she was alone, but had yet to hear anyone else in the block since her arrival.

All the walls were an ugly muddy gray, so dull they had likely once been white but had absorbed all the agony from wretched souls trapped within the walls before her.

Chimney Rock was City 7 in comparison to the prison.

After an eternity, the alloy wall finally parted, and Ana's cell was opened. A man in a vaguely official-looking gray uniform stepped inside, and the paneled wall closed behind him. Unlike the Watchers, he wore no helmet. The man was tall, with a long, square face, and looked close to her father's age. His hair was cut short and severe up top, with a splash of silver on either side highlighting his jug-like ears. His jaw jutted from his face like a hardback book, and his nose was long and sharp like the blade of a knife.

He was both the ugliest, and scariest, man she had ever seen.

He entered her cell and his icy dark eyes met hers. A chill ran through her body.

"My name is City Watch Chief Keller. Perhaps you've heard of me? I was once your father's boss."

"No," said Ana, shaking her head.

The chief was apparently in a hurry for answers. He cleared his throat. "How do you know Liam Harrow?"

Part of Ana's silence was defiance, but most was fear. The little she had left was simply because she had no idea what to say.

"What do you know about Liam? And most importantly, Ms. Lovecraft, *where is he*?"

Duncan had told her to tell the truth. But the preacher could be dead for all she knew, and Keller wasn't wearing a helmet to help him detect her lie — though his icy eyes promised a gaze that was probably enough.

"I've known Liam forever. We went to academy together years ago, before he went to the orphanage."

"How *well* do you know him?"

"Not well." She shook her head.

"But you know him well enough to attend church together, is that correct?"

Ana couldn't swallow, or speak. She could barely breathe. "What do you mean?" she finally managed, choking on her saliva and coughing, surely giving herself away as a liar.

"You know exactly what I mean, Ms. Lovecraft. The church where you were seen together is a known sanctuary for anarchists." Keller said it like a fact, leaving no room for defense.

Ana shook her head, then stared into his icy eyes. "You have me confused with someone else. Maybe a friend of my father's."

Keller held her stare, still calm. "I don't know why you're protecting him, Anastasia. Your friend is an anarchist. He killed eight people in the church, including a child. In cold blood. You must know that your friend is a murderer?"

Ana tried to hide the anger that must've been painting her face. Keller was lying — Ana had been there when the Watchers opened fire. That was NOT a planted memory. Her upper lip twitched, begging her mouth to cry foul on his lie, hating him most for using the word anarchist to define the Underground, something her father had been part of.

Her father wasn't an anarchist. He believed in the law. But perhaps not the City's.

"I don't know him well. But that definitely doesn't sound like Liam from the little I know." Ana held his eyes.

"Ah, well then," Chief Keller said, his voice pleasant. "You must not know him that well at all. For he, and all the rats who scurry beneath the hard-working feet of the citizenry, are precisely what's wrong with the world. They are the vermin who destroy the City from within. Their corrupt thoughts, their evil deeds, and their devotion to anarchy, no matter the cost."

Keller pursed his lips, turned, and left her cell, returning a few moments later with a thin, sleek black pad in hand, the kind that people with homes read, played games, and watched TV on. The pad began to display photos of dead bodies from the church — starting with the Watchers, their helmets all removed, displaying the faces of young men who didn't look nearly as sinister as their helmets suggested.

Ana wondered if the Underground had removed the helmets to eliminate any video recorded by them — a smart move she'd not considered.

"Anarchists have no respect for rules, or doctrine, or laws. Democracy, totalitarianism, socialism, capitalism — everything is 'evil' to them. And order is *always* wrong.

Anarchists abhor rules, Anastasia. But no rules means no safety, and in the year 2134, no safety means certain death."

As he said *death*, the final photo showed Iris, turned up, clothes stripped, and a huge, gaping hole in her chest. Her eyes were open in a permanent gaze.

Ana looked away.

Keller cleared his throat. "So, you *do* have a heart, then? You don't agree that any action is worth the cost, right?"

She said nothing.

"Anarchy will never work because humans will never *earn* their Utopia, and all ideals ultimately end in selfish exploitation. Nine years ago, my eight-year-old boy Joshua, my only son, was murdered by Underground rebels — a bomb blasted shrapnel into his skull, killing him and sixteen others instantly. We had been watching the parade but a moment before; he was squeezing my pinky like he always did when he couldn't wait to see what was about to happen."

The horror of Keller's memory, frozen in his icy eyes, made Ana wish she were anywhere else in the world, maybe even outside the Wall.

"Joshua would be seventeen now," he continued, the emotion gone from his voice, fading as fast as it had appeared. "That's how old you are, correct?"

Ana nodded.

Keller cleared his throat, and the inner interrogator was suddenly back. "You were seen going into the church. Do you deny this truth?" He cut Ana with a second question before she could respond to the first. "People are willing to testify that you were there, and that you were with Liam. Do you deny this truth?"

Ana held his eyes, hating herself for trusting monsters

more than her father. She shook her head. "That wasn't me."

"We're not interested in keeping you here, Ms. Lovecraft. Do I have to beg you to keep you from making this difficult? Tell us what you know, and you can return to Chimney Rock tonight. Or don't." He shrugged. "But then we have a problem. A big one." Keller held both palms in the air. "So, what's it going to be?"

"I don't know what to tell you." She shook her head. "I wasn't there. That wasn't me."

He leaned down, and his head thrust forward like a striking snake. Keller was suddenly centimeters from her face, close enough for Ana to smell the sour stink bubbling up from his throat. In a low growl, he said, "I'm giving you one more chance to save yourself. *Don't lie again.*"

His vinegar-like breath made Ana want to vomit.

"Were you at the church with Liam?"

She shook her head, holding his eyes even though fear ran cold through her blood. This time she replied in what was almost a whisper. "That wasn't me."

Keller smacked her so fast across the face, Ana had no idea his large hand was on its way until pain splintered her cheek and screamed through her left ear.

She shook her head, reeling, trying to blink through the stars, as fat hammers punted through the walls inside her head.

She fell hard against the wall on her tiny bunk, where she lay curled up, staring up at Keller, determined not to cry.

He pulled her up roughly by the hair, forcing her to stand.

"Let's try this one more time, okay, dear?"

Ana was dead if she told the truth.

The only thing keeping me alive is their uncertainty.

"I really don't want you to be here. I want you to have a hot meal, and I want to help. You and Adam both." Keller shook his head. "But I can't help either of you if you are unable to tell me the truth."

He's going to kill me.

His mention of Adam worked like a screw of doubt, twisting away at Ana's plan to keep quiet.

"Were you at the church with Liam?"

She paused, then shook her head again. "That wasn't me."

Keller gritted his teeth, then squeezed his fingers into her arm, pinching hard into her flesh. He stood above her, glaring down. "You know, you and your mother have a couple of things in common. You're every bit as pretty, and just as stupidly stubborn."

"How do you know my mom?" Ana was suddenly twice as scared and three times as angry.

Keller ignored the question, then leaned in, giving her nostrils another blast of his rancid fog as her eyes swallowed the icy heat of his burning stare. "I'd hate for you to end up just like her, too."

He'll kill me, no matter what.

"I'll give you until lunchtime to consider."

Then the door opened and Keller was gone, though the chill he left in the room only grew chillier.

IT WAS several hours past lunch before Keller returned.

Ana spent the entire time swimming in indecision, wondering what she should do, whether there was any way out, and most importantly, what would happen to Adam if there wasn't.

Keller smiled as he entered the cell, his hair slightly

damp and his face freshly shaved. "So, have you given any thought to the truth?"

Of course she had, though Ana was certain her definition of the word *truth* was a sun to Keller's moon.

She shook her head. "It wasn't me."

Instead of growing angry like Ana had been picturing through most of the many hours she'd been kept waiting, Keller simply laughed.

"Okay, then." He fell onto the bunk beside her and rested a hand on his knee. "It's decided. *This* is how it shall be."

Each word sounded more threatening than the one preceding it. By the time Keller whistled the end of the *be*, Ana was shaking.

Change your story.

Tell him what you know!

Save yourself — it's not like you know where Liam is. He's a big boy. He can handle this a hell of a lot better than you or Adam!

Just tell Keller what he wants to know!

Ana, suddenly proud to be her father's daughter again, for the first time since the bottom of his boots were covered in her mother's blood, shook her head. "I told you everything I know."

"Okay, princess." Keller stood. "Looks like we have our newest Darwin Games player. And good thing, you're just in time. A new game starts tomorrow."

"What?" Ana said, falling back in her bed.

"You don't want to cooperate with us. That's fine, we understand. But there are examples to set, and we must set them. So we'll be putting you somewhere where your poor decisions are on full display for the benefit of the entire City to learn from."

"I told you!" Ana screamed. "I don't know anything. I wasn't in that fucking church!"

"I'm sure." He turned away from her and stepped through the sliding door.

"You can't just put me in the Games, you have to try me in court first!"

Keller turned back, smiling. "Suspected traitors can't be put on the stand without compromising City security. You're guilty as charged, declared by me."

She screamed, "You can't do that!"

He held his smile. "I can and did. Enjoy your final night of freedom, Ms. Lovecraft. Tomorrow we have a daughter following in her daddy's footsteps for the first time in the history of City 6. Fans are going to love it. Who knows, maybe you'll even make it to City 7, so you can reunite with your murdering daddy. I bet you two have *so much* to catch up on."

Keller left laughing, while Ana stayed inside her cell screaming, at first into her pillow, and then at the walls, which echoed her righteous anger back at her.

But even after she stopped screaming out loud, Ana still couldn't silence her mind.

Who will protect my brother?

EIGHT

Jonah Lovecraft

Two days earlier ...

JONAH IMAGINED the clean efficiency of the City 7 hospitals and smiled. No waiting, no assembly-line medicine — true rest and whole-body healing was just another short van ride away.

His body ached from its inside-out beating, but there was solace in knowing that was now part of yesterday's worry. City 7 had soft beds and strong medicine. Jonah would be healed, back to himself, and better than ever in no time. He might even feel something close to normal — or as normal as he could following the murder of his wife and the destruction of his family.

Jonah was thrilled that he'd won the Darwin Games, but not entirely surprised.

He had seen enough Games from beginning to end to believe he would make it to the middle rounds at least, and had believed it from the second he was tossed outside the Walls. After making it to the middle, Jonah figured there was a reasonable shot of his seeing the Final Six. And once there, Jonah *knew* he'd eventually face off against Bear.

But he'd never believed he could kill the giant, at least not until he knew for sure that there wasn't any choice.

He had, and thus earned a new dawn at City 7.

It's what he had fought for, bled for, and deserved.

But he sure as hell didn't deserve the reputation that would follow him into the coveted City, where he would be forced to live the remainder of his life without any hope for repair. He could never return to City 6 or prove to his family, friends, and loved ones that he wasn't a monster.

That made City 7 a prison, despite its presentation as a paradise. No one ever left City 7. You lived in luxury but never returned. Leaving was impossible, at least according to legend.

Jonah had never been to City 7 himself but knew its history well, same as everyone else. Much like the Australia of the old world a half millennium before, City 7 was initially settled by convicts — all of them former winners of the Darwin Games.

Rehab facilities inside City 7 were the best in the State, turning many of the City's convicts into productive members of the almost-Utopian society.

The entire City was practically one giant Arcade, and despite the one-time criminal population, or perhaps because of it, City 7 was said to be freer than any other City even though there were some rules and it still operated within the State. It was such a paradise that many lined up to willingly enter the Darwin Games in hopes of winning a new life in City 7.

But Jonah was heading into City 7 carrying a handicap none of the other winners had to tote behind them. Being former City Watch meant that he'd put thousands of citizens away during his decorated career. Some of those citizens had entered the Games, and a few even made it out alive and into City 7. Jonah had lost track of the winners over the years, mostly because he didn't want to think about them.

But now as a marked man he'd be forced to.

He figured the Darwin Games were aired in City 7, and word of his exploits, and past, had undoubtedly made their way to prior City 6 winners.

They saw him battle.

The saw him nearly surrender.

They saw him finally triumph.

Some of the people in City 7 would love Jonah. Most would hate him. Some would wish him dead. Perhaps City 6 winners would be so pleased with their new lives, far better than their old lives, that they'd be thankful for his part in their destiny.

Or so he could hope.

But Jonah would need to make friends. Because he had big plans. Plans to expose City corruption, and perhaps bring City 7's freedom to all the Cities.

The van finally stopped and Jonah smiled, now just scant seconds from laying eyes on a new life he never thought he'd see. The door opened, and he stepped from the van, spinning in a circle, confused.

He expected to see the rising spires of City 7, like he'd seen at the beginning and end of every Darwin Games broadcast since he was a boy. But there were no rising spires or wide asphalt streets dipping like gleaming black knolls from the near horizon to the ocean vista.

Instead, they were in the middle of a sprawling forest, same as they'd been since leaving the Walls of City 6. A small shack, maybe an outhouse, lay about a hundred feet away — the only unnatural structure in sight.

Jonah turned to the first driver. "Where are we?"

Before he could answer, the second driver pulled the trigger on his dart gun.

Jonah dropped to the dirt, his eyes already woozy.

"Welcome to City 7," the second driver said.

JONAH WOKE WITH A START, lying on the cold floor of an empty-feeling room, draped in darkness. His heart pounded as he braced for impact of anything or anyone, living or undead.

He rose from the floor, woozy and head spinning, then realized from his movement's echo and his foot brushing the base of a wall in front of him as his hand hit the side wall, he was in a narrow, confined space.

Jonah's mind was surfacing from its bog surprisingly fast, considering he'd been shot with a coma dart, as the drugged darts regularly used by both Watchers and Darwin Games producers were not-so-affectionately called. He flashed back to the last thing he'd seen as he was passing out: the small wooden building.

He wondered why he'd been brought out to the middle of nowhere instead of City 7. One of the men had said, "Welcome to City 7." Jonah wondered if that was the driver's way of saying that City 7 was all a lie. The hopeful part of him, the part that had been clinging to the beautiful paradise on TV since the second he was sent outside the Walls, refused to even consider that City 7 was anything less than reality.

It has to be real.

This has to be some other part of the show or something.

Or maybe they just couldn't let me *into City 7. Maybe they knew what I was planning for when I got there.*

But that didn't make sense. If they knew his plans, they

would have simply killed him. They'd shot him with a coma dart instead, then stashed him in a relatively safe place out of the elements.

Why take the time? Why make the effort?

They could've simply shot him dead or left him on the ground where zombies would've eventually found Jonah and finished him for good.

If they didn't kill him, then they didn't want him dead.

But they didn't bring him to City 7.

Why?

Because it's a lie, you idiot. You, and everyone else, have been duped.

He thought back on all the countless hours of City 7 footage he'd seen throughout the years. The shots of Kirkman standing in front of the sprawling beaches, the montages of people having fun, splashing in the water, relaxing on the beach, or strolling along the city's clean streets in its shopping district with their seemingly endless credits.

They couldn't have faked it all, could they?

Jonah was certain that he had seen them show past winners arriving at City 7. Not often, but at least a few times. The show had always explained that there was an adjustment period before fresh denizens were allowed to mingle in the new city to help keep the peace. Jonah wondered if this was some part of his "adjustment period."

His head swam as he silently turned around in the shack's thick curtain of black. He kneeled to the floor, then swept his hand along it. It was cold and hard, a bit of debris — dirt, twigs, and small rocks — moved beneath his fingers.

He was cold, hungry, and confused.

Jonah leaned forward, carefully positioning himself on

his knees as he reached out into the darkness, feeling the wall in front of him as his hands searched for the door.

His right hand slid across the cold metal knob, and he twisted it slowly. He pushed at first, then realized that the door opened inward and pulled it open.

The door creaked much louder than he'd wanted, spilling dim moonlight into the wooden structure. As his eyes slowly adjusted to light, he made out the snow-covered clearing where he'd been dropped off, and beyond that, a wide copse of trees lining every side of the forest.

He listened, trying to discern anything above the sounds of the haunting wind and occasional animal noises that he'd grown used to during the Darwin Games. He heard nothing unusual, so he slowly opened the door all the way, then turned back, casting his eyes around the small structure's interior in hopes of finding food, supplies, or weapons.

There was nothing.

Shit.

He stepped out of the building and looked around. A cool breeze bit into his skin, and he wished he'd been wearing something more than the gray coveralls and boots the network had given him.

He was even thirstier than he was hungry. Jonah had been given a bit to drink after being declared the winner, but it was barely a swallow, and there wasn't so much as a morsel of food. Already that seemed like a lifetime ago. He couldn't remember the last thing he'd had in his stomach — probably a handful of the wild juniper berries two days ago, which had seemed a million times sweeter than anything behind the Walls.

Jonah scanned the snow for tracks, but fresh snowfall had smoothed the forest floor. He had to find something soon.

Shit. Shit.

He reached down and scooped fresh snow into his hands, brought it to his lips, and swallowed, savoring the moisture. He took one more scoop, then stopped at the sound of a branch *snapping* in the distance.

He waited for a second snap, but none ever came.

The woods were pitch black on every side, like a wall of darkness as impenetrable as the Walls of City 6.

Going into the woods at night was stupid even when armed. Crossing the tree line and stepping into the blackness empty-handed was begging to die and getting your wish.

Jonah looked back at the wooden building, figuring he should go back and wait until morning. The shack offered little protection from the cold, but it would at least get him free of the wind and snow and keep him hidden from any hungry zombies who might catch his scent in the outside air.

Jonah turned and was starting to walk back to the ramshackle shelter when a sudden ear-piercing shriek split the night.

He spun around and saw the zombie — a tall, lanky creature — at the edge of the woods. Its white eyes practically glowed against the darkness as it broke into a run.

Jonah raced toward the shack, nearly tripping on his third step, then reached it and pushed himself through the threshold, slamming the door shut behind him. He fumbled along the knob searching for a lock.

Nothing. Shit!

Since the door opened inward, he'd have to push himself against it and hope he could brace the door against the weight of a zombie assault.

Shit!

The zombie shrieked again, shambling footfalls growing louder and faster as it neared.

His heart pounded loud and with an insanity of speed that threatened to drown the sounds of the approaching monstrosity. A short moment later, its bulk slammed against the other side of the door with a thud, shaking the door in its frame.

Jonah leaned hard against the wood as the zombie screamed and shrieked from the other side, the horrible scrape of its scratchy voice reaching deep inside and twisting his gut into panic.

The doorknob rattled violently as Jonah squeezed it tightly in place. He wondered if the zombie was trying to turn the knob or simply pushing against it on repeat, as a phantom memory ordered it around.

The door shook harder with another thump. The sound of wood cracking in the darkness fueled the fear flooding Jonah's body and coursing through his veins. There was no way the door would hold much longer.

He racked his mind for a solution. He had no weapons and was trapped in a box, while a zombie gnashed at the door, waiting on the other side to devour him.

Suddenly the door stopped moving, and things grew quiet.

Jonah swallowed hard, wondering what the hell the zombie was doing. He dared to hope it had grown impatient and had simply wandered off in surrender. That seemed unlikely given that on his third morning in the Games, he'd woken to find four zombies waiting under the tree he was sleeping in. They waited nearly six hours for him, not leaving until they were distracted by one of the mutated animals, something that resembled a moose but was far larger and uglier, that wandered the Barrens.

Jonah wondered if something had also distracted the zombie outside the shack.

He waited, ear pressed against the door, listening for the sound of the creature's retreating footsteps, but heard nothing above the howling wind beating hard against the decrepit structure.

Jonah pressed his ear closer to the door, straining to hear anything useful.

Then he heard it, just barely, but it was there, in the distance.

No. No. No.

Whatever warmth was left in his body bled out the instant he recognized the moaning. Not just the one undead monster outside his door, but who-knew-how-many. The groans were accompanied by an even more terrible sound — zombies running across the clearing, so many it sounded like a herd of horses in full gallop.

Jonah wanted to open the door, just a crack, to see how many there were — sounded like at least a dozen — but he couldn't chance it. They were closing in around him, moments away from the shed.

He braced the doorknob tight in his hands, pushing his foot tight against the bottom of the door, shaking as he heard them drawing closer, surrounding him.

Something hit hard against the wall of the shack.

Fuck.

This is it.

This is it.

There's no way I'm getting out of this.

Another zombie smashed against the shack, much harder than the first time, as if driven by anger now. And then another.

Suddenly, the thumping was coming four and five hits

at a time, from all sides, and the shrieks and screams began to swell in an unholy cacophony.

Jonah thought again of Ana, Adam, and ...

Molly, his beloved wife.

He saw her dead eyes looking up at him.

Anger coursed through him again. Anger at the bastards who had set him up. Rage aimed at the bastards who had made his daughter testify against him. Pure fury for the bastards who had destroyed his family.

Jonah flashed back to both of his children as babies, as wide-eyed, trusting infants looking to their daddy with only faith and love in their eyes. The world had been so simple back then.

And now ...

More screams.

More splintering wood, followed by a deafening cracking.

Oh God.

One of the monster's hands shot through the wall beside the door, reaching in and blindly grasping at nothing, barely visible in the moonlight just inches from his waist.

The entire shack shook around him, and it seemed only moments until the entire structure collapsed under the mounting pressure.

The wails and screams grew louder, pounding of zombie fists going faster, reminding Jonah of excited electrons in an atom.

Again he thought of his children.

"I'm so sorry," he cried as the hand kept swiping, slapping the inside of the wall and inching closer.

Another sound, this one impossible, rose above the monstrous wailing.

Gunshots!

Jonah turned his head sideways, trying to be certain of what he heard.

Another gunshot followed, confirming the inconceivable cavalry, followed by a scream and the sound of a body hitting the ground.

Gunshots screamed into the night, sounding like semiautomatic rifles, old weapons long out of use within the Walls.

The arm reaching into the shack slipped back beneath the weight of a fresh round of fire as he deeply exhaled. Tears streamed down Jonah's face as his rescuers continued their assault.

I'm saved!

I'm alive!

As the last of the gunfire settled, and the only remaining sound was the footsteps of his saviors and the creatures' final dying cries, his heart pounded, wondering who had saved him.

Watchers?

The network?

The Underground?

Who?

"Come out!" The voice came from a young woman with either an unrecognizable accent or some sort of speech impediment. "Slow. No weapons!"

"I don't have any weapons." Jonah slowly opened the door and stepped out into the blinding light from a pair of light sticks.

"Thank you." He shielded his eyes, stopping just inches outside the door. "You saved my life!"

His saviors said nothing.

When they moved the lights from his face, he lowered his hands and squinted as his eyes adjusted to the light, to see who saved him. It wasn't Watchers, the Underground, or the network.

Jonah was staring at three children — two boys and one girl, none of them older than ten — standing a foot in front of him, clutching old assault rifles. Their faces were filthy, and their clothes thick with caked mud and dirt. They looked like some of the kids he'd seen in the Dark Quarter, lost in the system, pulled into the drug, sex, or slave trades.

"You're kids." Jonah couldn't bury his shock.

"No talk, Watcher," yelled one of the boys, jabbing the gun toward Jonah, anger turning his face into a vicious mask.

"Walk!" ordered the girl with an accent, not an impediment, as she glared at him with steely blue eyes.

"What?" Jonah said, confused.

"You're our prisoner, Watcher. Now walk!" One of the boys shoved his rifle hard into Jonah's lower back, nearly knocking him down.

He stumbled forward and considered spinning around, grabbing the gun from the little bastard, and shoving it in his face. But the other two kids were eyeing him with the icy, calculated intensity of seasoned soldiers.

Jonah had no idea who the kids were, or why they had saved him. But, as he looked around at the tiny mountain of bloody undead now lying still forever, the only thing he knew for certain was that underestimating the kids would lead to a bullet in his skull.

"She said walk!" the kid behind him repeated, louder, and with a sharper jab of his rifle.

Jonah met the girl's gaze and saw only hate in her eyes.

NINE

Anastasia Lovecraft

Before they were loaded into the van for their final journey, the four contestants were forced to stand on stage for the Farewell Ceremony, as their names and crimes were read out loud.

Ana was found guilty of being a traitor to the State and part of the Underground.

She was surprised that there were three other contestants, since there were usually only two from each City. Also surprising was that the others were also female, which she was fairly certain was a Darwin Games first.

This must be a Special Edition Game. I wonder if the entire Game will be girls.

Each person's name was read, immediately followed by a chorus of boos.

Ana spent the entirety of the ceremony scanning the crowd for either Michael or Adam. A line of City Watchers and robot sentries posted along black wooden barricades held the crowd back. Just as she was wondering if Michael had kept Adam away from the ceremony, she spotted them — standing in front of one of the barricades, about a hundred yards away. They must've gotten up early to secure a spot so close to the front.

Her eyes met Adam's, and she swallowed her rising tide of tears. She had to appear stronger than she felt. While she'd wanted to see Adam, if only to know he was okay and that the Watchers hadn't grabbed him up, she wished he didn't have to see her going off to her certain death.

He'd lost so much and had thus far managed to hang on. But to lose his sister might be the straw that finally broke him.

No, don't think about it. Be strong.

Michael stood tall behind Adam, his eyes meeting hers. She couldn't tell for certain, but it looked like he was working to keep his emotions in check as well.

Adam waved.

Ana swallowed, then waved in return.

"Ana!" Adam screamed, lurching forward.

A Watcher moved toward him, stick raised.

"No!" Ana cried out.

Everyone on stage looked at her, then followed Ana's gaze down to her brother, about to incur the wrath of the Watchers.

Michael was fast on his feet. He grabbed Adam, yanking him back before her brother was beaten. He tried to break free from Michael's grasp, but Michael held tight, apologizing to the Watcher repeatedly and begging the officer's mercy.

"His sister is up there, please, please!" Michael yelled above the growing noise of the crowd to the two closest Watchers.

"Go home, Adam!" Ana called out. "Go home!"

Michael pulled him into the crowd, then vanished from sight.

The last thing she saw before she was ushered away

and into the waiting van was two Watchers following Michael and Adam into the crowd. She screamed, trying to draw as much attention as she could toward her and away from her brother, to allow Michael time to get him away before things really got ugly.

Someone screamed in the crowd.

More Watchers moved forward, sticks swinging.

The van door slammed shut as the sound of the rowdy crowd got rowdier.

Ana looked at the other girls staring at her as if she'd incited a riot. She wasn't sure what to do, or say, so she sat back against the rear wall and looked down at the floor, hoping Michael was able to usher Adam away in time.

As Ana sat in the van with the three other girls, silence cloaked the air.

She thought more about the possibility that they might be playing a Special Edition Darwin Games, where the network changed the rules seemingly at random. A Special Game could be shortened to a single day or extended to months. It was anybody's guess, and they might never be told the rules until they needed to know them.

She tried to keep her rising terror in check, not wanting to be seen as an easy target, or too strong and therefore someone to eliminate immediately. It was far better to fly right down the middle and under the radar for as long as she could.

Ana wondered if the additional contestants were a blessing or a curse. More players meant her odds of her winning were slimmer, but it also increased the chances that someone else would be targeted at the Halo when the Games began, meaning she might be able to slip away, as most smart players did, before chaos erupted.

She tried to avoid eye contact while discreetly sizing up her competition. None of the girls were familiar, which wasn't surprising. City 6 was the second-largest of the half-dozen Cities, but social circles behind the Wall were small.

An oversized brunette sat across from her. She looked mid-20s and was large enough to have been Bear's daughter. Beside her was another brunette, tall and skinny, who wore a smile that said she knew more than everyone else in the van added together even though she looked all of fourteen. Last was a raven-haired woman, in her early 20s, sitting beside Ana. A stranger who looked oddly familiar.

Ana wanted to know her story.

"What's going to happen when we stop?" asked the raven-haired girl.

She earned no answer the first time, but her second attempt saw a response when the partition between the driver's cabin and the cargo bay opened and an older man with longish hair stared at the girls through the slit with his shadowy tired eyes. "Haven't you girls ever seen the Games?"

"Of course I have," Raven said. "But everything happens so fast. What are the rules? Why do some people fight and others run?"

The man laughed. "Are you kidding? Sweetie, there are no rules." He shook his head. "You run or you fight, that's up to you. Just don't let those zombie fuckers near you; they're faster than they seem onscreen."

Ana swallowed. "How do *you* stay alive?" She stared past the partition and into the man's eyes. "I've never heard of TV crew members getting killed."

"We're producers for the show. They give us body armor when we're in the Barrens." He patted the thick, layered body armor that made him look like the dog trainers Ana had seen when her father took her to visit the K-9 Unit, back when she was ten. "Mostly, you learn to stay away, and to never miss a shot when you need to take it."

"You kill the zombies?" Raven said.

"We're not supposed to, and we usually don't. But sometimes it's them or us, and we do what we gotta. All producers have a mandatory two-week training, twice per year. I've been taking mine for twenty years, so I'm used to the ugly fuckers. But I assume none of you have ever seen a zombie up close?"

No one answered.

The old man shrugged, then with no warning or ceremony, the partition closed and the back of the van was draped in a fresh pall of silence. Ana circled her worst fears for another hour or so, waiting until they finally arrived at the Halo.

The giant circular clearing was usually littered with so many fallen bodies, and so frequently, the zombies had learned to hang around, like birds at a feeder, waiting for the next drop-off of fresh meat. One Game didn't even last an hour because after the initial scrum for weapons, there were only three people left — with forty zombies to manage.

Ana shivered, wondering how long she would last.

Would she even get a chance to reach the woods?

Or would someone in the van, or perhaps someone from one of the other Cities, target her immediately?

Being a girl in the Games was doubly worse. You not only had to worry about murderers and zombies, but sometimes the male contestants would rape the females. Ana hoped this was an all-female edition of the Games.

The van stopped, and with barely a pause, the man from the other side of the partition — or perhaps the driver, it was hard to tell since they were both now wearing helmets and fully armored — threw open the door and yelled, "Get out, and when you hear the cannon fire, get to running if you want to keep living!"

One of the men grabbed Ana by her arms and pulled her roughly from the van.

The City 6 van was the first to arrive, parking a hundred yards from the tree line that marked the Halo's perimeter.

Other vans were pulling up to join them.

The man yelled again, pointing to a shed about two hundred yards off, in the center of the clearing, stacked with boxes of supplies and a small swarm of zombies in front, feasting on the raw meat set there to bait them. "Head over there if you want weapons and food" — he jabbed his finger toward the forest — "or over there if you wanna live a few minutes longer. Choose the latter, you'll need to forage and hope you find something. You'll either need to get lucky and find a fallen contestant's weapon or craft your own."

He spun from the girls, then turned his eyes to a small glass card in his palm and swiped his fingers across the top. A pair of orbs flew from on top of the van, then hovered high in the sky above them.

There were perhaps two dozen zombies scattered across the Halo, with most lingering around the meat and all the supplies, with many more pouring into the Halo from the forest to the right.

Five other vans were letting contestants out beside them, forming a line in front of the field, surrounded on all sides by thick woodlands. To her disappointment, Ana saw that the other groups varied in sex and age.

As the contestants eyeballed one another, and some even started shouting threats, trying to psyche out their opponents, another van pulled up and drew the crowd's attention.

Z2134

What's going on here? Another surprise for the Games?

Ana wondered what the producers had in store. Would they open the door and free a group of already-armed contestants, like they had a few years back?

She braced herself as the passenger-side door opened and a producer jumped from the van, his helmet already on. He ran up to the two producers who'd driven Ana and her fellow City Sixers, moving his arms wildly through the air. They must have been talking on radios inside their helmets, which no one else could hear.

Whatever was happening, the excitement was thick.

Once the new producer finished speaking, one of the men who had brought them to the Halo approached their group.

"We've got a last-minute addition from City 6. Any of you wanna go back?"

The youngest ran forward, crying, "Please, can I please go back?"

"Hop in." The man jerked his thumb toward the back of the van.

The girl climbed inside. The producers closed her door and then got into the front.

All eyes turned to the new van as the producer opened the doors, then reached inside for the replacement player.

Ana gasped as she saw Liam shoved to the ground.

"Good luck, anarchist," said the man behind him.

Ana met Liam's eyes.

She hadn't seen him since they got into the argument and he told her to get out of the apartment. She wondered if his anger was enough to paint a bullseye on her back.

Or did it make more sense to stick together and fight as a unit?

They looked around the clearing, taking in the other

clusters from each of the Cities as the vans kicked dirt into the air at their departure.

Six groups, four people each.

And an army of zombies surrounding the weapons stash.

Though it seemed so close to the forest on TV, now the stash seemed a quarter mile away, at least.

A long way to run in the snow.

Ana eyed the weapons in the center of the field, then Liam.

In the distance, a cannon fired.

And the Darwin Games began.

TEN

Anastasia Lovecraft

Run, girl, run!

The cannon blast erupted in the distance, sending the players onto the field known as the Halo. Ana was thrown to the ground in the chaos, back first, as the girls she'd come with rushed toward the center of the Halo.

Ana cried out, throwing her arms over her face instinctively, but she needn't have done so, as the City Sixers were already gone.

She looked up to the cloudy gray sky, watching the orbs zipping by overhead, seeming to track individual players for the audience back home's viewing pleasure.

She rolled over, burying her elbows in the cold snow, and looked up to see as half of the twenty-three other players immediately raced toward the shed where supplies and weapons waited in the Halo's heart for anyone brave enough to battle their way through the zombies.

This was the Opening Rush, and usually one of the bloodiest parts of the competition. It was considered one of the true "can't miss" moments of each Game. Even as a viewer, she couldn't imagine that so many people were willing to risk their lives in order to reach the weapons first. Not only would they have to fight past the zombies, but they'd also have to contend with any other player who got ahold of a weapon. It was suicide.

In person, actually on the field, it seemed an even more suicidal feat.

There were at least fifty zombies around the center of the field. And as she watched, a zombie claimed its first victim, a chubby guy who should have headed to the woods with the remaining players who split up, some heading to the right of the Halo and some to the left, charging into the woods.

That's what the smart players did. That's what the weakest players, who wouldn't survive a scrum in the center of the field, did. That's what Ana needed to do — head for the woods. She got to her knees and then to her feet, and turned, desperate to find where Liam had gone off to, wondering if he'd left her alone when she got hurled to the ground.

She turned to her right and was surprised to find him standing just inches away.

She flinched, wincing, almost expecting him to attack her right there in the opening seconds of the Games.

She thought of one of the show's many taglines: *Keep your friends distant, and your enemies close.*

Their eyes met, and Ana felt foolish, even a bit guilty when she saw the deep concern in his eyes.

Darwin was a battle to the death, and that meant Liam would eventually have to kill her if he wanted to live himself. But for now, his eyes made a vow for her safety.

"What are you doing here?" Ana asked through panicked breath.

"Same as you!"

"You were arrested?"

"Yeah. I'll go get us some weapons." He pointed toward the Halo's center, where a handful of players were tearing through the weapon crates.

A gunshot thundered from the same area.

Wonder if it's someone shooting a zombie, or another player?

Liam must have had the same thought. He wrapped his body like armor to shield Ana, then spun his head around the Halo. "It's a player taking down a zombie. They haven't turned on one another. Yet.

"I'm going to get weapons now. I need you to run. I'll catch up, okay?"

Liam had already sat too long with her. She knew if he didn't get to the weapons soon, he wouldn't have a chance in hell of getting one from the stash. She wanted to argue with him, plead with him to go into the woods with her. They could get weapons later, somewhere along the way.

"Wait, Li—" Ana said, but before she reached her second syllable, Liam had already released his grip and launched himself toward the chaos. She stood frozen until a second gunshot sent her spinning around and racing toward the forest.

She wanted to vomit at the source of the second shot — a middle-aged bald man standing over the dropped body of the heavyset twenty-something brunette she'd ridden in with, her head busted open like a melon dropped on the floor.

Ana looked up to search for any sign of the people she had seen going right. She wanted to make sure she didn't follow them too closely into the forest. Nothing would be worse than running into them and getting killed five minutes into the Games.

Not seeing them, she ran toward the trees as fast as she could, ignoring the sounds of gunshots and the screams of players and zombies alike.

She reached the woods, her heart pounding as she scanned for signs of others, not daring to stop or even slow until she felt as if her lungs were on fire. A lifetime of nowhere to run behind the Walls of City 6 turned a few hundred yards into a gauntlet she was not remotely in shape for.

Ana made it a hundred or so yards into the forest before she halted in her tracks to recover her breath. She leaned forward, hands on knees, looking around. The snow gave way here and there to bits of brown earth, branches, rocks, and undergrowth, with the trees spaced closer and the canopy casting the woods into cold shadows.

On the plus side, there were plenty of places for her to hide while she waited for Liam to return. On the negative, that meant more places for the other players to hide, and perhaps attack her from.

As if worrying about the other players wasn't bad enough, the woods were always crawling with zombies. A lifetime of previous games strobed through her mind as she pictured one gory surprise kill after another. The network loved gruesome finishes, routinely airing specials such as *The Top 10 Most Surprising Kills!* or *Darwin in Action: Dumbest Deaths of The Games* during downtime of the live Games.

Ana didn't want to make any of the highlights shows.

After watching who knew how many seasons of Darwin, she was certain the producers had ways of keeping zombies from the forest and elongating tension. Her father had speculated a few times that he was sure the network had laid out hidden gates, false walls, and other obstacles, which it used to funnel zombies and players to the spots where they most wanted them.

When the games began, most of the nearby zombies were already in the Halo, meaning players were usually safe in the woods until after the initial battle for weapons took place. If everyone died right away, that meant six days without The Games on TV — which wasn't good for network or the viewers starving for entertainment and death.

Still, the most consistent thing about the Games was their inconsistency.

Ana looked around, trying to decide where to go. She could head back toward the Halo, but that seemed like the stupid option considering the speed at which she had run from that direction. She could climb a tree and hide, which might keep her safe while waiting for Liam, or keep going just in case he didn't make it out of the Halo with weapons.

The longer she stayed put, the more danger Ana was putting herself in. Soon enough, other players or zombies would start heading into the woods. And without a weapon, she was as good as dead.

Paralyzed by indecision, Ana begged her body to move.

Most of her wanted to wait for Liam. He said he'd find her and she believed him, but it wasn't like they'd coordinated a plan. The Barrens were sprawling, and sudden danger could send anyone running in any direction, and at any time.

A thought bubbled to the surface, which made it even harder for her to decide.

What if Liam was lying? Maybe he just told me to go so he wouldn't have to be saddled with me. Maybe he's already off on the other side of the Halo.

The Games were about survival of the fittest, with exactly one winner. People formed alliances, especially in the beginning, but all alliances ended in bloodshed. Maybe he was doing her a small mercy by leaving her now, before it was too hard.

Run.

Forget about Liam.
Cut the cord and run, girl.
NOW!

Her mind flashed back to hiding under the floorboards in the church as the Watchers stormed in and murdered a woman and child. How Liam had held his hand over her mouth to keep her safe.

If he was risking his life to get weapons, she owed it to him to wait like she said she would. *FUCK!*

Ana shook her head, feeling stupid, as she ignored her first instincts and began to trace her path back toward the Halo.

He's not gonna be there.
He's probably gone.
Or dead.

Ana ignored her inner voice and pushed herself forward until she reached the edge of the woods, staying hidden behind a cluster of bushes, as she peeked out at the Halo.

The shed at the center was on fire, smoke pouring from it and trailing into the sky. She could make out several players surrounding the shed and fighting off zombies, of which there were even more than when the cannon fired. There were at least thirty surrounding the players, not including the twenty or so lying dead in the snow.

By Ana's count, there were only three player casualties so far, and Liam wasn't among them. But she also didn't see him among the survivors, though there were some people on the other side of the fire that weren't visible from her angle.

Ana scanned the field, spying a heavyset man swinging a two-handed sword at four zombies who were backing him toward the woods. He made several wide-arcing swings amid his retreat.

After a half-dozen steps, the man suddenly roared, then charged the swarm, bringing the edge of his blade crashing down into the nearest zombie's head, raining blood like a bucket of dark-red paint over the others. Then with a second bellow, he swung the sword in a wider arc, shearing a pair of zombie heads from their shoulders before pulling the blade back, then plunging it deep into the fourth zombie's chest like a knife into pie.

The final creature twitched on the ground as the heavyset man thrust the blade back into its body. Ana stared in horror and a sort of admiration, wondering how the man had grown so skilled with a sword.

And then she saw something the man had not — a small red-haired girl, who couldn't have been an hour older than twelve, the earliest age allowed into the Darwin Games, racing from the woods toward him. She held a wooden board overhead as she ran. The man must've heard her because he turned back, but too late.

The girl swung, and her board smacked into the man's head, then stuck there as the man fell face first into the snow, wounded but not yet dead.

The girl ran to grab the man's sword, but it must've been too heavy because she dropped it, then went back and started yanking the board from his head. It must have had nails in it.

She finally yanked the board free and began bashing the man until he finally stopped moving. She looked around and froze for a moment when it seemed like she was staring right at Ana.

Ana's heart leaped into her throat, suddenly afraid the girl would come after her next. But instead, she scurried off from whence she'd come, board in hand.

No matter how many times Ana had seen the brutality on live TV, nothing prepared her for the in-person gore, or such a young person unleashing it. She stared at the crimson-soaked corpse, stunned.

Just beyond the burning shed, Ana spotted a handful of players working together to stave off a sea of approaching zombies streaming in from the north end of the woods. It looked like there were as many as forty, the entire swarm seeming to move with more speed than normal, though she had no idea if they were actually faster, or if it was the difference between living it and seeing similar events playing out onscreen.

Ana wasn't sure if the rest of the players were among the dead, had taken off into the woods, or what, but it seemed like these were the last humans on the Halo. She squinted to see past the flames and billowing smoke.

She gasped at Liam's long hair whipping back and forth as he came into view, swinging a machete with abandon. Seeing him fight for his life, with a machete, no less, made Ana think of her father, flooding her with an aching guilt she couldn't afford.

Liam cut four zombies to nothing in twice as many seconds. Helping him was a large, black-bearded man swinging an oversized mallet into one of the zombie's skulls, sending it to a twitching heap on the ground.

A horn brayed in the distance, and though she'd heard the horn countless times before, it still filled her with icy panic.

The Fire Wall!

Ana stood frozen, not knowing what to do next. She'd completely forgotten about the Fire Wall.

Between ten and fifteen minutes into each game, a massive wall of fire erupted through a seam in the earth. The seam, which was made of a six-foot-wide metal pipe, ran north and south for miles in both directions, across the Halo and through a charred clearing in the woods. The surrounding snow was already melting, and Ana watched as the thaw created a dark line that split the Halo into halves.

From her angle, it seemed as if Liam's group was practically on top of the seam. They would have to pick a side — right or left, east or west — and get there immediately.

Ana was on the right side of the seam by a hundred yards, at least.

The Fire Wall was meant to divide players early on. She couldn't risk being on the wrong side of the seam once it came on. The Wall lasted for at least a full day, and if she wasn't on the same side as Liam, she might never see him again.

She'd have to get closer, and quickly, in order to determine what side of the seam Liam and his group were on. She was too far away to tell with certainty. But she'd have to risk being seen by the zombies and being too close to the seam once it erupted.

She ran out of the woods, feeling the cold air burn her lungs.

Racing into the Halo, she saw that Liam and his group had killed all but ten or so zombies. They were, however, down to just three people. Liam, Black Beard, and a skinny, curly-haired male with a pistol. They were, to her delight, on the right side of the seam. But they were also perilously close to the seam.

Liam and Black Beard worked in tandem, slicing through the remaining zombies as the third man felled a parade of approaching zombies with nearly perfect precision using only his pistol.

The group kept drifting toward her, now fifty yards away, close enough to see her, if any of them bothered to look toward her.

She stopped, not daring to go any closer and risk being

seen by the zombies. Once they'd killed all but four of the monsters that had yet to reach them, Ana waved her hands, trying to draw Liam's attention.

The horn's second blast warned of thirty seconds to go before the Fire Wall burst upward from the seam.

Suddenly, the skinny man with the gun turned the pistol at Black Beard and Liam, who were looking away from him, at the oncoming zombies.

Liam was in the lead, closest to the zombies, with Black Beard just behind him, holding his mallet, preparing for another round of deadly swings, both oblivious that their partner was about to betray them.

"Liam!" Ana screamed, earning the attention of all three men, along with several of the surrounding zombies.

The moment froze, and several things happened at once.

The skinny man fired point-blank at the back of Black Beard's head, sending the big man to the ground in an instant.

At the same time, Liam had spotted Ana and was frozen as their eyes locked onto each other. He opened his mouth and screamed at her, waving her toward the forest as the zombies began to run after her.

Oh God!

The skinny guy turned his gun on Liam, who was still looking at Ana and waving her away. She wondered if Liam hadn't noticed him murdering Black Beard. Maybe he'd heard the shot but figured the man was still helping them.

Ana tried to scream and warn him.

But as the enemy took aim, Liam surprised both the gunman and Ana by swinging his machete without looking.

The blind swing sliced through the man's gun hand,

lopping it off at the wrist in a swoop and sending his hand with the gun sailing through the air and down to a patch of charred earth where the snow had already melted away.

He screamed, his left hand clutching the bloody fountain spraying from his stump.

Liam thrust his blade through the man's chest, then yanked it back out, grabbed the gun from the man's dead hand, and looked up at Ana.

The horn screamed again as the four zombies raced toward her, now fifty feet away.

Liam fired twice at them but missed both times.

No way he could kill all four zombies before they reached her; there wasn't time. The undead monsters rarely fell from a single bullet unless you hit them in the head. Even if he had more than a few scant seconds, there was an excellent chance he'd wind up shooting her instead.

The zombies were a dozen yards away, and Ana was again frozen with fear.

The horn brayed a final time — five seconds until the Fire Wall ignited.

Ana looked down. She was practically on top of the seam and would be fried in moments if she didn't move one way or another.

To the right were the zombies, fast approaching.

To the left and all those endless miles of forest.

Liam was twenty yards ahead, racing toward her and firing shots as he ran. She moved without thinking — racing across the line, glancing back long enough to see that three of the four zombies were following, but still on the other side of the seam.

She closed her eyes and pushed herself to run even faster, hoping she had managed to lure the zombies into the path of the coming fire.

Then the line bisecting the field erupted in a wall of

ungodly heat behind her, hissing loudly, charring the debris that crossed the seam. Something nearby exploded so loudly, she thought for a moment that the detonation was closer than it was.

Ana dared to look back and stumbled, falling face first into the snow.

She rolled over onto her back to make sure the zombies weren't still on her trail.

Then she saw them, blackened bodies caught within the fiery curtain, screaming as they died again. But one of them refused to perish, stumbling out from the screaming blaze, still on fire, its arms reaching out and waving madly as it shambled toward her.

Ana forced herself to stand and run toward the woods as the burning monster gave chase. But before she'd made it twenty feet, she heard the creature hit the ground, surrendering its charred remains to an inevitable fate.

Ana stopped in her tracks and turned back, desperately scanning along the Fire Wall for any sign of Liam.

A lump hardened in her throat.

Oh God, what if he was caught in the flames?

Ana swallowed, feeling sick to her stomach when she spotted a dark shape in the fire, a body.

Oh God! Liam!

Then she heard a scream above the fire. "Ana!"

"Liam!" she screamed back, looking up and down the flaming wall for him.

"Are you okay?"

"Yeah, they're dead!" Ana shouted over the loud flames.

"Face the fire and look to your right! Are you?"

"Yes! Why?"

"That's south. Stay in the woods and head south. I'll find you where the fire ends!"

"Okay!" Ana cried, swiping at her stinging eyes.

"Be careful! I'm going now, moving away from the fire. We won't be able to hear each other again!"

"Okay!" Ana screamed. "I'll meet you where the fire ends!"

She waited for a reply.

But none came.

After ten seconds, she retreated into the forest, glad to know Liam was alive and looking to help, however temporary that assistance might be.

Trudging deeper into the woods, Ana tried to ignore the constant buzz from the network orb, hovering above and broadcasting her every move.

ELEVEN

Adam Lovecraft

THE TV HALL inside Chimney Rock erupted as the horn signaled the coming Fire Wall.

Adam's emotions were balled up and thick in his throat, trapped among fear, terror, and numb humiliation as the many spectators inside the orphanage's TV hall had one eye on the spectacle onscreen and the other on his reactions. Some pretended they weren't watching him, but most didn't bother to hide it.

He refused to give them anything more than the blank mask he gave the TV while chewing on his inner cheek and digging his nails into his leg.

Even managing to hide most of his emotions, it wasn't like they weren't tearing him up inside.

Ana was barely gone, and Adam would never see her again. Every time the camera closed in on her face, he saw the fear and terror, and it tore right through him.

His new friends were all around him. Tommy, Morgan, and Daniel, each dividing his attention between the oversized monitors blanketing the long length of the wall and trying to talk to him. Fortunately, they were also talking to some girls in the front of the hall, which kept most of their attention.

Adam kept his face blank, showing them nothing as one side of each monitor had Ana running from the fire, with a near-frantic Liam running behind her on the other.

Ana cleared the Fire Wall as Liam's feed went temporarily dark, heightening tension as the producers liked to do. Ana had just barely escaped, momentarily safe as flames swallowed the three zombies. Then one of the monsters emerged from the Fire Wall, consumed by flames but still walking.

Adam sank into his chair, glad he was near the back corner of the room. He sighed, still trying not to cry as he watched his sister narrowly escape both the zombie and fire.

Once Ana was safe, the surrounding whispers grew louder. Adam could see several kids staring from the far sides of his peripheral vision and felt the bristles of others watching.

Being observed was worse than being invisible — how he had spent his time at Chimney Rock, and most of life, thus far. When he and Ana first arrived at the orphanage, Adam was happy to wear his usual cloak of invisibility. The last thing he wanted was what he'd always had — people laughing at his expense, ridiculing him and his "weirdness." He was content to attend class, spend time with his sister, and keep to himself.

But now with his entire family gone, he felt truly alone for the first time in his life. And he wished that he'd been wired differently so he would have an easier time making friends.

He thought of his father and how easy it always seemed for him to speak to strangers, even when he didn't want to.

Z2134

Adam watched the screen as it shifted to show a girl with long black hair climbing out onto the wide branch of a tree, then lying flat against the bark as a couple of zombies passed below.

I hope they see her.

Come on, stupid zombies, look up.

He felt terrible immediately.

While others openly rooted for the zombies against players they didn't like, or hadn't bet on, Adam had never wished for a player to die. But every death that wasn't his sister put her closer to City 7.

He wondered what the odds were that Ana could actually make it. He smiled, imaging both his sister and father living in City 7, happy and free. But even in that scenario he would still be stuck in City 6. His smile faltered.

If Ana somehow wins, maybe I should get myself arrested. Maybe all three of us could live in City 7, happily ever after.

He watched as his new friends laughed with the girls. He thought about his father again. Three years ago, Adam first realized just how different he was from other kids. He suspected that his parents had always known. It would explain the frequent whispers when people thought he wasn't paying attention. But he'd never really thought much about it until the kids started picking on him more harshly, calling him names like freak, Quarter Boy, and stupid.

It was three years ago when he nearly broke down in tears and asked his father why it was so hard for him to make friends.

"Wanna know the secret?" his dad had asked.

Adam nodded.

"Double I and F," he'd said with a smile. "Remember that and you'll always be fine."

"What does that mean?" Adam had asked.

"It means be interesting, interested, friendly, and funny. That's the formula for making friends. It's never been more complicated than that."

Still trying not to cry, Adam had said, "How can I be interesting if I'm actually boring?"

Adam's dad had shaken his head. "No one's boring unless they think they are. So maybe it's time you stopped sentencing yourself to the lie." His father had then smiled and winked, like he always did when trying to cheer up his son. "Being interesting doesn't mean making stuff up in the hopes that people will like you. It means framing who you are in a riveting light. You know all those books you love to read?"

Adam had nodded.

"Well, those books should give you an endless list of things to talk about. People love stories, Adam, and they always will. Keep reading and you'll never run out. Beyond the stories," his father had put his arm around Adam's shoulder, "lies the other side of interesting, and that's being interested. As much as people love stories, every beating heart wants another ear to listen to theirs. Treasure their words like they are your own and respond to what they're *truly* trying to say, and not just that surface layer. Any time you're talking about things that are interesting to someone else, you're instantly more interesting to them."

"What about friendly and funny?"

His dad had laughed. "You're already friendly." He'd punched Adam lightly on the shoulder. "Problem is, you're too shy. There's nothing wrong with that, really, but it does make it harder in the making-friends department. If you don't have the courage to say *hi* first, that's fine, you might grow out of that. Even if you don't, you can always smile with your eyes. But no matter what, you have to genuinely enjoy meeting new people, or they'll see through your smile."

Before Adam could push the next protest from his mouth, his dad had said, "Being funny doesn't mean being a comedian, it means being able to recognize life's regular humor. And if you don't think something's funny, at least try to see why someone would. The more you see humor in your world, the easier it is to draw it into conversation." He'd tightened his embrace. "Truth is, son, making friends is about being yourself more than anything else."

After a few months in Chimney Rock, Adam finally listened to his words and was shocked when he found that his father was right. For the first time ever, Adam had friends. Tommy, Morgan, and Daniel all seemed to genuinely like him. They thought he was neat, seemed interested in what he had to say, and laughed at his jokes. Well, most of them.

Still, even with new friends around, nothing replaced the familiar comfort of the people who really knew you — *family*.

"Holy crap!" Tommy cried. "Check out the black-haired bitch!"

"Don't call her a bitch," Daniel said. "You'll get us in trouble."

Everyone turned to the screen as it showed a slow-mo replay of the girl with black hair dropping from the tree and launching her heel hard into a lone zombie's chest. The zombie hit the ground, screaming as the girl smashed her heel repeatedly into his face.

Morgan leaned into Adam's ear and whispered, "Hey, Adam, let's hit the mess hall. There's something we wanna show you."

Adam shook his head, then turned to Morgan and met

his blue eyes. "I don't want to leave the hall. I need to see what happens with Ana."

"You kidding, man?" Morgan ran his hand through his curly blond ringlets. "They're going to rebroadcast this shit a billion fucking times!" A whispered hiss, low enough that none of them could possibly get in trouble for his dirty mouth.

Daniel said, "Nothing ever happens the first day, not after the Halo, anyway, and we'll only be gone for a minute or two."

Tommy's hand fell on Adam's back. "Come on. You don't want us to do this without you. Trust me, it might even make you forget about what's happening to your sister on the outside."

After another two minutes of pressure, and the creeping fear that he might lose his only friends in the world, Adam finally agreed, then stood and followed Tommy, Morgan, and Daniel out of the TV hall, then down the long hallway toward the mess hall, which they reached in less than a minute — but walked right by as if they were never aiming for it at all.

"I thought we were going to the mess hall," Adam said.

"Nah," Daniel shook his head, "we're going somewhere cooler."

Morgan grinned. "Patience. We'll get there."

Adam swallowed, suddenly nervous and wishing he were somewhere else. They walked for another minute until they reached a section of the hallway that was farther than Adam had ever been. The area was roped off for repairs, with a black plastic curtain hanging behind the rope, running from ceiling to floor. A sheet of parchment was stapled to the black plastic with the single word *REPAIR* written in all caps.

"Where are we?" Adam wondered out loud.

"Don't worry about it." Morgan parted the plastic, then ducked behind it.

Tommy followed, then Daniel, with Adam taking tentative steps at the rear.

"We're not supposed to be here," Adam said, shaking his head as he stepped past the curtain and then through an open doorway.

Morgan laughed first, but Tommy and Daniel were both only one breath behind.

"Don't be such a bitty baby bitch," said Morgan through a cackle of laughter.

"Yeah," Daniel agreed. "Live a little. You can't obey all the rules all the time."

Adam kept quiet as they crept through a darkened room, filled with a ton of heavy-looking furniture, all of it draped in filthy, dust-covered sheets. Adam wasn't sure whose room it had been, but it seemed as if it had been there forever, and it had been just as long since anyone had occupied the place. Adam wasn't even aware that there were living areas on the same floor as the TV hall.

They crossed the shadow-filled obstacle course and found a quiet stairwell on the farthest side. Adam hedged, falling a step back where the dark shadows grew darker.

Morgan laughed, louder than before. "Peas or grapefruits?"

"What?" Adam twisted his grin, trying to figure out what Morgan was trying to say without looking scared.

"Peas or grapefruits?"

"What?" Adam repeated, as he slowly realized what he *thought* they were saying. He took a second to chew the probability in his head, since being wrong meant laughing, and always at his expense.

What if they're not talking about my testicles?

"Grapefruits," Adam said.

Morgan grinned. "All right, then, let's go." Then he waved his arm forward and stepped into the dark stairwell.

Daniel and Tommy followed, with Adam another three steps behind.

A new surprise waited one floor below — another room just like the one above.

Jayla was sitting on the middle cushion of an old couch, with her legs crossed, and wearing the cutest smile Adam had ever seen.

Jayla was the prettiest girl in Chimney Rock. With olive skin, dark chestnut hair, and golden eyes, her look was unique and intoxicating. Adam could hardly stand to look at her.

He noticed Jayla for the first time on his second day at the orphanage. She smiled at him while waiting for her spoonful of lunchtime slop in the mess hall. Judging by the width of that smile, she'd been living at Chimney long enough to maybe not realize how sour the food tasted.

Jayla grinned at the four boys. As she opened her mouth to maybe say hello, a trio of giggles surfaced, followed by three girls, emerging from an adjoining area, maybe a bathroom.

"Hey Tommy," said one of the girls. Adam recognized all three as friends of Jayla's, though he didn't know any of their names.

Adam smelled the smoke before he saw the cigarette, curling into his nostrils and reminding him of the Dark Quarter — the only place kids were said to openly smoke, not that Adam had ever been there.

The middle girl blew a plume from her mouth, then held the cigarette in front of her. Tommy reached to take it, but she quickly drew it back, shaking her head. "It's for him," she said, then nodded to Adam.

Adam shook his head. "No thanks."

Adam's friends all laughed. The three girls joined them. He was used to boys laughing at him, but the girls cut even deeper and made him feel even dumber.

Jayla, to her credit, was silent.

The middle girl shrugged, then handed the cigarette to Tommy and turned to Adam. "Pretty cool, your sister being in the Games. Did you get to watch the opening?"

The girl's question was innocent enough, but a current of rage raced through Adam anyway. He yelled before he could stop himself. "You wouldn't think it was a fucking game if it was *your sister* running from zombies!"

The middle girl shrank back, her eyes wide and startled.

Tommy laughed.

Daniel said, "Whoa, did you hear Bilbo? He said *fucking*."

The guys laughed, though it seemed to be a more genuine laughter, instead of the kind that mocked him.

Adam, who often talked of *The Hobbit*, had never said the F word anywhere outside of his own head. He swallowed, shocked by how good it felt, first on his tongue, and then as it left his lips.

"Chill." Morgan set his hand on Adam's still-shaking shoulder. "It's cool. Melissa didn't mean anything by it."

"She's just trying to make conversation," Jayla said, making Adam feel like he'd been reprimanded by the one person whose opinion he cared about.

"I know," Adam said, then stuttered, knowing he couldn't take it back, but having nothing else to say.

"It's my fault," Jayla replied. "I asked Morgan and the boys to bring you down here."

Adam was stunned into silence. "What? Why?"

Morgan and Tommy each finished their turn with the

cigarette. Daniel drew a final drag, then passed it back to the girl standing to Melissa's right.

Jayla smiled. "Because it can't be easy to have both your parents gone, then wind up in here, only to have your sister sent outside the Wall. We all have our stories, but your story seems worse than most." She shrugged. "I thought it might cheer you up."

Adam was trying to decide what he should say. He was surprised that Jayla had even thought about him, let alone considered his hardships.

The girl who had taken the cigarette from Daniel dropped the butt on the floor, snuffed it out with her heel like a scurrying roach, then bent to the floor, scooped up the evidence, dropped it into her pocket, and turned to Jayla. "Let's show him."

"Yeah," Morgan agreed. "Let's get out of here."

Adam swallowed, terrified, wondering what it was they wanted to show him.

"Okay," Jayla said, swinging her feet to the floor, then standing. She held out her hand and the girl to Melissa's left filled it with one of the pillowcases.

"Let's fly." Morgan slapped Adam on the back again, then stepped in front to take the lead. Tommy and Daniel both edged their way by, following the four girls into the shadows, with Adam just behind, trying not to appear as scared as he was.

They left the room and walked a long hallway without a single light, so dark it may as well have been outside the Walls on a moonless midnight, their footsteps echoing back to them. Adam found it odd that none of the hallway seemed familiar. If it was the floor beneath the TV hall, it *should have* been one of the teaching levels, not some dusty living quarters.

But the walls here weren't black, they were a faded

brown stone. It seemed like an entirely different building — a secret wing in an ancient mansion or castle from one of his books.

"What is this?" Adam whispered. "These aren't the classrooms."

"It's one of the secret floors," Jayla whispered back. "There's a few of them between the other floors, places the elevators don't stop."

"Wow! How did you know this was here?"

"When you grow up in the Rock, you hear things," Jayla said, smiling.

Somewhere, behind one of the many doors in the hallway, something made a loud groaning sound.

Adam jumped, startled, and everyone laughed, way too loud. Someone would hear them and they'd get in trouble, but he didn't dare whine — not in front of Jayla.

"Relax." Tommy slapped Adam on his back. "It's just the pipes. Haven't you ever heard the pipes before?"

Adam laughed, feeling foolish.

Jayla caught his eyes and grinned.

They reached the end of the hall and ran into a second set of stairs leading up.

They climbed the narrow stairwell, then opened a black wooden door with faded peeling paint that led to a gleaming, white kitchen.

"I told you we were going to the mess hall," Morgan laughed.

Adam gasped as he stepped into the light. He had never seen the world on the other side of the cafeteria line, but everything in the kitchen seemed shockingly clean and surprisingly new. Everything else in Chimney Rock was ancient and dingy, but the white tile and gleaming aluminum inside the kitchen reminded Adam of the high ceilings and wide-open rooms of his father's office at City Watch.

He swallowed his hesitation and stepped into his bravest voice. "Why are we here?"

"Because," Jayla chirped, "they're about to show the Top 10 Opening Games Moments, and *everyone* goes out to the hall to watch. Starla noticed it about seven Games back."

The girl who must've been Starla — the blonde who had said nothing so far, the one who had been standing to Melissa's left — smiled and gave Adam a tiny wave.

Daniel, Tommy, and Morgan were already in the kitchen's middle, kneeling beside a giant metal cabinet and digging through the second-to-bottom drawer.

"Let's load up," Jayla said, shaking her pillowcase.

Adam joined the huddle and stared down into the drawer, packed high with various-sized white boxes marked *City 6 Rations* over a listing of each box's contents: cereal, crackers, jam, cookies, dried fruits, nuts, puddings of chocolate *and* vanilla, beans, soups, and dried meats.

"Oh my God. There's so much food," Adam whispered.

He salivated, then fell to his knees and started scooping rations into a pillowcase that had fallen into his hand without his even realizing it.

"Not too many," Jayla warned. "We have to be careful. If they notice, we can never come back. Let's move to that one." She pointed to a second stall on the far side of the kitchen.

"Good idea." Morgan pulled a pillowcase from Starla's hand and crossed the kitchen. Halfway there a loud clang rang from behind them.

Adam's heart nearly stopped beating.

"Hey!" a woman shouted into the silence. "Who's in here?"

Without any words, the bottom drawer slammed shut and they ran back the way they'd come. His heart pounded as he followed — at any second they'd run into an adult.

"Hello?" the woman shouted from far behind them.

They reached the door to the stairwell and ran down the stairs, back down the hall, and then into the room where they'd been smoking.

Adam was the last through the door and was surprised to find Jayla waiting for him, a big smile on her face, eyes wide and alive.

She pulled the door closed and locked it.

"Oh my God!" Starla said. "That was soooo close!"

Adam collapsed on the couch, his lungs on fire, adrenaline coursing through him, mixing with fear, exhilaration, and then, to his surprise, laughter, which burst from his mouth almost like a bark.

Everyone turned, looking at him, as shocked as he was by his laughter, and then they all joined him.

Jayla sat next to him on the couch, and their eyes met. "You're pretty cool, Adam."

"Balls like grapefruits!" Morgan shouted, ripping into a box of cookies.

Adam was too excited and nervous to eat. "Shouldn't we get back to the TV hall?"

"We're gonna wait until right before the show is over and they go back to live footage," Tommy said.

"Relax." Jayla put her hand on Adam's. "Everything's gonna be okay."

Adam sat there with his new friends, next to the prettiest girl in the world, happier than he could remember being in a long time. He wished his father could see him.

Dual blades of guilt. Happiness while his sister was fighting for her life, and wondering what his father would think of his thievery.

TWELVE

Jonah Lovecraft

Jonah woke with his head throbbing hard enough to make him wonder whether he'd been out all night or half-dead for a month. His throat was dry, and his mind was a fog thick enough to cut through.

His arms and legs were bound to a chair.

He yanked at the bindings, but they wouldn't give, and pulling was agony on his arms. He blinked several times, trying to move his mind into motion while casting his eyes across the dim room, lit only by an old tube light in the ceiling. He sniffed the air, wrinkling his nose at the musty scent.

How long had he been out? And where the hell had the kids brought him?

The last thing he remembered was them walking toward a tunnel ... then nothing after that.

They must've drugged me with a coma dart or something.

The wavy lines in front of his eyes finally straightened, and Jonah found himself blinking at an ancient-looking poster announcing some sort of high-speed train. As the poster swam into focus, Jonah saw an illustration of a gleaming silver train soaring through a tunnel and out onto a track high above a city. Giant bold type announced:

The Bullit: The Maglev Across America! Tomorrow's Train TODAY! Debuting in the Winter of 2030.

He *was* underground, in the old Maglev station, which had been turned into a subterranean habitat for many banished from City 6. He'd never been to the station and had only heard of it from Duncan, though most people didn't know of its location. The Cities didn't care much about anyone beyond the Wall, but there were no doubt people living in the Barrens that City Watch would love to get its hands on — to question, torture, and exact some ounce of flesh for offenses, real and perceived.

Had the people who'd taken him known he was Underground and that he'd helped get so many people to this very place, he'd be a hero, not a prisoner. But neither the City nor the network had exposed him as an Underground operative. They didn't want to make him a martyr — so they made him a crazed wife killer instead.

To these people he was a disgraced former Watcher, someone they'd hold responsible for their treatment within the Walls of City 6.

Jonah was an enemy without a state.

He twisted his head to the right, gasping in a surprise when his gaze fell onto a man whose shoulders were broad enough to be dangerous, though he was short enough to be considered a dwarf.

"Nice to see you awake," said the dwarf.

Jonah tried to hide his shock. Dwarves were among those forced to live in the Dark Quarter, lives consigned to freak show or sex trade, assuming they weren't murdered at birth as most were. The Cities allowed only one child per couple unless you could afford a ticket for a second.

Parents rarely wanted to "waste" their child credit on anything less than a perfect clone of themselves.

The dwarf seemed to be around thirty-five or so, with long brown hair and a matching scruffy beard. His eyes were ice blue, though weary from experience. He was wearing all black from his coat to his pants to the belt and the sheathed blade hanging from it.

"You're probably wondering how long you've been out." The dwarf's voice was smooth and eloquent, not at all Dark Quarter brusque.

"How long?" Jonah asked.

"A few days. You must've really needed your rest." The dwarf smiled, *almost* friendly. Though Jonah couldn't allow himself to trust his captors just yet.

"What is it you want from me?" Jonah asked after the silence lingered too long.

Jonah had been on the other side of countless interrogations. He recognized an interrogator when he saw one.

"Only answers. Nothing more. You are safe here, and that's how you'll stay, so long as you cooperate. If you don't …" He shrugged, still smiling. "Well, you can imagine."

"Ask away. I've nothing to hide."

There was something disarming about his interrogator not hovering above him, being at eye level, despite the fact that Jonah was seated. As he paced in front of Jonah, seemingly in thought, he felt a chill run through him.

"Very well, then. My name is Father Truth, but you can call me Father."

"Father Truth?" Jonah repeated. "Your parents give you that name?"

"My parents gave me nothing, including my name." He cleared his throat. "So, Watcher, why were you banished?"

Though every other word sounded pleasant, *Watcher* may as well have been *Satan*.

"If you know I'm a Watcher, and that I was banished, then you obviously saw me on the Games. So what are you really asking?"

"I'm gathering background. But if you're ready to dig into the details now, then so be it." He leaned closer to Jonah, inches from his face, then whispered, "*Is it true? You murdered your wife?*"

"No." Jonah shook his head, barely keeping his emotions in check.

Father's even tone neither rose nor fell, but seemed to mine glee from Jonah's discomfort. "Then why would City Watch say you did? Weren't you found guilty?"

Jonah tried not to growl.

"Yes, I was found guilty, but that doesn't mean I *did* anything."

Father Truth looked puzzled. "Are you saying your own people set you up? The *esteemed and honorable* bastions of justice, City Watch, could do something like that?"

Jonah wasn't sure if he could trust Father until he was certain that the man was Underground himself. For all Jonah knew, these were State operatives, looking to get information from Jonah through an elaborate ruse that included child savages and a dwarf. Jonah couldn't give up Duncan or any of the others. The entire resistance could crumble if he did.

"Yes. I was set up."

"And *why* were you set up?"

Jonah couldn't answer Father directly. Same with every other question volleyed across the next fifteen minutes. His history of interrogation probably wasn't too different from Jonah's. He knew when he'd hit a wall. Eventually his smile fell into a frown that tugged at the corners of his mouth, and he shook his head as if disappointed.

"Just so you know, I never prefer doing things this way."

Jonah refused to satisfy the dwarf by asking him which way that was — he'd find out soon enough. Sure enough, Father reached inside his pants pocket, withdrew a slender strip of leather folded neatly in half, then opened the small pouch and pulled out a syringe. He pulled off the cap and stuck the needle into a small glass cylinder, withdrawing a clear liquid into the needle.

Father squeezed the air out of the syringe as he met Jonah's eyes, smiling almost pleasantly, like a kindly doctor visiting his patient.

"What's that?" Jonah hated himself for wanting to know, and even more for asking.

Father smiled wider, as though appreciating his captive's inquisitive nature. "Oh, nothing much. Just a little something to help loosen your lips. I find that this works so much better than the violent ways that your brethren utilize at City Watch."

Father Truth was an inch away. The needle pinched the flesh of his neck before he'd even had time to register what Father was doing. He was either deceptively quick or Jonah's senses had already been dulled by whatever they'd given him while he was passed out.

"You fucker." Jonah glared at the man for violating him in such a way.

"Ah, there's the Watcher charm I remember so well," Father said sarcastically, grabbing a chair to sit in front of Jonah, then twiddling his thumbs as he whistled. "It shan't be long now."

And it wasn't.

Jonah felt instantly better. For the first time since the unthinkable became normal, he was almost ... *happy*.

"Wow, this shit is good," Jonah said, smiling, despite his efforts not to.

Father wasted no time.

"Why were you set up?"

Jonah longed to say nothing, and tried keeping his lips pressed tight to keep his words inside. But they fell out anyway, slightly out of order, and slurred.

"I knew they think," Jonah said, giggling as he heard his words come out wrong.

"Knew what?"

Jonah shook his head, almost violently, wanting to say nothing, though the pleasant tickle inside him swore everything was okay, and that there was no reason to keep things inside any longer. An intoxicating happiness glowed within him, warming him, making him feel as if Father were his oldest and most trusted friend.

"Wow, so this good." Jonah looked at Father, feeling tears of joy well up in his eyes, wanting more of whatever this was.

Father leaned in again, whispering in Jonah's ear. "Tell me the truth. Relieve yourself of this burden. You want to be free from the pain, don't you?"

The idea of being free, of going back to life before all of this, was all he wanted. But it was also a cruel impossibility, no matter what this man promised.

Jonah growled, "People who are you?"

"Who do you *think* we are?" Father sat back in his chair and folded his hands.

"Underground? Agents Watcher trying to get me to speak? I dunno ..." He shook his head, confused.

Jonah settled into a long silence as Father Truth sat, rocking back and forth, arms across his chest.

The dwarf looked like a petulant child, and the image sent Jonah into a sudden fit of hysterics. He tried to stop, worried that Father would think he was laughing at his physical stature, like many City 6 citizens did when passing the broken rabble hunched in the Dark Quarter's gnarled shadows.

Then, as suddenly as the laughter had started, Jonah collapsed into an even deeper fit, guffawing so hard that he started to choke before sucking a gallon of air into his lungs and slowly returning his breathing to its regular rhythm.

Jonah was desperate to apologize but failed when he tried. "You're funny!"

Father Truth smiled, obviously not taking the insult personally. He cleared his throat and said, "Until later, then."

Father stood, spun on the balls of his feet, and headed toward the door.

"Don't leave me alone," Jonah screamed, suddenly insecure and afraid, surprised by the flurry of emotions ripping through his brain. He yelled louder as Father Truth's right hand grabbed the doorknob. "Please, come back. I'm sorry!"

Father Truth turned around, lightly nodded, then returned to stand in front of Jonah, arms still folded, still no taller than a hunched and sitting Jonah.

"Tell me. Were you a good Watcher?"

"What do you mean?" Jonah asked, confused, and happy that he could finally string some coherent words together, despite the drug.

"Watchmen come in all sorts, as you must well know. So, what sort of officer were you, Mr. Lovecraft? Good? Great? Corrupt? Depraved? Tell me."

"Good."

"Do good cops kill their wives?"

Jonah scowled, then tried not to yell. "I didn't kill her."

"Of course you didn't," Father said, placing a small but patronizing hand on the back of Jonah's head before patting him like a dog.

He broke down into the first of several heaving sobs, confused by Father's kind smile and comforting hand.

"What did you give me?" Jonah asked, furious that he had been drugged and suddenly reminded of the night Keller had picked him up with a six-Watcher unit for backup.

Father ignored his question, so Jonah repeated it with a scream, anger replacing his earlier euphoria.

"I already told you, Jonah, I've given you something to loosen your lips. It's harmless, and the side effects, as I'm sure you'll agree, are quite pleasant. Now, you answer a question: Do you remember a man named Charles Egan?"

The name was a far-off, painful memory, but quick to surface once summoned.

Jonah said nothing.

"Allow me to jog your memory." Father uncrossed his arms and put his hands in his pockets, then rocked harder on the balls of his feet, swaying back and forth like a pendulum, inching closer to Jonah. "Ten years ago, I believe this very month, a man named Charles Egan was found guilty of conspiring against the State. He was tried and found guilty, of course, then sent outside the Walls to play in the Darwin Games, which he eventually won. Does any of this ring a bell for you?"

"Of course I remember Egan," Jonah said, smiling as he recalled Keller's disappointed face when Egan won the Final Battle.

"Why are you smiling?" Father asked.

Jonah felt a fresh wave of guilt, barely a flutter, until

enough seconds passed to shatter the dam. A surge of memories tore through him, and Jonah remembered how the man, Charles Egan, had been found guilty — based almost entirely on Jonah's falsified eyewitness account placing him at a known Underground meeting place.

It felt like a million years since Jonah last thought of the man he helped to set up and send outside the Wall. He wondered how he could have excised something so awful from his mind. From nowhere, Jonah felt a second wave of guilt, closer to a tsunami, as the truth of what happened after Egan won found him again.

"So you *do* remember, then?"

Jonah nodded.

"Why did you set Egan up?"

Though he didn't want to confess, Jonah's mouth moved faster than his mind. "I was ordered to."

"By whom?"

"Keller. He said Egan was guilty, but that he'd been too careful. A witness had seen him, but the witness had protected status and couldn't testify."

"Who was the witness?"

"I don't know." Jonah shook his head. "Keller never said. Protected status and all; he didn't have to."

Father stared at Jonah for a long moment before he said, "Are you sure?"

"They didn't tell me," Jonah repeated, his voice cracking, wondering if he would ever be himself again. "I never thought about it, until …"

"Until when?"

"Until after the trial, when Egan stared at me as the Watchers were taking him away. The look in his eyes, the anger as he begged and pleaded with me to tell the truth and say it out loud. He screamed his throat raw, swearing that I was a liar. I could hear him screaming even after they led him from the chambers."

Jonah's voice broke as he started to cry at the memories. "That's when I first thought that maybe something was wrong."

"So, why did you smile when you heard Egan's name?"

He smiled again. "Because I remembered him winning the Games, and how pissed off Keller was."

"And how did *you feel* when he won?"

"I thought *good on him*. He deserved some good news after being set up."

"What else did you feel?"

He wasn't sure what Father was asking. "I'm not sure."

Jonah wanted to say more, but his mind wouldn't make new words.

"Perhaps relief that the man you set up wasn't killed in the Games?" Father suggested.

Jonah nodded.

"And what about Egan's family? What happened to them?"

Jonah shook his head, not wanting to revisit those memories.

"So you know?"

Jonah nodded.

"That's all for now." He held Jonah's gaze for another half-minute before turning away and heading to the door, even as Jonah screamed behind him, begging him not to leave. Jonah wanted to follow, but he was bound, unable to go anywhere.

"Please," he cried, wanting anything other than to be left alone, cursing the drugs that made him so needy. "Please don't leave, Father!"

But his footsteps faded down the hall until the last lonely echo fell into nothing.

Z2134

JONAH WASN'T sure how long it was before he passed out, but euphoria had turned to despair, circling him until he finally did, forcing him to revisit his every sin and all the pain of the past few months.

Who knew how long later, he opened his eyes to a girl standing three feet away, staring at him. He blinked several times to make sure she was really there. It was the girl from the other night, one of the kids who had saved him.

The one with hate in her eyes.

Jonah couldn't speak since his throat was so dry, so he nodded at her hands, filled with bread in one and a cup of something in the other.

She opened her mouth as if to speak, but one of the boys from the night before — the one who had jabbed him — appeared behind her in the doorway before she could speak.

"Hurry up," he said.

The girl turned back, glared, then looked at Jonah.

"Y' hungry?" she asked.

"Yes." He managed to push the single word through the desert in his mouth. "Thirstier, though."

She brought the cup to his lips, and he swallowed a cool gulp of what tasted like the cleanest water he could imagine, and had certainly ever experienced.

She tore a piece from the hunk of bread and shoved it roughly between his lips. He slowly chewed, feeling numb, then swallowed and opened his mouth for more.

The girl tore another piece of bread from the hunk, her hand now shaking as she brought it closer to his face.

The boy seemed like he was standing guard behind the girl. Her eyes could barely meet his. Jonah wondered why she was so frightened.

"I'm not gonna hurt you," he said.

"I know." Her eyes met his, still burning with the same hate. "Tis you who should be worried about me hurtin' ya."

"Why?"

The girl brought the cup of water to Jonah's mouth before he was ready, spilling it past his lips and down his shirt.

"Calla!" the boy called out, shocking the girl to attention.

She yanked the cup back, spilling more water on Jonah, then retreated, leaving the room without another oddly accented word.

The boy wasn't guarding the girl from Jonah, he was guarding Jonah from the girl. He stood there, glaring.

"What was that about?" Jonah asked.

"Her name is Calla Egan. And you're the reason her mother died."

THIRTEEN

Anastasia Lovecraft

TWILIGHT THREATENED darkness as Ana crept through the forest, too scared to slow her pace but too timid to keep from worrying through every other step.

She inched her way south as Liam had directed, following the Fire Wall and trying to remember how long it ran, racking her brain as she replayed the insufferable song of Kirkman's annoyingly chipper voice from any one of the prior games, where he proudly announced its length.

Ana felt a stab of guilt for the many times she had enjoyed watching Darwin, especially the parts with the Fire Wall, which were always especially exciting. The bright blue at the bottom of the seam, where plumes of screaming orange ascended twenty feet into the air. Ana had to admit, the fire was more alluring when watching from the safety of City streets, the comfort of their flat, or even the horrible wall of monitors in Chimney Rock's TV hall.

In person, it was nothing more than a hissing promise of death.

Ana was wondering if the Fire Wall would ever end

when she spotted a swath of shadows in the distance, dark enough to make her certain there wasn't a flame anywhere near it.

She walked faster, nearing the end of the fire and allowing herself to feel suddenly hopeful. She doubled her speed, almost racing toward the end of the seam, running so fast that she nearly crashed into a cluster of zombies swarming between her and the end of the Fire Wall.

She bit her lip hard enough to draw blood but managed to keep the scream inside her mouth. She dropped to her knees, then looked to the cluster, confident that between her speedy drop, the forest's many shadows, and the zombies' near-complete stupidity, she was, and would be, free from their sight so long as she stayed careful.

After a minute of zombie watching, her confidence doubled. Ana rose to her feet and slowly moved to her right, deeper into the woods, to navigate around the zombies. She inched through the darkness one tentative step at a time, careful, scared, and half-certain that every foreign sound was her swan song hummed by a zombie beside her.

Well past the writhing undead, and ready to circle back toward the Fire Wall, Ana was startled into a scream too sudden and fierce to hold inside.

She brushed by a lone zombie standing as still as a tree, almost as if it had been waiting for her to pass.

It growled as she screamed, then thrust its arms out, reaching for her, its fingertips grazing the edge of her arms as it moaned.

Ana somehow slipped away, and ran as fast as she could, racing blindly into the belly of the woods and farther away from the Fire Wall, hoping like hell she wouldn't lose the seam that could lead her back to Liam.

She kept running until the sounds of the monster

disappeared behind her. Just as she nearly settled into the comfort of quiet, she heard more moaning.

It was coming from in front of her, behind her, and to her left.

Shit, shit, shit.

She moved farther from the seam and spotted a cave to her right, the white of its rocky face reflecting a glimmer of moonlight.

No way I'm going in there. Gotta find a way back.

Moans multiplied in number and volume, seeming to come from all four directions, pushing her closer to the cave, even as she desperately searched for anywhere else to go.

Zombies moved among the shadows. There were at least a dozen surrounding her, save for her only path of escape — right into the cave.

She looked around and thought there was a small chance that the zombies had yet to see her. She prayed the cave would offer a safe harbor until the threat had cleared. She hunched over, trying to make herself as small as possible as she quietly ran toward the cave, ducking her head and crawling into its wide-open mouth.

She was inside only a handful of seconds before the whoosh of a network orb followed behind, throwing bright blue light against the black walls. Its light helped to illuminate the cave, while shining a giant spotlight on her to the zombies outside.

The orb would get her killed.

As if to punctuate the threat, Kirkman practically screamed: "And here's City Six's Anastasia Lovecraft, daughter of murderer and winner of our most recent Darwin Games, Jonah Lovecraft, seemingly trapped inside a cave! What *was* she thinking?"

Kirkman filled his delivery with the usual dramatic pause, then:

"What *will* Anastasia do next? Will she display her father's derring-do and inventiveness? Or will she die a vicious death like her poor, dear mother?"

"Shut the hell up!" Ana growled.

A handful of zombies ambled into the cave as Ana fell several steps back, terrified, wondering how deep the cave went and how many minutes — if not seconds — she had before her inevitable death.

Ana kept backing into the depths as the tunnel grew musty and murky and wet all around her. She turned around, staring into the darkness beyond the orb's glow, then took a step forward as the orb floated beside her.

She managed one more step before the floor disappeared beneath her.

Ana screamed, fell flat on her ass, then spiraled down a sliding metal chute, spinning faster and faster, round and round for what seemed like forever before it finally spit her hard onto the ground and into darkness.

Ana tried to stand, rubbing her head with her right hand while massaging her bruised ass with the left. Halfway to her feet, a row of red lights flickered above, then turned brilliant, fully illuminating her long and narrow glass-box prison, the bridge in front of her, and the enormous cavern she'd fallen into.

Two orbs dropped from the darkness, one of them coming closer to her and the other moving ahead of her into the darkness.

The box was placed on one end of a long and narrow bridge. A second light clicked on at the far side of the expanse, where the second orb had gone, about 200 yards away, bleeding crimson light on a second glass box. Inside the box stood a young man, whom she saw on the orb's monitor, no more than a few years older than her, wearing the blue coveralls they wore in City 3.

The guy on the other side looked like one of her old friends, Barnum, enough to make her uncomfortable. She swallowed the thought as a third row of lights lit a wide, round platform in the middle of the bridge. The center of the platform had a wide pedestal with a big red button atop it. A short sword leaned against the pedestal, glowing red from the glimmering light above.

Oh God, not the King of the Bridge.

She peered down as bright white lights flared to life beneath the bridge, and immediately wished she hadn't.

One hundred feet below them was the Pit, well-stocked with vicious mutant boars, many of which were said to weigh more than six hundred pounds. Even through the glass box, Ana could hear the boars grunting, waiting to feed.

She remembered cheering as Jeffrey Ramirez was torn to tatters, after his expulsion from City 6 following his verdict of guilty for six counts of rape. The memory made her shiver. Ana hoped that if she lost her balance, the fall would kill her before the boars got the chance.

The orb continued to hover beside her.

"That's right, folks, it's the King of the Bridge Challenge! What are the odds that two players would trigger the trapdoors so close together? How fortunate they are that they didn't have to wait for the other player!"

Kirkman read the rules, which he probably knew by heart. "The rules are simple, but the challenge is anything but. In the center of the bridge is a platform that is actually an elevator to the surface. Whoever reaches the platform first gets the sword, which they'll need to defend the platform once they press the button. Because in the King of the Bridge Challenge, there can be only one king! But be careful, contestants, because the bridge is narrow, and the fall is steep. And then, of course, there are the boars!"

Kirkman paused as a third orb's camera zoomed in up close to a particularly ugly boar with sharp, disfigured fangs. She heard the sound of an audience somewhere roaring in applause, which made her stomach lurch and roll.

"Anastasia Lovecraft, are you ready?"

Ana said nothing, but Kirkman laughed as if she'd cracked a joke.

"Like father, like daughter; not very talkative, eh? Well, let's ask our other player, Cody Samuelson, playing for City 3.

"Cody Samuelson, are *yooouuuuu* ready?"

The orb's screen lit with the image of the boy who resembled Barnum. Scrawny, with curly brown hair, just like her old friend. Ana swallowed, wondering if it would be harder to eliminate someone who looked like a friend than it would be to kill a stranger.

The boy who wasn't Barnum said nothing, so Kirkman loudly repeated: "Cody Samuelson, are *yooouuuuu* ready to kill?"

His face twisted into an angry scowl. "Death to the murderer's daughter!" He raised his fist as if in mock tribute to the "To Jonah" Ana saw all too often while her father was playing the Games.

She would have liked another minute, or even thirty seconds, to assess her situation, but both boxes raised into the rocks above as the lights burned brighter and the sound of an uproariously cheering audience filled the cavern, almost in sync with the screeching and squealing from the monstrous boars below.

"Run!" Kirkman shouted.

Ana and Cody took off at the same time, tearing from

their glass boxes, then moving as fast as they dared along the narrow bridge. Ana kept telling herself not to look down past her feet on the narrow bridge, knowing that if she allowed her focus to shift to the beasts below, it would undo her.

Kirkman kept talking, but Ana ignored his every word. She wished she could ignore the strobing light from an orb above casting dizzying shadows onto the bridge, making it even more difficult to focus on her footwork.

She held her arms horizontally to her side, turning her body into a T, focusing only on the certainty of her steps as she set one foot in front of the other, maintaining momentum and forcing herself to ignore Cody's progress on his side of the course.

Don't look at him. Don't look at him. Just keep your mind on the path ahead. One foot in front of the other.

Her mind raced faster with every step, wondering if she could reach the platform before Cody, and if she could actually bring herself to murder someone.

Yes, it was in self-defense. But still, it was murder.

Don't look, don't look.

Nearly there, Ana succumbed to temptation and was shocked to see Cody was almost twice as close as her. Realization fueled her doubt; doubt nearly caused her to fall.

Ana gasped, windmilling her arms, swinging wildly to recover her balance as her left heel planted itself hard against the bridge, righting her body just seconds before she could tumble off the precipice and into the pit of ravenous boars.

The orb hummed beside her, lending Ana mercy with silence, allowing her to focus. Unfortunately, her reprieve lasted only seconds. Once Ana had righted herself, the Orb's screen returned to vibrant life, the crowd loudly chanting.

"Die! Die! Die!"

Clearly, Ana wasn't the crowd favorite her father had been. Being labeled a traitor in the Underground gave the audience fuel to hate her, and they were clearly rooting for her ruin. Her father *was* in the Underground, but the network had said nothing of the sort, not even mentioning rumor, revealing only his wife's cold-blooded murder, which, Ana supposed, was somehow more acceptable to the audience than treason.

She glared at the screen, hating the orb and the horrible world inside it. Cody was maybe six seconds from the platform. Her death a given unless she started to run. Ana planted her heel harder against the bridge, then launched herself forward.

Just then, Cody reached the platform, then slipped, screaming as he fell out of her view behind the pedestal. Ana wasn't sure if she heard him scream, or if his cry was lost amid the squealing from the boars below, but she figured he must be dead. She took another long step toward the platform, feeling the pedestal within her reach.

The moment her feet found the platform, she saw Cody hanging onto the edge of the platform by his fingers, his eyes and mouth both open wide in horror. Then he saw her, and his eyes narrowed in anger as he somehow managed to swing his leg onto the ledge.

She considered running toward him and shoving him off, but was terrified that he'd either get up before she reached him or grab her leg and yank her over the edge.

Instead, she grabbed the sword.

As she raised it, Cody found his footing on the other side of the pedestal and brandished a knife he must've had before falling down the chute.

He swiped the blade at her, but his reach was too short.

She stepped back, then remembered she only had a

few feet to move before she'd fall into the pit. She jabbed the sword forward, trying to scare him back before committing to murder.

"Go!" she shouted, gritting her teeth. "Go, and I won't kill you."

"No way!" he sneered. "You go, and I'll let YOU live!"

"I've got the sword." She took a swing, again purposely missing. Part of her reason for not striking him was a fear that if she missed and the sword was close enough to him, he'd be able to wrest the weapon away from her. Then she would be a dead girl.

"Yeah, but I don't think you'll use it." He took a brave, or maybe stupid, step forward.

"Just go! I swear I'll kill you!"

"You know I can't do that." He shook his head, holding his knife out in front of him. "If you go, they'll leave me down here to die! We both know how it ends for whoever doesn't take the platform back. So get off and let me on. You can take your chances with the boars and your sword."

Maybe Cody is right.

Maybe she *could* make it up without the platform. It wasn't impossible, though she would still need to get through the boars and find the alternate route.

But Cody charged before she could even question her logic.

She shocked herself by raising the sword, waving it in a wide arc, swiping her enemy with a long gash across his chest, and painting the already-red button with a spatter of blood.

He fell a step back, eyes wide and dazed, his mouth open in a capital O of surprise.

"Finish him!" Kirkman's voice cheered from the orb.

Ana's uncertainty was gone in a blink. She shoved the

sword deeper, then hefted it up and through his guts as he screamed.

She pulled it free from his body, as if his skin were its scabbard, then fell another step back, expecting him to fall, maybe even over the edge. Instead, Cody did the impossible by lurching forward, blood drooling from his mouth, and waving his knife madly through the air.

He missed, but his surprise attack sent her sword to the ground.

"Uh-oh!" Kirkman said as the audience gasped.

Ana ducked, then jumped at Cody, aiming for his waist and sending him hard onto the ground. She straddled his prone form, curled her fingers into his hair, then lifted his head and sent the back of his skull into the platform's metal bottom repeatedly as she unleashed her pent-up rage.

Rage at City 6.

Rage at the Games.

Rage at the orb and Kirkman's incessant chatter.

And rage at Cody for forcing her to kill him.

The orb hovered beside her, filling the air with a play-by-play.

"You've got to be kidding me!" Kirkman said, clearly giddy. "Little Miss Jonah Junior is ninety-something pounds of RAGING FURY! Look. At. Her. *GOOOOO!* City 6 might want to consider laying odds on our brand-new favorite!"

Tears streamed down her face as Cody's blood spilled out, soaking the knees on her coveralls as Cody's dead eyes stared up at her.

Applause filled the cavern, the fickle fans suddenly finding their new darling underdog. She didn't dare turn to the orb and let the vultures see her tears.

She allowed her hair to fall into her face, masking her

pain as she climbed off Cody and turned back to the pedestal and smashed her fist down onto the button.

The platform lurched upward with an angry grinding sound as she headed back to the surface, sword in hand, hoping she could find Liam.

After a long moment, she finally raised her eyes and met the orb's unblinking stare, with Kirkman's smiling face filling the screen.

"What do you have to say for your fans back in City 6?"

Ana stared into the orb, and then, to her surprise, she raised her fist. "To Jonah!"

And, of course, the audience erupted in cheers.

FOURTEEN

Jonah Lovecraft

JONAH OPENED his eyes just as Father's needle pinched his neck again.

A sudden rush, followed by a swimming mind, led to seconds that fell into minutes while he searched for a focus that didn't want to be found.

When his vision finally cleared, a man from Jonah's past was sitting across from him — Charles Egan, who was staring at him with heavy lids over red-tinged eyes. Jonah wasn't sure if the color was due to rage, tears, alcohol, or all three. Egan was thin, his dark hair thinning, face gaunt and haunted. He looked like a shell of the chubby man he knew a decade ago.

Jonah flashed back to the last time he'd stared into the man's eyes, as Watchers dragged him from the courtroom. Egan had been begging Jonah to just do one thing — tell the truth. The truth that Jonah had sworn to uphold as a Watcher. A truth that Jonah had turned his back on, no different than his corrupt bosses.

Egan's unfortunate end in City 6 ran in miserable parallel to Jonah's own, honing a blade of guilt so sharp that Egan didn't even need to wield it for Jonah to feel its edge.

"I'm sorry." He swallowed hard and wished he could disappear, almost willing to die if it meant not having to meet this man's eyes. It wasn't as though he had anything left to live for, not with Ana and Adam and all of his life still stuck behind City 6 Walls.

Egan said nothing, keeping his gaze fixed on his enemy.

Jonah tried again. "I swear, I had no idea. I thought I was doing the right thing."

Egan started in with his line of questioning instead, as Father Truth stood behind him, arms again folded across his chest. "Who set you up?"

"I don't know," Jonah said, telling the truth, knowing that whatever was rushing through his veins would prevent him from lying, and that he no longer had any reason. There was no way on earth that Egan was a City Watch spy.

He made Jonah stew in his guilt for another minute before asking his next question. "Why were you set up? Why would they need to silence you?"

"I don't know." His earlier euphoria was nowhere to be found, only a thousand pounds of shame and guilt as he simpered, "I'm so, so sorry."

"How does it feel to watch your life get torn apart piece by piece? Oh, but I don't need to ask you, do I? Tell me, Jonah, why did you set me up? How could you lie, knowing your actions would tear a family apart?"

"Because I didn't know. I *thought* I was doing the right thing. They told me, Keller told me, that you were part of the Underground."

"I wasn't," Egan snarled.

"I didn't know! I wouldn't have lied if I had known you

were innocent!" Jonah couldn't get his head to stop spinning. "I'm sorry."

"Tell my wife and son you're sorry," Egan said. "Except that you *can't*. My house was seized, and they were banished to the Dark Quarter. We all know what happened then, don't we?"

Jonah shook his head, not wanting to remember, or stare into the eyes of his past.

"Say it," Egan said, his voice rising almost into a scream. "Say it, you coward. Tell me what happened to my wife and daughter!"

"You already know ..."

"I want you to say it. I want the truth from your lying lips."

Jonah swallowed, then drew a fresh breath. "Your wife was raped and murdered."

"And?" Egan met his eyes. "My son?"

Jonah swallowed a lump, tears streaming from his eyes as the drugs continued to wreak havoc on his emotions. "Your son was sold into sexual slavery. He killed himself one year later. No one knows what happened to your infant daughter ... Is that her? Calla? How did you get her back?"

It took Egan forever to speak, and he neglected the questions. "I've hated you for so long, wished you dead for so long that it had become as automatic as a daily prayer."

Egan fell silent while Jonah struggled to maintain eye contact.

"I wanted to find you and kill you. What I finally chose instead, with the help of Father," Egan gestured toward the dwarf standing to his right, "was to focus on the life we had together, before *you* conspired to take it away. Father helped me see that blaming you would never bring them back. And so I went, going about my life, almost forgetting you. Imagine my surprise when fate conspired to bring you here! What poetic justice, that you would be framed for your wife's murder. That you'd be thrown into the Games as an outcast, then 'win' to end up here, as if God Himself delivered you to me."

He laughed, though the cackle sounded brittle and forced. A swirling rush of drugs, thick inside Jonah's blood, forced a ragged laugh from his mouth. Egan held his stare.

Jonah suddenly longed to hear Egan condemn him further. He deserved it all. He wanted to hear how awful he was and how he had it all coming. He was ready for whatever punishment the man thought he deserved. It was time to pay for his sins.

Egan stood, set a hand on Father's shoulder, then left the room without a word, leaving Jonah alone with the dwarf.

Father stood before Jonah, arms still crossed, saying nothing as Jonah wallowed in his guilt and misery.

Egan returned a few minutes later, carrying an orb in his right palm. "Look familiar?" He sat across from Jonah. "It doesn't fly or record any more, I saw to that. But what it does do, it does wonderfully."

Dread slivered down his spine. Jonah wondered how they would use the orb to torture him. Egan cracked a panel on its back, then flicked a switch inside the robot. Moments later, its screen lit like a parade, showing the familiar, always-on feed of the Darwin Games.

The display showed a green nighttime image of a young girl with long dark hair, crouching low behind a tree as a group of zombies ambled by in the midnight black.

"Why are you showing me this?" Jonah asked, confused.

"Patience." Egan smiled for the first time. "Just watch."

Jonah waited another minute, wondering what the hell

could be so important on the Darwin Games that Egan had to show him.

Suddenly, the scene changed, showing him what Egan wanted him to see — his daughter, in the Games, racing along a bridge.

Jonah screamed, bucking and shaking, trying to tear himself from the chair and its bindings. "What the fuck! Why is she in the Games?"

"They said she was with the Underground." Egan shrugged. "Isn't that ... *interesting*?"

Jonah stared at the screen, his mouth wide open as Ana hopped on top of a kid and bashed his skull in. Jonah was equally horrified and relieved as she screamed, slapped her hand on the button, then took the elevator platform to the forest above.

"Congratulations." Egan raised his eyebrows. "Looks like the apple doesn't fall far from the rotten tree."

FIFTEEN

Liam Harrow

LIAM FINALLY ARRIVED at the end of the Fire Wall and was about to double back on the other side to search for Ana. Then one of the network orbs hovered down directly next to him. He turned, wondering what the orb's screen was going to show him. A sense of dread began to fill him, certain he would be shown a recording of Ana's slaughter.

The screen flickered on, and Liam swallowed, preparing for the worst.

Kirkman's face filled the screen. "Well, well, well, it's Underground Scum, Liam Harrow."

Liam kept his tongue in check, waiting to see what Kirkman would say next.

"Liam Harrow is one of the oddest competitors in the Games, folks. Most people try to *avoid* the Darwin Games, but Crazy Liam practically begged for entry, isn't that right, young man?"

"I don't know what you're talking about," he lied through gritted teeth.

"Really? Maybe this will refresh your memory."

Kirkman's face faded from the screen, replaced with a recording of Liam storming into Keller's office.

"What the fuck?" Liam shouted, swiping his gun at the orb.

The orb zipped up, then back down, just inches above Liam's reach, forcing him to watch the recording:

"I'm done. I want out," Liam had said.

"What?" Keller replied.

"I'm through spying for you! You got—" The video conveniently lost audio when Liam accused Keller's goons of killing the woman and child in church. "I won't be your spy anymore. It's over."

"No," Keller said, standing up and glaring at Liam. "You've got a job to do, and you're gonna get your ass back out there and do it."

"Find someone else!" Liam swiped at Keller's desk, violently knocking his paperwork and mug of coffee to the floor.

Keller jumped from his chair and slammed Liam against the wall, barking into his face. "Are you out of your fucking mind, boy? You get your ass back out there now, or I'll hold you for treason!"

"Do it!" Liam shouted.

"Don't tempt me, child."

"I'm not tempting you, I'm daring you! Because otherwise, I'm walking out right now, and I'm going to tell everyone that I've been spying for City Watch. How do you think that would affect your operations?"

Keller spun Liam around, slapped handcuffs on his wrists, and shoved his face into the wall. Then the video cut back to Kirkman.

"What the hell were you thinking, kid? It's almost like you wanted to be in the Games or something."

Liam ignored Kirkman and kept walking, closing in on

the end of the Fire Wall, then racing to the end of the seam before turning back up on the other side of the Fire Wall, searching for any sign of Ana.

"Who are you looking for?" Kirkman asked. "Oh, wait a second ... you're looking for Anastasia Lovecraft, aren't you?"

Liam ignored the carnival barker and kept walking, searching for any sign of Ana. The orb floated behind. "Ah, I think I know what's going on here, ladies and gentlemen. Our young Liam was spying for City Watch and had infiltrated the Underground, where he met the lovely traitor, Anastasia Lovecraft. And when she got picked up, our young lover decided to get himself arrested so he could be with her."

The audience oohed and aahed as Kirkman tried to play up a possible romantic angle.

Liam spun toward the orb, raising the pistol and taking aim at the thing. "You don't know the first fucking thing about me, so back the fuck off!"

"Aww," Kirkman said, syrupy sweet. "I think we found a love story here at the Darwin Games! Of course, as we all know, the only romances here are *tragedies*."

Liam kept walking, and Kirkman finally shut up. The orb floated back up to its usual spot, forty or so feet in the sky.

After fifteen minutes of walking, Liam wondered if it was possible for Ana to have beaten him to the seam. He stopped, looking in both directions, seeing only fire on one side and darkness on the other. He felt increasingly sure that she had run into trouble. That she was out there alone, vulnerable and unarmed.

He thought about calling out to her, but with no ammo left in his gun, Liam didn't dare risk drawing zombies to him. He was no good to her dead. He ran north, never straying more than a hundred or so feet from the seam, desperate for any sign of her, hoping that each new shadow would be her emerging from the woods.

Liam was running so fast, he failed to notice a small boulder that caught him off balance and sent him straight to the ground, hard enough to knock the wind from his chest.

He rose slowly, gasping for air, and was about to continue his search when he found himself surrounded by a trio of players: a blonde-haired young woman with a crossbow; a six-foot-six guy with a unibrow, a large hanging jaw, and a metal pipe; and — a foot in front of the other two — a skinny, dark-haired guy, sleeved with tattoos running up and down his exposed arms where he'd cut his coveralls away. Blood covered most of the ink. The tattooed guy held a long, curved blade and a smile that said he knew just how to use it.

Liam pulled the gun from his waistband and aimed it in a circle.

"I'd put that down if I were you," said the man holding a pipe.

SIXTEEN

Liam Harrow

LIAM TURNED IN A CIRCLE, gun drawn on the three players, all with their own weapons ready — a pipe, a sword, and a crossbow. The pipe-wielding man was a giant with teeth like broken rocks in his open maw. His throat birthed a thunderous roll as he stepped forward, pipe swinging in slow arcs, readying to dispatch Liam's head from his body.

But instead of retreating, Liam stepped forward, gun right in the giant's face. Goliath didn't know that his chamber was empty.

"Back off!" Liam stepped into the giant's space and forced him three tentative steps back. As the big man stumbled off balance, Liam quickly bypassed him, then spun around, putting all three of the players in front of himself. He fell back, his gun still pointed at the big man.

The blonde kept her crossbow on Liam. "Think you're gonna shoot all three of us?"

Her snarl was so sexy Liam wanted to lick it. He tried to shake the image, surprised by his arousal, considering the danger.

Blondie was short but seemed especially so standing a

half-step to the side of Goliath. She could have been nineteen, or twenty-nine; it was tough to tell under the makeup, which she'd somehow maintained despite the conditions. The woman wasn't just a knockout, but she was rocking one hell of a swagger.

Liam couldn't remember the last time he'd seen a contestant appearing so confident or wearing her sexuality so obviously. In a game with criminals where rape was an ever-present threat — and practically a selling point for the premium-priced "uncensored version" of the show — women usually tried to stay relatively invisible, not calling attention to themselves with makeup and cleavage. There was something admirable about her raw confidence.

Blondie played to the three orbs hovering above her as if she were trying to woo the viewers back home. "You can try pulling your trigger," she purred. "But the second you flinch, I'm squeezing mine. You *might* get a shot off before my bolt slams into your forehead ... but I doubt it."

Her icy eyes were still on his, absorbing every detail. He knew the look well, and had his own polished version. Back in City 6, in a place like the Social, that first look would be followed by fast banter and teasing heat, then a long night of lust and thrust.

But he wasn't in the Social, or even behind the Walls. He was in the Barrens playing the Darwin Games, where thinking with your dick got you killed. While he hadn't seen many overtly sexual players, he *had* seen many femme fatales eliminate far stronger players by slithering into their best intentions, then striking like a serpent once a player dropped their guard.

Knowing your competition kept you alive in the Games. Even the best alliances were temporary and ever-shifting. No way Liam would be dumb enough to let any player get the drop on him, but that didn't mean Blondie had to know he was onto her game. No reason he couldn't play the dumb guy to buy himself a few minutes.

Liam grinned, ignoring Goliath and the guy with tattoos and a sword, while giving Blondie the same well-worn smile that had worked so well back home.

"Nope," he shook his head. "You're right. There's no way I can hit all three of you, and my daddy taught me to never be stupid when it's easy to be smart." His grin went wider. "But I sure as shit *will* shoot one of you, and since I've been practicing out in the hunting yards since I was six, I'm certain I'll manage to pop a couple of shots before I'm finished, and positive I won't miss either one."

As Liam expected, the men shifted uncomfortably on their feet. Neither wanted dialogue, and both wanted him dead. But they were following Blondie's lead, and she was clearly calling the shots, even if the men hadn't realized it or were lying to themselves that they were in control.

Liam laughed as Blondie held his stare and the two guys beside her blinked in confusion, wondering what sort of crazy bastard would be laughing while surrounded by three armed players.

Goliath moved in, pushing Blondie gently to the side as he stepped up to Liam, grunting and twisting the pipe in his hand as if readying another go at Liam.

Liam should have retreated, at least a step, but he didn't. Instead, he moved forward.

"Did you forget the gun already?" Liam screamed, thrusting his empty gun into the giant's face and freezing Goliath in his steps. "Ha," Liam said, testing fate and holding Goliath's eyes.

Tattoo looked back at Blondie for direction, but she was staring at Liam, her crossbow trained at his head.

Liam laughed out loud, further confusing his attackers. "Which of you is calling the shots?" He dared Goliath to claim the title. Then when he didn't, Liam turned to Tattoo: "Call off your dog, or I'll blow his head off!"

The giant snarled and took a step back without being ordered. "It's cool, Keb."

Tattoo nodded at the giant while keeping most of his gaze pinned to Liam.

"Thanks." Liam nodded at Keb. "Now if y'all don't mind, I'm gonna get outta here before shit gets ugly."

He took two long steps back, keeping his gun steady so everyone understood he was being smart rather than retreating — hoping the trio would see the wisdom in parting on friendly terms. He kept holding Blondie's eye like it was her hand, wanting to wink but feeling safer with his crooked smile. He took another two steps back.

"Wait," Blondie called, exactly as expected, turning to her teammates. "He has a gun. Maybe he can help."

Keb looked at Blondie as if she'd suggested surrendering their weapons and crowning Liam *King of the Barrens*. "We don't need no one else, least of all a pretty boy with a pea shooter."

The giant was still looking at Liam like an angry dog waiting to be unleashed.

"Maybe the ink from your tattoos messed up your hearing, so you didn't hear when I said it the first time," Liam laughed, "but I've been shooting my entire life. Dad and I used to hit the yards before I had hair on my balls, hunting game when rations thinned. I've killed more zombies than all three of you combined."

Goliath grunted again.

Liam figured he'd push his luck and play hard to get. Eyes still on Blondie, he shook his head. "But hell, I wasn't even looking to partner with anyone, today, tomorrow, or ever. I plan to win this thing, and figure I'm better on my own."

Z2134

Goliath seemed indifferent, Blondie curious, and Keb downright pissed.

"You're not going anywhere," he said. "If you're not with us, you're against us. That means you die. We're giving you one chance to keep breathing. I suggest you take it."

Liam stayed quiet as if contemplating the offer.

"Well, my daddy always said I ought to play better with others, and maybe walking the Barrens together isn't the worst idea." He shifted his glance from Keb to the girl. "And if Blondie's any good with that crossbow, I figure the four of us could lay a helluva lotta hurt on the rest of the herd." Liam shrugged but kept his weapon steady. "I guess I'm game if you are."

Liam smiled wider, his false grin now stretching far enough to break his face.

"The name's Chloe, not *Blondie*." Her expression was maybe a wink but likely a scowl. "Call me Blondie again and I'll put a bolt in your balls."

Something in Liam was begging for banter, but he wasn't about to risk pissing off the alpha male of the pack or the walking mountain. No use doing anything that could get him killed, especially if one or both men thought Blondie wanted to get with them, which was how Blondie, or Chloe, was likely playing it.

Keb nodded. "Way I see it, a team of four could go far. That gives us great odds if we stick together through the Final Four. I say we walk as one, then battle shit out at the Mesa."

Goliath seem unconvinced, probably still wanting a chance to swing his pipe at Liam's smart mouth.

Liam relaxed his gun and looked down as if thinking the offer over one last time. After a half-minute of nearly painful silence, he said, "I'm game if Goliath here agrees to shake and make up. I don't wanna be walking around wondering when the big man might snap."

Liam took a chance, in its own way the biggest of his life, and lowered his weapon with one hand while extending the other in peace. Goliath turned to Keb, then to Chloe as if seeking permission.

Just like a big dumb dog.

"Shake, and let's get on with this," Chloe said.

Keb went first, reaching out and shaking his hand, stronger than necessary. Liam stared at his arms, trying to untangle the patterns beneath the blood.

"I'm Liam." He met the man's eyes, appearing confident and respectful but not threatening.

"Keb," he said, dropping his palm.

Goliath went next, offering Liam a surprisingly relaxed shake. "The name's Marcus."

"Liam," he repeated, trying not to get lost in staring at the man's forest of misshapen teeth. Liam caught a kindness in his eyes as they shook, and realized he was probably only gruff due to years of abuse from others. He was the kind of guy who'd make a loyal partner once trust was earned.

Chloe lowered her crossbow and offered her palm. "Good to meet you, Liam. Don't make us regret this."

Liam shook Chloe's hand, her fingers gently teasing his skin as they parted. He turned, wondering if she could tell he was semi-hard. *Probably.* She was good at working people, maybe better than him. While Liam wasn't fool enough to fall for her charms, he'd play whatever game might facilitate his survival.

He hoped Marcus and Keb could hold their tempers once Chloe started flirting overtly, trying to turn them against one another once it suited her to do so. He'd bet his balls that was part of her plan. She would expect the stronger to eliminate the weaker, and it didn't matter who was left.

"I promise you won't regret it," Liam said to Chloe with a wink, then turned to Keb. "So, where we headed?"

"North." He nodded up and along the seam. "We heard from another player that there's a weapons stash near the river."

"Another player?" Liam asked.

"Yeah, he didn't make it." Marcus grinned awkwardly.

"All right, then, to the north," Liam said, grateful they were heading toward Ana's possible whereabouts.

Still, he had to figure out how to handle the situation once they ran into her. Without ammo, he had zero chance of stopping them from killing her. While it made sense for the trio to partner with Liam and his sharpshooting skills, there was no way in hell this would ever be a party of five.

SEVENTEEN

Anastasia Lovecraft

ANA HAD BEEN WALKING for nearly thirty minutes when she realized that she was lost.

She couldn't find any sign of the Fire Wall and wondered if she'd somehow shot past it and needed to turn around, or keep heading in what she thought was the right direction.

Panic fed her doubts faster and faster.

What if I went too far south and completely missed Liam? What if he went to the spot, saw I wasn't there, figured I was dead, and kept going without me? What if Liam is dead?

Standing in the cold, dark woods, far away from everything she'd ever known, it was all she could do to not break down right there. But she thought of the humming orb overhead, watching and broadcasting her every move.

I will not let them see me weak.

She looked up to the half moon, peeking down through the clouds, giving just enough light that she wasn't completely blind. She was traveling along a path that she thought would lead her back to the seam, with thick, dark woods on either side of her.

She tried not to think of the zombies or mutant beasts lurking beyond the dark walls on either side.

Just keep moving.

You'll find the Fire Wall.

You have to.

You'll find the wall. You'll find Liam. And the two of you will fight to the end.

But then what? What happens at the end?

Will he kill you?

Can you kill him?

The thoughts were too much and made her head hurt. She tried to push them down and focus instead on her surroundings. She heard a sudden crunch of snow to her left, just beyond the veil of dark forest.

She dropped to one knee, sword ready, tensed for attack, but nothing came. She stayed crouched, eyes scanning the darkness, her fingers wrapping tighter around the sword's hilt as her heart pounded against her chest.

Another unmistakable crunch of ice told Ana whatever it was had to be close, unless it was the whisper of the wind or her imagination. Silence followed as she leaped to her feet and spun slowly, sword in front, preparing for an ambush. After another minute of icy silence, she gripped the hilt tighter, lowered it to her waist, then took a tentative step toward the darkness where the sound originated from.

At least it's not zombies.

Zombies were too stupid to stalk their prey and rarely traveled in isolation, unless they happened to get separated from their herd.

It had to be another player, waiting to strike. Ana had enough fear and doubts circling through her mind without adding another player stalking her. Better to draw the player out and deal with them now than worry and wait for their strike. Taking the initiative meant she controlled the exchange. It didn't have to end in a battle.

It was still early enough in the game for an impromptu alliance. Calling out to her pursuer now could earn her a truce. Even if the other player didn't want to join her, they might realize that ignoring her and moving on might be the easier route. Ana had a sword. If the walking shadow was wielding a bow, gun, or any other long-range weapon, she would be dead already. She had an advantage if she handled it smartly.

Yet, she wasn't sure the best way to handle an invisible opponent. On one hand, calling out another player would make her seem bold and brave, but on the other it could make her seem weak.

In a game built on survival of the fittest, even the slightest show of frailty could get you killed. The network broadcast players' flaws whenever it seemed reasonable that a chink in the armor might make for aggressive battle, conflict, or anything to keep viewers staring at their screens. Ana wasn't sure if the orbs ever shared those flaws with other players, but she had to assume it was a possibility.

She had to appear strong, even if her strength was a hollow conceit.

Perhaps she could spout some nonsense words, loud and thick with rage. Maybe screaming something her attacker couldn't understand would scare them into retreat.

It had worked for Crazy Cal Moody — for a while.

Crazy Cal was a player from a few years back who pretended he was a lunatic. Whenever he got into a fight, he drew a perfect picture of insanity, biting people on the face, screaming at the top of his lungs — utter nonsense that sounded like he was speaking in tongues — along with anything else he could do to scare the living crap out of everyone around him, at least long enough let him reach the Mesa virtually unscathed.

Cal's false insanity was one of the best tactics Ana had ever seen. No other players, and few viewers, had figured him out. Her father called it early, almost immediately, though no one believed him.

"He's only acting crazy. You can see the cunning in his eyes," he'd said.

Cal made it to the Final Four, and then three, relaxing his guard only after befriending a 15-year-old named Ben Mallard, who faked a broken arm to earn sympathy. When Ben resisted Cal's offer of help, saying he was too scared to pair up with the man, Cal lowered his guard and told the kid he wasn't crazy and wouldn't hurt him. To this day, nobody knew why Cal would shed his successful strategy and befriend the kid. Some, like Ana, thought it was kindness while others believed it was the loneliness of playing a purely solo game.

Whatever the reason, it would prove to be his lone mistake in an otherwise flawless game. On the night before the Final Challenge, one early morning's walk from the Mesa, with just one other player left in the Games, Ben and Cal had settled in for their last evening's sleep, both knowing only one would make it to the end, but comforted that at least things were better together.

They had agreed to take shifts sleeping in case the Game's final remaining player, Jude Dawson, entered their camp. Cal had gone to bed, crazy enough to sleep soundly, believing Ben would keep him safe, and not for a second expecting the boy to slit his throat only seconds into his snoring.

Far better, Ana thought, to have other players fear you than to embolden them enough to attack.

Another crunch of snow split the silent night. She turned to the source, which remained hidden in the darkness now roughly ten feet away from her. "Show yourself."

Silence stretched for one minute too many as Ana stood frozen in place, icy blade hovering in front of her body. "I know you're there." She took a step forward and lied, "I can smell you."

Another several seconds of silence were followed by footsteps as the hidden player stepped forward from the darkness and into dim blue moonlight.

It was the red-haired 12-year-old girl, the one who'd taken out the big man using a board with nails in the opening of the Games. She stood eight feet away, her face caked with mud, blood, and an almost savage concentration. Her violet coveralls were even muddier and bloodier than her cheeks. Her eyes, wide and blue, were stuck somewhere between innocence and shock.

Ana stared without any words in her frozen throat. The girl held a knife, so small it may as well have been the jagged edge of an old tin can. The blade gleamed in the moonlight, casting fractured beams of secondhand moonlight dancing from the girl's hand into the snow.

Even armed, the child was tiny and unassuming. But looks were often deceiving. She had already proven herself with a vicious, and incredibly fast, sneak attack on the fat man with the sword.

Ana wasn't a killer, and couldn't imagine eliminating the child unless they were in the Final Battle. Right now they weren't, and Ana's life wasn't in immediate jeopardy. She couldn't kill the girl just because she *might* pose a threat at some point later in the Games.

But she *could* scare her away and avoid having to fight a child.

"I'll kill you," Ana said. "I already killed one guy, twice your size."

The girl stared, like she was savoring her next words on the tip of her tongue, or maybe waiting for Ana to say something else. She waited, hoping the girl would speak. It was too damned cold to stand still for this long.

"Go!" Ana yelled.

It was growing colder by the second, icy wind whipping through Ana's hair. Standing here forever didn't do either of them any good. If she was cold, the child must be freezing.

The girl stared at her, with a creepy expression that both terrified and confused Ana. Her teeth were chattering.

Ana had no idea what such a small child could have possibly done to get thrown in prison, much less sent outside the Walls and into the Darwin Games, but something about her made Ana think she didn't come from the Dark Quarter, or whatever equivalent stained the back alleys of City 2.

The girl stood, holding Ana's stare while Ana gripped her sword. She considered turning and running herself, but didn't dare. Surrender in the Barrens was always a mistake, and besides, the girl was probably faster.

The network orb that had been hovering above Ana for fifteen minutes suddenly descended as though dropped by a god, spinning like a top through the frozen air and spilling brilliant blue light into the forest below. Kirkman wasn't onscreen and was likely at home in bed, but the orb was prepared to broadcast whatever came next, with an audience watching, eager for bloodshed, even if it was a child's. Or Ana's.

She kept staring at the girl, wondering if her legs were

as frozen as hers, standing in the snow for what felt like eternity. The girl took a small step, almost tiny, slowly moving forward with one tentative foot in front of the other — bold, brave, and almost beautiful as she cautiously crept toward Ana, stopping a few feet in front of her, silent.

Is she trying to make peace or preparing to strike?

"Are you gonna say anything?" Ana asked, confused.

The girl shook her head, then opened her mouth.

Her missing tongue told Ana a long, horrible story in one short, miserable second.

Ana had never seen a cut tongue but had heard plenty of stories about the many atrocities that happened to the girls and women in the Dark Quarter, often used in sex rings. Their pimps cut their tongues off to prevent them from ever naming their "customers." This also served as a warning to any who might fight or flee — showing them how quickly a blade could change their lives.

Ana winced, then whispered, "Oh God."

She wanted to invite the girl to stay.

They could team up. Ana could keep her safe. She'd—

Blood erupted from Crazy Cal Moody's neck as Ben danced across the stage in Ana's mind.

You can't trust her.

You're not a team.

Even if you somehow make it to the end together, you'll have to kill her at some point if you wanna win.

Can you do that, Ana? Murder a little disfigured girl who's been through God knows what?

Ana lunged forward, twisting her face into an angry scowl. "GO!"

She swung her sword so close to the girl that her blade came back with a bloody tatter of coverall. The girl's eyes widened, then she turned and rushed into the woods.

Ana swayed in the snow, sick to her stomach as she listened for the final fade of footsteps from the girl's retreat. She felt horrible, but there was no time for feeling horrible. She had to get moving and find Liam.

Once the child's footsteps had trailed into the distance, Ana began walking so fast it was nearly a run, trying to spark her body back into warmth. She made her way through the darkness, still freezing, slowing every few hundred steps as her brain begged her body to pause. She rested for only a second, then pushed forward, knowing that to slow was to stop and to stop was to die.

Eventually, she found herself back at the Fire Wall, breaking into a smile, grateful for its promise of warmth. She was just about to run from the woods and to the fire when movement stopped her cold in her tracks. Four orbs floated in the distance. And below them, four players coming from the south.

Ana glanced up at her own orb, waving it back so as not to give away her location. To her surprise, the orb came lower, resting just inches from her, and powered down its lights.

"Thank you," she whispered as she dropped to her knees and waited for the players to pass her by. As they drew closer, so did their voices, chatter, and laughter.

She gasped in recognition of one of the voices.

Liam!

She wanted to run toward him but didn't dare. He was with others, and she had no way of knowing if the other players would see her as friend or foe. She waited as they walked past her. One of the players was a particularly pretty blonde who laughed at Liam's every joke. Ana felt a bitter taste in her mouth, a blend of betrayal and jealousy.

Did he even look for me, or did he just fall in with the first group he ran into?

As the group passed, Ana felt more confused than ever.
Should I follow? Or go my own way?

The girl's laughter carried back on the wind, bothering Ana more than she wanted.

Fuck that bitch.

Ana decided to follow.

EIGHTEEN

Jonah Lovecraft

It was Monday morning, by Jonah's estimations, and it had been many sleepless hours since Egan disappeared from the room here he was being held, leaving him alone in the darkness to ponder what was happening with Ana.

Why is she in the Games?
Is it to punish me, or is there something more?
Did she get in trouble?
Where is Adam?
Who is taking care of him now that Ana isn't?
Is Adam next?

Jonah waited for someone to come and turn on the flickering tube lights above. He'd had enough darkness to last a lifetime. In the Barrens it was a reminder that sleep meant possibly not waking up.

Now the darkness only served to multiply fears for his family. He had to get out and find Ana and Adam. Until then, nothing else mattered.

The same curse that kept him from sleeping poured memories forth, stacking the front of his mind with image after haunting image of a life with Molly, Ana, and Adam and the old world the four of them could never orbit again.

Remembering the holidays made him saddest, since that was when they had spent the most time together. Being a senior Watcher meant staying indoors while men with fewer credits, or no families, were obligated to clock double and sometimes triple shifts.

Nativity was a favorite holiday, though the Lovecrafts weren't religious enough to enjoy the long weekend for more than a light upgrade in rations and the exchange of simple paper-wrapped presents. As much as he loved Nativity, Fertility was the family's most loved, leaving them with a memorable week each year, starting April 1. The children enjoyed Fertility as much as he and Molly, though of course for an entirely different set of reasons.

The children loved their baskets, filled with two bars of chocolate and a bag of jelly beans each, left by the Fertility Bunny. And though Ana always proudly proclaimed that "this year" she'd be patient and make her candy last, it was always gone before nightfall.

He and Molly loved having an excuse to fuck like rabbits, even if they weren't allowed to conceive without a voucher.

Jonah closed his eyes, thankful for the memories, even if they were painful reminders of all that he'd lost, still able to remember the moment he'd opened the door to the end of his life as if it were yesterday.

He'd been working on an endless stack of forms to be filed when he got the call — Ana was sick and needed someone to pick her up from school. Molly wasn't answering the comm at home, and he'd figured she was likely sleeping since she'd stayed home from work with a virus and was feeling like hell that morning.

So Jonah had left work early, grateful for the chance to

care for his baby girl — for both of the women in his life. Ana was growing too fast, and time was flying by. Before long, she'd be married and starting her own family, so who knew how many more father-daughter moments they had left between them?

Jonah had thought about pulling Adam out as well, but knew Academy wouldn't like it, even if his rank as a Watcher kept them from argument.

By the time they were halfway home, Jonah had managed to make Ana laugh several times, even though she'd insisted that her stomach was hurting and kept begging him to stop. Jonah couldn't remember the last time it had just been him and her. Hell, he hardly remembered the last time it had been him and his whole family, considering how busy his schedule had become.

"I'm glad you got sick today," he'd said, as they walked down the hallway to their apartment. "Well, you know what I mean."

"Me too, Dad," she'd said, smiling back at him.

He'd opened the door to the apartment, still laughing, and called for Molly to see if she was awake. She wasn't in the kitchen, family room, or anywhere else in the front part of their small apartment. It wasn't until Jonah had made his way to the back of his apartment that he'd found her — crumpled in the doorway to Jonah's office, face down in a river of blood.

In reality, they screamed at the discovery together, but when the Watchers arrived on scene, Ana's story had changed, and she swore that her father had bashed her mother's skull in with his shock stick.

The Watchers, sure enough, had found the bloody shock stick in his office and arrested him immediately.

Though Jonah had known he could get caught working with the Underground, he'd never thought the government would murder his wife, frame him, and somehow implicate his daughter in the cover-up. The only explanation that made any sense in the insanity was Duncan's theory — that the City had somehow planted false memories in Ana's head via an implanted chip.

In all his years as a Watcher, Jonah had seen, and done, many illicit things in the name of justice, but he'd never seen an implanted memory.

And yet it was the only explanation that made any sense. Someone had discovered him helping "the enemy," and rather than expose him as a traitor and admit that one of their best and most trusted had been compromised, they set him up for murder.

And if the City could do that, what else were they capable of? What lengths would they go to preserve their power? What other "crimes" had people been wrongly accused of?

His wife was dead. His daughter hated him, his son probably did too. If they could get Ana, of course they could get Adam.

But now she was in the Games. Had she discovered their deception? Perhaps the false memories weren't permanent, and now they had to clean their mess before it got ugly. Revealing him as a traitor to the State might embolden their enemies, or worse, cause other Watchers to question their allegiance. If a kind, trusted man such as Jonah Lovecraft had turned his back on the State, there might be a good reason.

But to set Ana up as a traitor was easy. She was young, and youths were easily implicated because the elders feared them, and the change they represented. Plus, she had legitimate reason to be angry with the State. It had, after all, locked up her father, even if he was supposedly guilty of murdering her mother. It seemed plausible that she'd be angry with those who put him behind bars.

So they set her up, sent her off to die. No more witnesses to their lie.

Except they hadn't killed him.

And Ana wasn't dead ... yet.

He had to find his daughter and reveal all of the government's well-crafted lies. As he began to drift off, he wondered how long his children had pledged allegiance to a deception.

Did Ana now know he was innocent?

Was that why she was put into the Games?

And if so, was Adam also in danger?

MOLLY WAS WALKING TOWARD HIM. Her footsteps echoed in the halls of his memory, each one triggering a new flash of their past, which came and went quickly, as memories are wont to do in dreams.

The footsteps crossed into reality, and Jonah woke to find he wasn't alone.

He looked up, light blurring his eyes and splitting his head. It took him a minute before both were working well enough to focus on the girl, Calla, standing three feet away, waiting to feed him.

His lids had barely lifted before Calla was roughly shoving bread between his lips, then pouring water down his throat, her smile just shy of laughter as he tried not to choke. Liquid dribbled down his chin.

"Doncha like?"

Jonah tried to shed his guilt, forcing himself to stare into her angry eyes. He was responsible for the loss of her mother. For Egan's wife. He was no better than the monster Keller. And no less responsible than Keller was for Molly's death.

"Thank you," he said, chewing the bread. "It's quite good. Did you bake it?"

"I helped, yes," she said, her eyes softening a bit.

"I know you hate me."

Calla stared, less angry-looking than curious. His voice fell an octave, moving from pleasant to compassionate, hoping she could hear the honesty in his words and maybe understand that he never meant her or her family harm.

He was one of the good guys, even if it had taken him too long to get there.

"You have every right to hate me. Your father does too. What I did was wrong. But I only did it because my boss told me your father was bad, and I was stupid enough to believe it." He dropped his eyes along with his head. "They lied to me so I would hurt your family, but I never would've done it if—"

The door burst open, and Egan stormed into the room, yelling at Calla. "Don't listen to this liar!"

Calla turned to Egan, startled, her eyes wide and watery with a million things at once. She squealed, making noise with no words, like a wounded animal. Jonah's food and drink fell from her hand and crashed on the floor. She took off running from the room.

Egan stared after Calla, then turned and glared at Jonah for several seconds before curling his fingers around the metal bar at the top of an ancient crimson chair. He dragged it over to Jonah and sat. "What kind of lies are you telling my little girl?"

"I was apologizing." Jonah explained. "So she wouldn't keep trying to kill me."

Jonah figured it was better to portray the girl as being

mean to him rather than kind; otherwise Egan might send someone else to feed him.

Egan looked down at the food and water on the front of his coveralls, then laughed.

"What happened?" Jonah asked. "Why is Ana in the Games?"

Egan smiled. "Tell you what, Watcher, how about you answer *my* questions first?"

"What do you want to know?"

"Everything."

"Sure," Jonah said. "I've nothing to hide. Like I said, I'm on your side. But please, just tell me, is Ana alive?"

The words burned from his throat.

"You talk. Then *maybe* I answer." Egan paused, drew a flask from his coat and put it to his lips, then began. "Tell me why you don't take responsibility for your crimes."

"That's not true," Jonah said, fighting his anger. "I *do* take responsibility. I know things I did as a Watcher were wrong, horrible, unconscionable, unforgivable. But I never did anything I *thought* was wrong, and once I knew I was being lied to, I stopped and did everything I could to make amends. I didn't know you were innocent, Egan." Jonah shook his head. "I had no idea who the good guys were."

Egan stared.

"You're part of the reason I joined the Underground." Jonah's admission was relieving but awful on his tongue, betrayal and honor sharing space in his mouth. "It was years later before I finally saw the State's lies for what they were. But once I knew the truth, I helped from the inside and never stopped until I was sent outside the Wall."

"You?" Egan laughed. "Underground? Yeah, right!"

"I was." Jonah held his stare. "I trafficked intel so the Underground knew when armory and food shipments were arriving from City 1. I also helped citizens flee the City through the tunnels."

"You got them past the Walls?"

"Not directly. But I made sure they knew when sectors were thin, and I had the right guards posted, with orbs rerouted along the tunnels for two years straight."

Egan slapped his leg, cackling loud enough to turn his laugh into a scream. "Well, fuck me, Lovecraft. That's some real irony. You and your fellow fuckers at City Watch set *me* up for being Underground, even though I wasn't, and now here you are, City Watch *and* Underground scum!"

Jonah was suddenly, and rather stupidly, terrified that Egan was about to announce he was in fact a City Watch spy, that Jonah's confession had been recorded, and that now he was *really* in trouble — though Jonah couldn't imagine deeper shit than what he and Ana were already in.

"Please let me go. I have to find my daughter. She's not cut out for the Games."

Egan sneered at his prisoner. "Are you hoping for my sympathy? Did you want me to feel sorry for you because you finally saw the light and did a few good things after ruining so many lives? How THE FUCK does that bring my wife back? My son? TELL ME!"

Egan raged, his spittle spraying across Jonah's shrinking face. Egan's fists hovered, clenched at his side, shaking for nearly a minute before Egan finally lost it, lashing out and launching a right hook hard into Jonah.

The first shot sent splintering pain through his cheekbone.

The next, and every one after, unleashed a fury to Jonah's chest and head, leaving him bloodied, battered, and barely able to breathe.

"Fuck you, Lovecraft. You don't get a second chance! You're going on trial, and unlike the Cities, we don't banish. We put you to death and bake a fucking cake when we're done."

NINETEEN

Adam Lovecraft

ADAM STARED at the monitors in Chimney Rock's TV hall from the same spot he'd sat in since he and his friends robbed the kitchen. While the Games were holding everyone else's attention, all he could think about was the looming threat of being caught.

"Stop worrying so much!" Morgan punched him on the shoulder. "We're safe."

"What if they find the pillowcases?" he said, still staring at the screen.

Morgan shrugged. "What're they gonna do, lift every sheet in the storage room? They won't find 'em. Even if they do, so what? Not like they're gonna know *we* did it."

A collective *ewww!* rolled through the room.

Adam's eyes went to the monitor and caught the aftermath of some guy getting shredded by zombies. It wasn't Liam, and Ana wasn't part of the action, so he returned his attention to the hallway behind the hall's large open room, waiting for someone to come and jab an accusing finger their way.

"Would you relax?" Tommy said with a laugh. "Nothing's gonna happen. Shit, kid, you'd think we killed someone the way you're acting. It's just some stupid food that nobody's gonna miss."

The feast on the monitors grew louder, as did the cheering. Adam's friends were glued to every inch of the main monitor. Zombie strikes were bloody, sudden, and hypnotic. Adam turned his attention back to the TV so his friends wouldn't think he was too scared.

The gore onscreen made his stomach churn. All he could think about was his sister being attacked by the disgusting monsters. He was so engrossed in thought that he was caught off guard when Miss Abby, one of the only three grown-ups who were ever nice to him, though only barely, grabbed him roughly by the collar, then yanked him from his seat and onto the floor without a word.

Jayla and her friends were in their own corner of the TV hall, watching. Morgan, Tommy and Daniel all leaped back from Adam in shock.

"You're coming with me." Miss Abby's snarl barely sounded like her.

"Where are you taking me?" Adam whined. "I didn't do anything!"

Miss Abby dragged him away by the collar, drawing the attention of every kid in the hall and the laughter of about half of them. Adam stumbled and nearly tripped trying to keep pace and to prevent himself from falling flat on his face, which would *really* make everyone laugh.

They reached the end of the hallway, then stopped at the elevators. Miss Abby smashed her thumb on the bottom elevator button, still angry, then turned to Adam, glaring, and pulled the boy to his feet.

"Where are we going?" Adam asked again.

"To Schoolmaster Bertram's. You're in big trouble."

She shook her head. "I didn't expect this from you, Lovecraft."

The elevator dinged, the doors parted, and Miss Abby pulled him roughly into the box and pressed the button for the ground floor — the schoolmaster's floor. They rode in a silence as the elevator creaked and shook its way down, Adam terrified and wondering what he was in trouble for. Sure, *he knew* what he had done, but how could they? And if they did, why hadn't they grabbed up any of his cohorts?

The elevator was taking forever, making his first trip to the schoolmaster's office all the more horrifying as the minutes stretched, teasing him with a dozen different scenarios, each of them worse than the prior.

The elevator doors opened and Miss Abby dragged him forward, past several closed classrooms to a large red wooden door at the end of the hall that read *Schoolmaster Bertram*.

Miss Abby opened the door and pointed to an empty wooden chair sitting by itself in front of an impossibly large desk — black as midnight and twice as scary. Beside the large desk, two bookcases stretched across the walls, stuffed with books.

Adam marveled at the sheer number of *real* books, more than he'd ever seen in his life, all from before the Walling. But he didn't want Miss Abby to think he was enjoying his visit, so he hid his excitement.

"Sit there. The schoolmaster will be with you shortly." A faint note of compassion crept into Miss Abby's voice as she added, "Good luck, Lovecraft," then quietly closed the door behind her.

Adam wasn't sure if she had left him in the room all alone so he would feel especially guilty when the schoolmaster arrived, but that was definitely how he was feeling.

Adam's heart pounded as he waited. He whispered to

himself, "It's okay, it's okay, it's okay," over and over, just how Michael had taught him.

Adam had heard more scary stories than he could count since arriving at Chimney Rock, and many of the worst were set inside this very room. He had no idea which were fact and which were fiction. Tales of torture ran from simple spankings with wooden paddles, like the neat dozen hanging in a long row over a short black cabinet in the rear of the room, to beatings and assorted abuses administered in a small cell on the other side of the red door at the back of the schoolmaster's office.

While Adam had never given the stories much weight beyond the kinds of things that kids said to scare one another, the stories suddenly felt real enough to make him shiver.

He stared at the freshly painted red door, remembering one of the worst stories and wondering if it was true. Behind the red door, so said the story, was a black one. Behind the black one was a narrow closet's worth of space, about the size of a coffin. Guilty kids were forced to stand upright for anywhere from one to three days, depending on their infraction. Some had even died of fright inside, or so legend said.

The longer Adam stared at the red door, the harder it was to breathe. His chest tightened, and his heart felt like it might explode from his chest. If he didn't leave the office right now, he'd have a heart attack for sure.

Just as he was about to lose his composure, the schoolmaster's office door flew open, and someone who wasn't Bertram stepped inside: City Watch Chief Keller.

Adam had expected a scowling Schoolmaster Bertram, ready to beat him to within an inch of his life, or maybe take it from him, starting with three days inside the standing coffin. He certainly hadn't expected his father's old boss — smiling as if he had found a cure for the zombie virus and was mere weeks from tearing down the Walls.

"Hello, Adam, I'm Chief Keller. You remember me, right?" He extended his hand for Adam to shake.

Adam did so, nodding shyly. "Yes, Mr. Chief Keller."

While Adam's panic had subsided, it was only by a little, replaced with curiosity about why this man was here to see him.

"Just call me Keller," he said, smiling broadly. "You've grown so much. I remember when you were three and your father brought you to the office. Time sure does fly."

Adam nodded, relieved that Keller mentioned his father, but also sad.

"Are you okay?" Keller took a seat behind the giant desk, his voice softer than Adam had imagined, and kinder than anything he'd heard from any grown-up at Chimney Rock, including Miss Abby on her best day.

Adam nodded.

"Excellent. You've had a rough few months." Keller's smile was thin, but his words at least sounded sincere. "My heart bleeds for you, Adam. Now, before we get started, is there anything I can do for you? Anything at all?"

Adam shook his head, confused, but not wanting to admit his confusion.

Keller waited a moment, parted his lips, and sucked in his breath as though his next words were as painful for him as they would be for Adam. "I know about the rations."

Adam said nothing, but he wasn't sure if his face hid the lie.

He shrugged. "Someone ratted you out."

Adam wondered who Keller meant. Morgan, Tommy, and Daniel were all with him when Miss Abby came to take him, and had been since stashing the pillowcases. It had to be one of the girls. He hoped it wasn't Jayla.

"I propose we settle this," Keller paused for a second, dropping his voice like his words were a secret, "without any of the difficulties that normally accompany such unfortunate situations." He sighed. "There are too many problems in this place already, no need to add anything else to your difficult life."

Keller smiled an apology, then fell into a speech, with few pauses and not one interruption, detailing Chimney Rock's long and horrible history as a place where everyone was a victim of unfortunate reality, and how life's odds are stacked so high against its residents, it takes but one mistake for everything to crumble. According to Keller, the majority of orphans wound up in the Dark Quarter.

"Do you know what happens in the Dark Quarter, Adam?"

Adam swallowed, moving his head in an awkward circle that turned in no particular direction. He'd heard hundreds of stories, going back as early as he could remember, some true, most probably not, and not a single one he would say out loud, especially to an elder. "Sort of."

"I know how you feel." Keller smiled, his face filled with understanding. "Most of the stuff that happens in the Dark Quarter is too awful for words — the stuff of nightmares, right?"

Adam nodded, shifting in his seat.

Keller tapped one of the schoolmaster's pens against the top of his desk, then leaned back in the chair. "Well, I don't want to burden you with bad dreams, but I would like to tell you a little story. Is that okay?"

Adam nodded again, knowing that Keller wasn't really asking permission.

Keller smiled. "This story's about a kid named Alex.

It's an older story, since Alex has been gone from us for a few years now. But our tale starts when he was a boy about your age, give or take a year. Alex was moved to the orphanage after his parents were killed, getting involved in some things they shouldn't have been doing. You know how *that* goes. Eventually, Alex came of age and had to leave Chimney Rock. Without a proper foundation, his situation went from bad to worse. He fell into the Dark Quarter, then sure enough found himself in trouble with City Watch. He wound up getting to play the Darwin Games for a chance at freedom in City 7, but of course, he screwed that up, too, and wound up as a meal for a horde of starving zombies. The real horror of the story, Adam, is that not a single thing that happened to Alex was his fault. He was a good kid, fell in with some bad seeds, and got screwed by life's circumstances — a lot like you."

"What did he do?" Adam whispered through his trembling lips.

"What *didn't* he do?" Keller shrugged. "I don't know how many of life's atrocities you already know of, son, and I don't wish to put anything inside your head that doesn't need to be there or isn't already. My point in telling you this story is to make sure you don't end up like him."

Keller paused, leaning forward from his chair as he spoke in a conspiratorial whisper. *"You don't want to end up in the Dark Quarter like Alex, do you?"*

Adam swallowed, shaking his head furiously back and forth.

"Well, you don't have to," Keller reassured him. "You're not like these other deviants and lowlifes wasting God's good air in the orphanage. You're special. You weren't born in Chimney Rock or sent here as punishment. You're an unfortunate victim of circumstance. Just because your father committed an unconscionable act doesn't mean you should suffer. You, Adam, are not your father, and don't deserve to end up in prison, outside the Walls, or anywhere near the Dark Quarter."

Keller let his words sink in.

Adam's heart was racing again. The room felt even smaller with someone as imposing as Keller in it with him. Adam wished he could melt through the floor.

Keller leaned back again, setting the flat of his right foot on top of his left knee, quietly rocking.

"Before your father snapped, he was a good man and an excellent Watcher, one of the best Watchers we had. I was proud to have him serve my sector. He was a thorough officer, enforcing our laws proudly. But more than anything, your father was a friend. I loved how he always spoke of his family, like a schoolboy giddy for a pigtailed girl."

Keller laughed, then kept going. "His enthusiasm stayed fresh, even after many years. It was *you* he spoke of more than anyone, Adam. Of course Jonah went on and on about all of you, always telling me how proud he was. As much as he loved Ana, his firstborn, you were his *son*, and he had a special spot in his heart that was only for you."

Adam was doing his best to hold in his tears.

"You know how much he loved you, don't you, Adam?"

That sent him into a flood.

Keller didn't seem surprised by the tears or their heavy flow. "You wouldn't want to let your dad down, would you, Adam? So, please, do me a favor. Tell me who was with you."

Adam shook his head, sobbing as he repeated the word *no* over and over.

"I'm trying to help you, Adam. I owe that to your father. Help me help you."

He collected his breath, then spilled every bean in a sentence: "It was Daniel, Morgan, and Tommy. And Starla, Melissa, and Kim too."

He gave up everyone but Jayla, which he couldn't bear to do.

Keller smiled. "You know your friends say you're slow, don't you?"

Adam nodded, wishing Keller hadn't said that.

Keller waited for him to stop crying, then said, "Are you slow, Adam?"

"No, sir. I'm not." He shook his head. "Just a little shy, and my mind wanders sometimes. But I'm not dumb; not at all. I used to have trouble making friends, but my dad helped me through that."

Keller patted the top of Adam's hand. "I don't think you're dumb, son. Hell, you're already smarter than your sister and father. Know why?"

"Why?" Adam said, trying not to lose any more tears, though it was hard once Keller started talking about his family again, and insulting them.

Keller leaned farther forward and pressed his hand harder on Adam's. "Because *you* told me the truth. Tell me, Adam, do you want to be my friend?"

Adam nodded nervously, unsure what Keller was trying to say. He was scary-looking, but so were most adults, especially at Chimney Rock. Keller was the chief, the highest-ranking of all the Watchers — surely he was one of the good guys.

Keller's smile widened as he produced a delicate box from nowhere, setting it on the desk, lifting the lid, and filling Adam's eyes with a small pile of gold-wrapped something or others. He smiled, then whispered, "Chocolate, Adam. Would you like one?" Keller slid the box forward across the huge desk. "I think you deserve it. Don't you?"

Adam's hand inched tentatively toward the box, slightly shaking on its way. He reached inside, pulled one of the chocolates out, then looked up at Keller, half-expecting the man to snatch it away.

"Go on," Keller said, still smiling. "Enjoy it."

Adam unwrapped the chocolate, took a nibble from the tiny ball, then started to chew as Keller spoke.

"You know what courage is, Adam?"

He nodded.

"I'm glad you think you do, but I'm going to suggest that maybe you don't. Not your fault, of course. The same can be said for most children, though, since the schools are always teaching kids the wrong things about fear. Courage doesn't mean you're not scared. It means staring into the eyes of whatever terrifies you, then telling that thing to go fuck itself. Does that make sense?"

Adam laughed, then nodded.

"True courage, well, no one's born with that. I've known leaders and soldiers, son, and not a one of them was ever what you'd call fearless, and even if they were, that sure as hell wouldn't make them brave. If you're fearless, well then, you're probably reckless too, and reckless kids often end up in the Dark Quarter, and we both know you don't want to ever wind up there, right?"

Adam wasn't sure if he was supposed to agree or not, but since it seemed like Keller was waiting, he swallowed his nibble of chocolate and said, "Right," then pulled more of the sweetness into his mouth.

"Let's look at the men of Fire Watch, rushing into burning buildings to rescue people who need saving. Well, they're scared to death for most every second, but they run into the fire anyway because regardless of their fear, being a hero is who they are. We're making a big mistake teaching our kids that bravery is the absence of fear, and that being afraid is the same as being weak. Bury your fears, Adam, and they'll bury you right back. I say if you're afraid of dogs, it's time to get a puppy."

Keller smiled and tapped the box of chocolates, offering Adam another. "Do you think you can be brave?"

"Yes," Adam nodded, taking one more chocolate from the box.

"Good," Keller said with a smile. "We're going to take a little walk, together, just the two of us, back into the TV hall so you can show me everyone who was in the kitchen with you."

Adam froze. "What? But they'll be mad at me." He swallowed, then tried again. "I'm not afraid, but if I tell on them, then they won't be my friends anymore."

Keller closed the lid, made his chocolate box disappear, then leaned forward, closer than ever. For a moment his nostrils flared, and Adam was certain Keller was angry. But he wasn't. He set his hand over Adam's, the one without the chocolate.

"They'll get over it. Besides, as I said, it was one of them who ratted you out to one of your counselors."

Adam wanted to ask which friend it was, but was afraid he'd anger the chief.

"You and I are friends now, Adam, and when you're friends with me, people have no choice but to be nice to you."

"Really?" Adam asked as he stood from the desk to join Keller at the door.

"Really." Keller winked. "Now let's take that walk."

ADAM AND KELLER left the schoolmaster's office in silence, walking the corridor and then taking the elevator back upstairs before heading into the TV hall.

"Are you ready?" Keller asked, leaning into Adam as they approached his only friends in the world.

They stopped in front of Morgan, who turned to Keller with eyes so wide they looked like they might roll from their sockets. Morgan looked from Keller to Adam, then back to Keller and swallowed.

"Are these the friends who were with you in the kitchen?" Keller turned from Morgan to Tommy, then over to Daniel.

Adam nodded, avoiding eye contact with any of them.

"Anyone else?" Keller knew the answer. He wanted Adam to say it.

Adam slowly nodded, then pointed across the room toward the trio of girls, grateful that Jayla wasn't with them at the moment.

"Just to be clear, these are the thieves who helped you steal the rations?"

"Yes, sir," Adam said.

"Fucking liar!" Morgan screamed.

"SILENCE!" Keller roared.

Before Morgan could take a step back, Keller's hand struck Morgan's face, sending his knees crashing hard on the floor. His cheek was bright red, glowing from Keller's five-finger outline.

"Are you calling my friend Adam a liar?" Keller loomed over Morgan, glaring, his face red and scary.

"No," Morgan whimpered.

"No, what?" Keller backhanded Morgan across the top of his head.

"No, sir!" Morgan yelped, planting a palm over his newest bruise.

"I'd like you to apologize to my friend," Keller said, forcing Morgan to stand and say he was sorry right into Adam's eyes.

Tommy and Daniel shifted on their feet.

Keller turned to Adam, his face and voice suddenly calm. "We'll be speaking soon, Young Lovecraft. Thanks for being such a fine little Watcher."

Keller tousled Adam's hair, then turned to the group. "You can all come with me."

Keller then led the pack to the girls, instructed them to follow, and ushered the six of them from the TV hall as every accusing eye settled on Chief Keller's newest friend.

TWENTY

Jonah Lovecraft

JONAH TRIED PULLING FREE, but the rope bit deeper into his flesh, threatening to tear his wrists off if he continued.

His captors were smart, putting him in a room with no view of anything else and far from any identifiable sounds. He was underground in an old train station, but he had no clue where that was in relation to the parts of the Barrens that were sectioned off for the Darwin Games or City 6 hunting grounds.

Worse, Jonah had no idea what lay directly past the room he was in. Was he in a remote part of the subterranean refugee village, or right in the center of their version of a prison?

Even if he could break free from the ropes, Jonah had no idea what he'd be walking into. Nor did he have any idea which tunnels went back to the surface.

The tunnels went on for miles and were home to not only other refugees, but bandits, beasts, zombies, and hunter orbs closer to the City. Even if Jonah managed to break free, he had no guarantees of safety.

And even if he happened to run into Underground

rebels friendly to the cause, it wasn't as if they'd see him as a friend. He was a Watcher to them, his role in the Underground a secret they would have no reason to believe. They'd likely shoot him on sight.

Egan was his only chance at freedom, or of helping Ana.

A sudden crash pulled his attention to the doorway as Father Truth stumbled into the room and knocked a metal cart on wheels into the wall with a clang.

The dwarf was rubbing his hand on the side of his leg while righting himself from his fall, his face lightly flushed as he looked over to Jonah.

"Wasn't looking where I was going," he said, turning his embarrassment into a smile.

Jonah smiled back. It was hard not to like Father Truth. He was calm and made every word easy to believe. Jonah wondered how much his name had to do with trust. That was the sort of shit the State did. There was nothing safe about a safety stick, which most civilians called by its more appropriate name: shock stick.

"Damn," Father said, looking at Jonah's face. "Did you run into a cart, too?"

"Something like that."

Father reached into a satchel on his belt and removed a small tube, pressed some paste onto his hand, and then spread it over Jonah's swollen cheekbone.

He cringed at the touch.

"Hold on a moment," Father said, and left the room, leaving the door partly open.

Jonah's heart sped up as he pulled at his bindings again, to no avail.

Father appeared a few minutes later, dashing all hope of escape. He was followed by Calla, holding a tin bowl.

"She's going to wash your wounds. I hope you don't

mind. Meanwhile, I'm gonna give you something to ease the pain." Father pricked him with another of his needles and then stepped back as Calla approached him.

She dunked a gray rag into the bowl of water and brought it to Jonah's face. He flinched as her hand got closer, but her touch was surprisingly gentle, and her eyes focused so she would not accidentally press too hard in the wrong spots. The cold water felt good, even if it hurt.

She dipped the bloody rag into the bowl, then squeezed it out, leaving a cloud of red before bringing the cloth his face again, wiping away at his bloody lip.

"Did my father do this?" she asked, her eyes locked on his.

"It's okay, I deserved it. And thank you."

Calla finished cleaning his wound, then looked at Father Truth for approval.

"Good job, sweetie, thank you."

Calla nodded at him, then looked at Jonah again and gave him a subtle nod.

"Thank you." Jonah returned her nod and watched her leave, feeling overly emotional again. "She's a good kid." *The damned drugs!* "I thought you gave me something for the pain, Father, not more truth shit."

"Both, actually," Father said with a grin.

"Fine, fine. Could you please at least tell me what's going on with my daughter? Last night, did she make it? Is she still alive?" Jonah choked on the final question.

Father shook his head. "I don't know."

"Bullshit. That doesn't sound like *truth* to me, Father."

He smiled again, sadder than before. "You're right, and I'm sorry. Truth is, I'm not allowed to say."

"Well, what *can* you tell me?"

"What would you like to know?"

"Why are you here? To get me ready for my big trial?"

Father turned and pointed to the wall, at a slit running lengthwise beside one of the several faded train posters, so thin and draped in shadow Jonah hadn't noticed it before, even though he'd been frantically searching for signs he was being watched.

"We have a camera in the wall," Father whispered. "I came in to tell you to stop pulling at your restraints. You're making *my* wrists hurt." He turned from Jonah, then dragged a chair beside him and sat. "What else would you like to know?"

"Can you tell me about the trial?"

"Sure. What do you wish to know?"

"Anything? I mean, why have one at all? Seems like Egan's mind is made up already. Hell, I don't even know what I'm being charged with, but I know I'm guilty."

"Because sometimes doing the right thing when everything else is wrong is all we have left." Father crossed one leg over the other, and Jonah had to swallow a laugh despite it all.

"Nearly two hundred years ago, the Old Nation went to war with the East, and the president authorized leaders within the War Department to place all citizens from the East into detention camps. So they rounded up 120,000 citizens of the Old Nation and locked them away. Most had documentation, but the War Department granted themselves permission to evacuate and imprison any citizen they wanted, forgoing the time-honored right to a fair trial for the first time in the Old Nation's history. The war lasted a few years, I'm not sure exactly how long, but through its entirety, not a single spy was arrested or convicted."

Father shifted in his chair and continued. "Hard to say whether this was morally right or wrong. Who knows? The Old Nation was at war, and they probably figured they were keeping citizens safe. But back when my father told me those stories, before I escaped the Dark Quarter and the City, he spoke of a world where things like laws weren't thrown aside as soon as it became inconvenient to follow them. We're different here than inside the City. Laws aren't arbitrary, and justice means something."

"So, I get a 'fair trial' so you can say you gave me one to keep an illusion of what, exactly?" Jonah shook his head. "That's bullshit, and it means nothing. Egan's already decided I'm guilty, so what's the point? I'm just another prisoner in the camp, with formality to slow things down. I should be in the Barrens, looking for my daughter."

"Egan isn't in charge. We have a Council of Five. Egan is only one vote. Even if he's decided, that makes twenty percent of the vote, and honestly," Father met Jonah's eyes, "I think you do Egan, and yourself, a grave disservice assuming his mind is so easily tainted." He leaned forward. "Would you really be so unfair?"

Jonah shook his head. "Does the council know he's gonna try me?"

"They're aware of your crimes, yes."

"I want to talk to Egan."

"Why? Do you have new information? Would you like to confess to a crime? He won't be interested in seeing you if not."

"Yes. I have something I'd like to confess."

"Really?" Father replied, eyebrows arched. Something about his expression reminded Jonah of Duncan. He wasn't sure why, but the feeling was unmistakable.

"Yes," Jonah repeated. "I have something to confess."

"Very well. I'll be back."

He left, disappearing up the stairway before returning

moments later with Egan, as though he had been standing nearby waiting for Father to fetch him.

Father and Egan stood side by side.

Egan said, "So, you have something to confess?"

"I do."

"Then get on with it." Egan crossed his arms, waiting.

Jonah wasn't sure what he was going to say, only that he wanted to inspire Egan's humanity.

"I'm a bad man," Jonah said. "I deserve to hang for many sins. Some at the service of the City and State, ignorant of my wrongdoing. Others where I knew what I was doing wasn't right, yet I did them anyway because it was easier to follow than to question authority. Hell, I *was* the authority. And I wish I could take it all back. As a Watcher, I burned books because they contained forbidden knowledge, I actively pursued people I thought to be conspiring against the City, I torched people's homes and shops to teach them to obey the City, and I burned evidence that likely could have freed many people over the years. But the sin I regret more than all others combined was not telling the truth that day in the courtroom."

Jonah swallowed, partly for drama and partly to try to keep his voice from cracking. "When I saw your eyes, when you begged me to tell the truth that day, part of me knew right there that I should've done something. And yet I did nothing. It felt too late to put the genie back in the bottle. And then, when I was called onto the scene where your wife was murdered, it killed me to know that it would never have happened had I told the truth. You'd still have your wife and your son, and you'd still be living in City 6, happily ever after. Well, maybe not, if someone was setting you up. But perhaps I could've intervened and spared you some of the heartache. Maybe I could have made a difference. But I didn't. I was a coward. And for that, I am sorry, Mr. Egan."

Egan stared, emotionless despite Jonah's plea.

Is he waiting for something else?

Jonah continued, hoping to find the right blend of words to change his mind.

"I have no problem paying for my sins, and I tried making amends with years of service in the Underground, helping rebels behind the Walls. I probably made a bigger difference than anyone else in that time, at least when it came to raw numbers, constantly furthering the cause. I wanted to undo some of my wrongs."

Jonah didn't want to cry, even if it would help draw Egan's sympathy, and hated his eyes for welling up. "If my attempted amends aren't enough to pay for my mistakes, well ..." Jonah held his stare "... then I'm happy to pay with my life. But not yet. Not while my daughter's in danger, and not when I can still help her. Please, Egan. Let me go, let me find Ana and save her — she shouldn't have to pay for *my* crimes."

There was a glimmer in Egan's eyes. For a second, Jonah thought he had reached Egan, that maybe his words had slipped through some small chink in his emotional armor.

Then the glimmer was gone. His eyes were cold and dark as he leaned into Jonah. "My family paid for my supposed crimes against the State. So perhaps its only justice that yours do the same. An eye for an eye, two lives for two lives. *That* sounds just to me. In a few hours you can make your case at your trial. Maybe you'll find the mercy I was denied."

Egan turned and left the room without another word.

Jonah's eyes met Father's, seeing an expression he knew

all too well: the look one gave a dead man moments ahead of his sentencing.

TWENTY-ONE

Liam Harrow

Liam was careful to vary his walk, occasionally pulling ahead of the group, or falling slightly behind, making sure they saw him as a minimal threat, absorbing the inane chatter from the men while trying to ignore Chloe's siren song in his ear.

The longer he walked behind her, the more he wanted to fuck her. But each time he caught himself staring at her ass, he turned his attention to Marcus's giant caboose instead, splashing cold water on his libido. Thankfully, it was a trick that had worked each time over the course of the hour they'd been walking together.

"I prefer a blade," Keb said.

"Why would anyone *prefer* a blade?" Chloe turned to the tattooed leader, or at least the guy too dumb to realize the leader was actually Chloe. "A blade is only slightly better than nothing, and a great way to get yourself dead."

Keb shook his head. "You're only saying that since you're a girl, and hand-to-hand's not your thing. But Marcus would agree. Guns are too easy, a lot like your crossbow. A knife is up close, personal, and the only way to really taste the kill."

"You're an asshole," Chloe said. "Why would you want to get that personal? What in the hell is wrong with you? It's no wonder you're here."

Liam winced as she said it — the third such comment directed at Keb in the last half hour or so. Chloe's subtle personal attacks were designed, Liam was certain, to create some tension among the men — the sort of comments that were likely dormant before Liam entered the picture.

"Tasting your kill tells you who you are. And if you expect to survive out here and make it to City 7, you *need* to *know* who you are." Keb clenched and unclenched his fist as he walked, shifting his sword from left to right, whipping its curve against the wind.

"Why do I get the feeling you volunteered your way outside the Walls like an idiot?" Chloe said. "Seems like you get off on this."

Keb shrugged. "One man's idiot is another man's genius. We'll see who's stupid when I'm sipping cocktails in City 7. I've been waiting for this since I was a kid. I'm finishing this shit nice and alive. Sorry to let you three down, but none of you stands a chance. Sticking with me, though, that'll definitely get you living longer than you would've otherwise."

Keb winked. Liam wasn't sure whether it indicated that he was just trying to rile Chloe up, or making a veiled threat and hoping he'd take the bait.

Marcus piped in. "You might be good with that blade, but you weigh less than a girl, man, so I don't think you're gonna win shit if I'm still in this thing."

Chloe laughed. So did Keb, though his was a horrible icy cackle. The hairs on Liam's neck stiffened as Keb stopped walking mid-stride, then turned and stared up into the giant's eyes. "You must have me mistaken for someone who can't kill a fucker a minute after he thinks it." He laughed again, louder. "You ever come across someone, and about a second after you stared into their eyes you knew they was the one person you shouldn't have fucked with? Well, that was me behind the Walls, you big ape, and I'm a hundred times more dangerous out here."

"Show, don't tell, asshole," Chloe said, with a light laugh with just enough charm to keep Keb in a smile.

Marcus held Keb's stare, then surprised Liam by getting more articulate by the minute. "I'm not much for saying my thinking out loud, since folks don't usually expect me to say much. But the truth is, all of us are going to die, and probably none of us will make it to City 7, *if* it even exists, which it might not. My kid brother Johnny won the games about four years back, and I've not heard a word from him since. Whether we make it to the end or not, all that matters is that we stand against the enemy with our feet unmoving for as long as we can. Nothing is certain in these games, and most times people win by accident. I'm glad to live a little longer with the two, and now the three, of you by my side." He turned to Liam, smiled, then added, "That is all."

Liam liked the guy more and more the longer they walked together, even if he did have an ass like an anvil.

Keb said, "You haven't heard from anyone from City 7 because they're not allowed to communicate with the other Cities. That's a fact, Mack. And here's another one: I've been ready to make my way to the end since I was fourteen, and I guarantee I will."

Marcus started walking. "Only reason Johnny wouldn't find a way to send word to his brother, allowed or not, would be if he was dead. Like I said, City 7's probably a legend. Why don't you think they ever show past winners on TV?"

Keb said, "I dunno, it's some policy thing or something, who the fuck knows, but City 7 is real. If it's not, then we would've known by now. And we'd all be fighting in these Games for nothing."

The group fell into silence. Liam figured they were each contemplating the discussion and whether or not they truly were fighting for nothing. Or maybe they were each trying to figure out the best way to make it all the way, and who they'd have to kill first.

Liam wondered what Chloe was thinking. She kept looking from one of them to the other, acting like she wasn't looking at any of them.

They trudged through the snow, thinning it to sludge. The wind had died down to practically nothing, which made it easy to hear the first zombie nearly a minute before they saw it shambling from the woods.

Keb started laughing, hysterical and almost out-of-control, like a kid about to run out and play hit ball.

He then stood still, body tensed, waiting for the zombie to come closer. Fifty yards away, Keb raced toward it screaming, arm hovering high, where it stayed until he was three feet from the undead monster, and he lowered the blade in a low swoop, landing deep into its shoulder, drowning both metal and snow in buckets of blood.

Still laughing, he yanked his sword from the zombie's shoulder, then swung it around, making stupid sounds like he was having way too much fun, or showing off what a badass he truly was with his blade.

Keb swung the sword in a wide arc and chopped the zombie's head clean from its neck, sending it into the snow.

The zombie crashed to its knees, swaying for a moment

before falling forward and spurting more dark blood into the snow like a busted spigot.

Keb turned in a circle, holding his arms to his side as though he were a T, waiting for applause that wasn't ever going to come.

Silence stretched until it made Chloe laugh.

"Fuck you, people," Keb said with a chuckle. "That was some ninja shit right there."

"Yeah. You're a reg—"

Chloe's comment was clipped short by a high-pitched scream from the woods behind Keb, followed by what sounded like at least a dozen more.

Oh shit!

Immediately, Liam thought of his gun with no ammo. Not only was he unable to fight the zombies, but should they survive the attack, he'd be exposed, and likely killed for bluffing his way onto their team.

"What are you waiting for?" Keb hollered without turning. "Attack!"

Liam ran toward the zombies, two steps behind Chloe and Marcus, hoping Keb would die. He was clearly skilled but a danger to all. If Keb dropped, then Liam could "lose" his gun and grab the sword, and do some damage and continue his deception.

Liam reached the swarm counting nine zombies total, fewer than he feared, but not exactly a light load considering their speed, regardless of the snow.

They were nearly surrounded as Liam entered the fray with his fists. Three zombies leaped on Keb, dragging him to the ground.

"What the fuck?" Chloe screamed at Liam as she fired a bolt into a charging zombie. "What in the hell are you waiting for? Shoot the fuckers!"

"My gun is jammed." The words were sour on his

tongue. As if to pay for his lie, Liam ran straight into the swarm, pulled an attacking zombie from Keb's body, then snapped its neck and dropped it to the snow before diving back inside for another.

Keb screamed for help beneath the pile, mostly profanities, as more zombies piled on top, teeth gnashing. Liam was doing his best, but without a weapon, he could only take on one at a time.

Keb's screams turned to muffled mumbles, then died entirely, drowned by the thunder of ripping flesh and the sloppy, soaking-wet sound of their feasting.

As Liam broke a second zombie's neck, another two came toward him.

He spotted Keb's sword lying a few feet behind them on the ground.

He raced right at the two zombies, diving to the snow just seconds before they collided into one another.

He grabbed the sword by the sticky handle, and leapt to his feet.

A female zombie ran at him, a scream like gravel spewing from her throat, hands stretching toward him.

Liam only had seconds to position the blade before she ran right into him. If he fell, he'd be buried in a pile like Keb.

He thrust the blade at her skull, impaling her face, destroying what was left of her brain.

Her arms went limp seconds before her legs did, dropping her to the ground as he pulled the sword from her head.

Liam spun around to see how the others were faring.

Keb had managed to kill three zombies before they ended his chances of making it to City 7 forever. Chloe took two before the crossbow was knocked from her hand.

She was fighting another hand-to-hand, but was too

timid in her battle and getting pushed back toward the Fire Wall.

To Liam's surprise, Marcus had only managed to kill one, but was now wildly swinging his pipe and keeping the remaining zombies away from Chloe.

Marcus bashed one zombie's skull, then immediately moved to the next one, almost as if the first motion gave birth to the second. He laughed, growled, then ran at another pair of moaners, ducking low and bashing them at the knee.

Once the zombies were down, Marcus turned back to help Chloe. But he'd failed to finish them off, and seconds after he turned his back, the zombies were on him.

Chloe screamed, running away from two zombies grasping at her as she ran, defenseless.

Liam rushed to intervene, swinging the sword into the first zombie's head, lopping it clean off.

The second zombie ran straight into his blade, almost like suicide, which made Liam laugh unexpectedly before as he finished it off.

Liam raced toward Marcus, who was fighting the last four zombies as Chloe retrieved her crossbow. He swung at the creature closest to him, and she sent a bolt into the open-sored skull of a second zombie.

Liam reached Marcus, who was pushing back two zombies as a third one came at him from behind.

Liam drove his sword into the back of the monster's skull.

As he went to yank it free, the zombie fell to the side, taking the sword with it to the ground. Liam leaned over, grabbed the hilt, and wrenched it free.

He turned back to Marcus, sword in hand but too late.

Marcus toppled over with one of the fuckers gnawing

at his throat, as the other one chomped into his arm, causing him to drop the pipe.

The big man fell, screaming as the zombies feasted.

Liam felt a flush of anger even though he knew he'd have to kill the giant eventually. Nobody should have to die like that.

Liam swung hard, the sword splitting the creature's skull open, then thrust the blade into its brain.

Chloe finished the final zombie, then they paused, surveying the dead and scanning the woods for danger.

Orbs hovered above them, watching and recording their every move.

"Fuck!" Chloe screamed, despite the danger.

She walked away, then bent to retrieve something Liam couldn't see, before spinning around and glaring at him.

Chloe was holding his gun. She threw it to the ground and raised her crossbow. "Jammed? You didn't have any ammo!"

Liam raised his sword, though it wouldn't do shit if she pulled the trigger.

"Drop it," she ordered, coming toward him.

"No way!" Liam gripped it tighter.

"Drop it or I'll put a bolt between your eyes!"

He met her eyes: *She wasn't fucking around.*

He dropped the sword and she lowered her crossbow.

"You lied to us! You cost me two players, you bastard!" She swung before he could stop her, hitting him hard in the head with the butt of her crossbow.

He fell to the ground, his head feeling like a dropped melon. He managed to laugh, using a bulletproof tone that had diffused countless situations.

But Chloe was glaring at him.

She pointed her crossbow first at his heart, and then

raised her aim to his forehead. Liam, still lying on the ground, didn't dare move, or laugh again.

"Listen Chloe," he said, palms open, eyes pleading, "I'm still an asset. Let me help. You don't have to do this."

Chloe twisted her voice into the tune of mockery, so tight it sounded almost evil: *"Listen Chloe, I'm still an asset. Let me help. You don't have to do this."*

She took another step toward Liam. "Sorry, but I don't need you anymore. Now you're only in the way."

She blew him a kiss, then pulled the trigger.

TWENTY-TWO

Anastasia Lovecraft

ANA STARED in horror at the battle erupting before her.

Liam and his new teammates were outnumbered, and the creatures had already claimed two, a skinny guy and the huge, giant guy.

Ana moved nearer to them during the battle but didn't get too close, afraid the players might see her as a threat instead of a potential ally.

When the zombies were all dead, the blonde girl turned on Liam and screamed, "You lied to us! You cost me two players, you bastard!"

Liam was on the ground, trying to weasel his way out of the jam, as Ana had often seen him do. But this girl was angry, and Ana had only seconds to intervene.

The girl stepped toward Liam, her face red with fury. She aimed her crossbow, moving from Liam's heart to his forehead. He held his ground.

Ana raced toward them, praying the girl wouldn't hear her coming.

"Listen Chloe, I'm still an asset," Liam said. "Let me help. You don't have to do this."

"Listen Chloe, I'm still an asset. Let me help. You don't have to do this," the girl repeated, her voice cruel. She took another step, then said, "Sorry, but I don't need you anymore. Now you're only in the way."

She blew a kiss and pulled the trigger as Ana plunged a sword through her back.

The bolt flew at Liam, barely missing his forehead but coming close enough to leave a line of gushing blood.

The girl crashed to the ground, bleeding out as the life left her wide-open eyes.

Liam slowly rose, wobbling in the snow, clearly woozy.

"Are you okay?" Ana said, scared.

"My head … It's pounding like—"

He crashed back to the ground. Ana kneeled down to help him, lightly slapping his face until he finally began blinking his eyes. Once fully open, they widened in horror.

Ana heard the horrible groaning coming from behind her. She looked up to see the giant rising, oblivious to the blood spilling from his open neck. His eyes were white, his mouth open and moaning.

He growled as he began walking toward them as the tattooed guy shambled to his feet with a scream that sounded like death being born.

Ana turned and saw her sword sticking out of the blonde girl, now standing beside her, mouth chomping for flesh.

TWENTY-THREE

Liam Harrow

LIAM BLINKED, almost believing the abominations lumbering toward them might be a side effect of Chloe's hitting him in the head.

No way this is real.

And yet, it was.

Chloe, Keb, and Marcus — all dead seconds before — had risen as zombies, snarling as they clomped through the snow, looking to devour them.

Liam had seen plenty of undead raging their way across the Barrens, through a lifetime of staring at the ubiquitous screens inside the City, yet he'd never seen players rise again so quickly.

While his former teammates' flesh had not yet started decaying or reeking of the putrefied stench of the undead, there was no mistaking that Chloe, Keb, and Marcus had become zombies. They had that familiar haunted white horror in their vacant eyes. Their mouths were open, with awful, elongated moans stretching from their lips, kissing the air with garbled bits of nothing.

And they appeared singular in their purpose — to feast on the living.

Why are they up so quickly? Marcus, maybe, he was bit. But the others?

Liam couldn't help but feel he was witnessing something new taking place, something with horrifying implications, yet he couldn't quite put his finger on what those implications were just yet. First he had to figure out how to kill his former comrades for a second time.

Liam leaped to his feet, head still throbbing from Chloe's attack, trying to find his balance and assess the situation. Zombie Chloe was closest, with the other two zombies on the way. He grabbed the sword he'd been forced to drop.

But before he could take a step, Ana sprang into action, racing past Chloe, then grabbing hold of the sword still impaled in her back. She stumbled back and as she yanked at it, but managed to stay upright as Zombie Chloe growled and turned to swipe at Ana.

Ana swung the sword in a wide arc, lopping Chloe's head off with a sickening *thunk*.

Chloe's head smacked the ground a second ahead of her body. Liam looked at her splayed fingers, opening and closing as if in search of her head.

Ana and Liam's eyes met, frozen for a moment.

There was movement behind her. He screamed to warn her, too late.

Zombie Marcus hit Ana in the back of her head, knocking her toward Liam's sword.

He pulled the sword back and leaped sideways, barely avoiding her.

Zombie Marcus barreled forward, his dead eyes on Ana, mouth open and growling.

Liam ran shoulder-first into the behemoth, but *Liam* fell

backward, pain splintering through his shoulder as if he'd run into a brick wall.

He fell back in the snow and stared up as Zombie Marcus bellowed. His rock-like teeth seemed all the more menacing now as a vow to rip the skin from their bones if given a chance.

Liam scrambled backward, slipping and sliding in the snow, trying to gain space as Zombie Marcus reached down with both hands, pawing through empty air.

The monster misjudged his timing, either not expecting Liam to move so fast or was too broken in brain and thought to calculate any moves.

The zombie swiped hard at nothing, then slipped and fell forward with an angry grunt.

Liam jumped back to his feet and thrust the sword through Marcus's side, spilling his guts and releasing their steaming contents to the snow below.

He was about to finish Marcus off with a stab to the brain, but Ana screamed and his attention was instantly on her.

Ana was on the ground, Zombie Keb on top of her, chomping jaws held barely at bay by Ana's skinny fingers gripping his larynx.

Liam ran to help, sword drawn.

Her panicked eyes caught Liam's, flickered with relief before going wide-eyed with horror. He felt the thunder behind him, too late to recognize the threat.

Pain exploded in his right ear, tearing through his skull as Zombie Marcus's fist clobbered him sideways to the snow, sword spilling from his hand.

He hit the ground rolling and sliding, trying to gain distance from the beast. If the zombie's full weight fell on Liam, its jagged maw would surely tear into his flesh.

The zombie growled, angry and agitated, charging forward.

His head was pounding, vertigo tilting the world on end. Yet, somehow Liam was able to barely dodge the giant with its slashed gut and oozing insides hanging from its torn coveralls.

Zombie Marcus slid past Liam, and hit the ground with his face.

Ana screamed again, shrill as her grip on Zombie Keb's neck slackened and the monster's teeth opened and closed, trying to bite her arms.

Liam thought of Jonah's battle with the zombie at the end of the last Darwin, and how he'd managed to grab an orb and bash the undead fucker over the head. But the orbs observing their scuffle were hovering too high, and Liam doubted Ana could manage Jonah's nearly impossible feat even if they weren't.

Liam spotted the sword on the ground, six feet away. He threw himself forward, on clawed hands and bruised knees, scrambling for the weapon.

Fingers inches from the hilt, something grabbed tight around his right ankle and yanked. Liam screamed, twisting around to find Zombie Marcus dragging him back with one hand. Even braindead, the zombie saw the danger of Liam reaching the weapon.

He twisted and turned, trying to wrangle free from the giant's grip, but Zombie Marcus was squeezing Liam's ankle hard enough to make it feel like it might snap off.

Liam grabbed a handful of snow, squeezed it into a ball, then hurled the snowball into its face.

Zombie Marcus let go of Liam to swipe at his eyes.

Liam's foot dropped and he seized the moment to slip away, diving again for the sword.

But Zombie Marcus grabbed his feet again, this time both of them.

"Shit!" Liam screamed.

Zombie Marcus pulled harder, dragging Liam even farther from the sword. He tried, but failed, to get a grip of anything on the ground to hold onto. He looked up just in time to see Ana losing her battle and Zombie Keb bearing down, just inches from her face.

Liam screamed, kicking wildly, trying desperately to break free as Zombie Marcus kept dragging him away to do God knows what to him.

Someone raced past him — a tiny red-haired girl, holding a pistol and heading for Ana.

"Ana!" Liam screamed, alerting her to the contestant trying to capitalize on their weakened positions by picking them off.

She hadn't noticed the girl, but Zombie Marcus *had*.

He let go of Liam and barreled toward the girl.

The red-haired girl stopped, standing two feet from Ana, then raised the gun and fired, shooting Zombie Keb from behind, blowing a chunk of its skull into fragments.

Ana screamed and shoved the zombie's body off of hers.

Before Liam could determine whether the girl was helping or about to shoot Ana, Zombie Marcus was nearly on top of her, swiping his massive arm at her tiny head.

She was small and agile enough to duck beneath his swing. She dodged a giant fist, fell to the ground, and rolled through the snow, right between his legs, popping out on the other side right behind him.

The tiny thing fired once, twice, then a third time, until her gun clicked empty.

Zombie Marcus turned, slowly toward the girl, growling.

Shit! Run, kid!

She stared down her empty gun, frozen as the monster faced her.

Marcus swayed, then fell to his knees, stunned.

The undead wasn't down, even if broken.

She fell a step back, grabbing the sword and swinging it in a wide circle, severing the zombie's head from its massive body.

Liam approached the girl, shaking as her eyes widened, looking up at him down the barrel of an empty gun.

The girl took a step back, followed by another three as she eased her way toward the tree line in terror. She threw her gun to the ground, pulled a knife from a sheath at her waist, then held it out, eyes darting back and forth between Liam and Ana.

"It's okay," Ana said, kneeling to the ground and laying her sword in the snow. "We're not going to hurt you."

The girl stared at Ana, then Liam.

He was still catching his breath, nervous that she would do something stupid, like try to stab one of them with her tiny knife.

She was too young to be in the Games, even if technically eligible. She was small and shivering, and Liam wondered how she'd made it this far. And why had she decided to help them? Was she looking for safety in numbers? Considering how the Games had to end, he didn't want to team with another player, especially a child. That was heartbreak waiting to happen.

Liam smiled to let her know that he wasn't a threat, palms facing her. "Thank you. You saved our lives. My name is Liam, and this is Ana."

The girl just stood there, the knife shaking in her hands.

"She doesn't have a tongue," Ana said.

"What?"

"She's a Quarter kid, I think. Someone cut out her tongue."

Liam swallowed, shaking his head. "I'm sorry. I promise, we won't hurt you." After a long pause, and an exchanged glance with Ana, "You're welcome to come with us, if you want."

She pointed at Ana, mouthing something Liam couldn't make out.

But Ana seemed to have understood the girl. "Yes, it's okay — I won't hurt you, either. Promise."

THEY'D BEEN WALKING for a half hour — mostly in silence as the girl followed several steps behind them — when Liam spotted a cave.

"I don't know ..." Ana shook her head before explaining how her last entry into a rocky black mouth had thrown her into a mini-game.

Liam told the girl to wait, then crept inside the cave to investigate. He held a pack of matches he'd taken from Keb's fallen body. He struck one of the dozen matches, then held the flame in front of his face as he peered into the black.

Liam could never know for certain, but it seemed — and more important felt — safe enough. The cave was slightly off their present path and twisted into an ever-narrowing hollow. While uncomfortable, the recess seemed like an unlikely spot for a zombie, giving them a decent hiding place with only a single entrance to guard.

It was the best rest spot Liam had seen, and if they

didn't stop for rest soon, they would all be dead within a day. Dulled instincts were a bigger threat to players than the opponents themselves.

"We'll take shifts," Liam suggested, starting a small fire in the back of the cave. "I'll stay up while you two get some shut-eye. Tomorrow morning, I'll grab an hour."

"An hour?" Ana repeated.

"That's all I need."

"You sure?"

"Positive."

The girl furiously shook her head, stepping back toward the entrance.

Liam turned to Ana. Allowing her to leave the cave would leave them vulnerable.

"It's okay," Ana assured her. "We're safe in here. We won't hurt you, and all of us need sleep. Do you understand?"

She nodded, then shook her head as if to erase it.

Ana kneeled, then slowly crawled across the cave floor until she was a few feet from the unmoving child. She pulled the girl's hands into her palms. "I promise, we won't hurt you. Would you like to sleep with my sword?"

The little girl nodded, then shook her head again.

"We're going to be okay. It's better in here with no zombies and maybe a little sleep, than for us to be out there with all of one and none of the other." Ana smiled and pointed to the mouth of the cave.

The girl made a face that looked surprisingly like a smile, and nodded.

"Why don't you two girls huddle together. It's freezing in here, even with the fire. Cuddle so you can keep each other warm."

"I'm going to put my sword in the corner," Ana held her eyes, "but you hold onto your knife, okay?"

She nodded.

Ana thanked her again for saving them and apologized for what had happened in the forest before, then she turned to Liam and spun their earlier story, letting her hear as she explained that she hadn't been trying to hurt her. She was scared and didn't know what else to do.

The girl yawned, seeming seconds from a full collapse, then finally nodded and crawled to a spot near the fire. Ana came up and huddled beside her. The girl was asleep in seconds, Ana followed her lead in minutes.

Liam stared at the girls as they slept, sorting his thoughts around the unexpected doubling of his burden. He didn't mind looking after Ana. He owed it to her, and to Jonah even more. Betraying the Underground left Liam with a debt he intended to pay — even if it meant settling the tab with his life.

Liam was prepared to get Ana to the Final Battle unharmed, then kill himself before it started. But also keeping the child alive would be impossible. The Darwins had one winner. If Ana lived, the girl died. So what was the point in prolonging the inevitable?

While staring at the child, still beneath a heavy sleep, Liam wondered about the cruelties that had eaten through her life in City 2. He had never been to any City outside of City 6 and therefore had no comparison, but since human cruelty knew no bounds, so surely their Dark Quarter was equally horrific.

He felt a chill, wondering how many atrocities had been visited upon people he loved because of his betrayal, and fell asleep wishing he'd been more faithful to the Underground.

HE TRIED STAYING awake until one of the girls opened her eyes, but Liam's eyelids grew too heavy to lift and he finally fell asleep not long before dawn. He slept for maybe an hour, though it felt like seconds, and woke to the hum of several orbs growing suddenly louder.

Blue light bounced everywhere as Kirkman's voice echoed through the bottled air. "Are you ready to wake up, contestants? I hope so, because it's *tiiiiime* to play! And we'll be starting this morning with a brand-new mini-game!"

Liam sprang to his feet and looked around. He was standing in a clear plastic box in an old barn that was surely older than the Walling.

Morning light poured through a gaping hole in the roof, illuminating heavy vegetation creeping into the barn.

Liam looked for his companions and found another pair of plastic boxes, one in the middle and another across the barn, one holding Ana and the other the child.

"No!" Liam pounded his fist against the plastic walls. He was trapped; they all were — likely gassed and dragged from the cave before getting tossed into the old barn.

He had never seen producers get so involved in a show. At least when watching from the monitors, the Games seemed to unfold naturally enough, but this was an outright manipulation of events.

He wondered if the audience had seen what had happened, or if they were lied to, a witness only to Liam, Ana, and the child waking in the boxes and believing that they had somehow stumbled inside the barn on their own.

"What did you do?" Liam screamed into the monitor atop the box.

Kirkman smiled. "Are you prepared for another challenge? We have a **BRAND** *new* mini-game, added to the Darwins! And you're lucky enough to play it first! It's called The Killing Choice. Are. You. Ready?"

The barn doors slid open wide on their tracks, spilling more bright light inside. And with the light came rapidly moving shadows, along with their undead owners.

Liam looked up at the monitor, screaming.

TWENTY-FOUR

Jonah Lovecraft

THE ROPE BIT deeper into Jonah's flesh as he pulled harder against his restraints. His flesh felt like raw meat. He tugged with more force, sending a shock of pain through his body as the cord bit into his tender skin. He winced, then hung his head in defeat as he realized he couldn't break free of his bindings.

Even if he had, Father Truth told him that he was being watched. So, how far would he really get? Again, it seemed that working on Egan was his only chance of freedom.

When he looked up, Jonah was surprised to find himself staring at Egan, though he'd not heard the man enter the room.

He sat in the chair across from Jonah and stared at him for minutes without words.

Jonah's head screamed as his flesh burned. "What?"

"Have you given any thoughts to your defense?"

"I don't even know the crime I'm charged with." Jonah swallowed, trying to keep from covering Egan in spit.

"Murder, of course. Someone must pay for the deaths of my wife and son."

Jonah said nothing, certain Egan wasn't searching for an apology. He was on a safari for something else, though Jonah couldn't begin to guess what that might be, and he felt too beaten to try. He sat quietly, waiting for Egan to speak.

"I've been thinking," Egan finally said, nibbling on a fingernail while narrowing his eyes at Jonah. "You said you were set up for your wife's murder, right?"

"Yes," Jonah nodded.

"And you're sticking with that story?"

He nodded again.

"So, how was the State able to manufacture such damning proof against you? The evidence had to be airtight, right? They couldn't throw you out like they did me. No, you were a Watcher. So, what did they have on you, Jonah?"

"My daughter testified against me."

His mouth split into a wide smile. "Oh, *reeeeeally?*"

His cheeks twitched, but Jonah refused to satisfy Egan by revealing his anger.

"Your own daughter testified *against* you? She must have really hated you."

"No." Jonah shook his head. "She didn't."

"So, what was it, then? Why would she help set you up? Was she corrupt like her daddy?"

"I don't know how they did it. I suspect the State planted memories in her mind. A good friend of mine swears there's a secret chip, besides the ID chip, inside every citizen, and that the Cities can use these chips to plant false memories at will."

"A mind-control chip?" Egan said, clearly trying to

suppress a skeptical laugh as he raised an eyebrow. "And who is this friend?"

"Someone in the Underground. Name's not important."

"How could this friend possibly know about such a chip, if it really did exist?"

"I don't know whether he knows or suspects." Jonah shrugged. "He has plenty of conspiracy theories and no shortage of outlandish ideas, so it's hard to know what to take seriously. I thought it was farfetched until I stared at my daughter in the witness box, listening to her swear she saw me murder her mother in cold blood."

"So you think they somehow corrupted your daughter's memories?"

"I don't know," Jonah said, hoping honest answers would color him as cooperative or at least sympathetic, and that Egan might be more willing to grant him leniency. "I can't see any other reason why she'd testify like she did. She seemed so certain during the trial, so filled with rage — the sort of anger that could never be faked. I don't think she was intentionally lying. She believed that she saw me murder Molly."

"Hmmm ..." Egan stroked his chin as if considering Jonah's situation. "Why would the State want your wife murdered?"

"I've no idea." Jonah shook his head.

"Did you have any information on the State, or Keller? Did they somehow discover your role in the Underground?"

"They questioned me on the Underground. I don't know if they knew, someone told them, or perhaps it was just another one of Keller's witch hunts."

"Are the tunnels still open? Can the Underground still get people in and out of City 6?"

"They were working when I was arrested, but without me there, I don't see how they could keep them running unless they had someone else — someone I didn't know about — on the inside. They might be open, might be closed. Your guess is exactly as good as mine."

"Could you find the tunnels now?"

Egan's people had to know many, if not most of the end points. There were catacombs and abandoned tunnels running beneath most of the land from the Barrens to the City, a winding maze few people knew well enough to navigate, but if Egan had been living here and receiving new citizens to his underground city, then surely he was aware of at least some of the tunnel locations.

Something wasn't adding up. But Jonah had to hide his suspicions in hopes that Egan would spill information that might shed some light on the confusion.

Jonah looked him in the eyes. "I'll tell you anything you want to know about my involvement with the Underground. But I'm not willing to give away any information that might compromise the organization or put anyone's life at risk. I'm sorry."

"No, I'm sorry," Egan said, then stared, just long enough for Jonah to squirm.

Egan stood up and looked down at him. "The Underground sounds like quite the noble enterprise, helping people escape the treachery of the City. Yet, when *I* was forced into the Games, no one thought to help my family, no one came to retrieve my wife or children and usher them to safety. Why do you think that is, Lovecraft? Any theories you'd like to share?"

"I wasn't part of the Underground then. Maybe the tunnels weren't operational, or only used on rare occasions. I don't see how my speculation helps either of us."

"So, if you *had been* with the Underground then, you're

saying you would have helped my family escape to the outside? You would have laid your life on the line for theirs, made sure they were spared, kept safe outside the City?"

Jonah was walking into something, blind and empty-handed. Egan's logic was spinning, but Jonah had no idea what it was revolving around.

He *should* say that yes, of course he would have helped. But that wasn't the truth — that wasn't how it worked. Jonah didn't always do the *right* thing because sometimes the *right thing* was wrong for the greater good. He had interests to weigh, and things were never as simple as the needs of one family. The cause was *most* important, and protecting the interests of the Underground, or maintaining his cover at City Watch, meant worthy people were often denied passage.

The truth wasn't kind, but in his seat, it was all he had. "I don't know what I would've done."

Egan chewed on Jonah's response, pacing in small circles around his chair, looking like he wanted to sit. "Why do you think no one helped your children escape?"

Jonah was confused, and uncomfortable with the edge in Egan's voice. "What?"

"When City Watch came for you, you were finished. You and everyone else had to know it. Have you ever known City Watch to make a high-profile arrest, then let their prisoner go?"

Egan paused, as if awaiting his answer, though both knew there wasn't any need. City Watch arrested plenty of citizens, often for questioning, hoping to turn neighbor against neighbor, or even better, sibling against sibling or child against parent, but if an arrest made the monitors, suspects were guilty of *something* — regardless of the truth.

"The Underground must have known you were arrested, and been aware that your children could be used against you or would be shuffled off to the orphanage, right? So why weren't they spared? Why not get them out of City 6?"

Jonah whispered the same answer he'd turned in his mind so many times. "Because my children were under watch. They had to be, especially Ana. The State needed her testimony, and they weren't willing to let anything stand in their way."

"Ah," Egan sneered, "so now that she's outlived her usefulness, it's off to the Games with her? Maybe they had to get her out of the City since those false memories don't last forever. They had to destroy evidence, which is, after all, what you Watchers are so excellent at doing — besides manufacturing the lies from scratch, of course."

"What do you mean the memories don't last forever? What are you talking about?"

"Do you know what I did for credits before my inconvenient arrest?"

"You were a factory worker, making circuit boards for the orbs, right?"

"Wow," Egan said, grinning. "They really didn't tell you anything, did they? Perhaps you weren't as complicit in my framing as I suspected."

"What are you talking about?"

"I didn't work on the orbs. Well, I did when I started, but I'm great with code and was quickly moved to the seventh floor. By my third year at the factory, I was with a small team — six of us working full-time on their chip program."

"The identity chips?"

"No." Egan shook his head. "Chips used to alter your reality, to control you."

"They're real?" Jonah nearly gasped, relieved to understand his daughter's betrayal, and sick that the State would go to such lengths to control its citizens.

"Yes, they're quite real, though far from perfected. At least they *were* far from perfected."

"What do the chips do?"

"Initially, they were designed to control violence by turning citizens docile, making and keeping them happy. That was simple enough, but the older developers, most of whom loved to whisper, said it was barely a minute into development before the State started looking into other applications."

"Like what?"

"Finding *other ways* of controlling people — to manipulate memories and even bloom new ones from a seed of suggestion. I was involved in the earliest stages, though. I've no idea where development is now, or how advanced they are now."

"Lord," Jonah whispered, as many pieces of the unseen puzzle started snapping into place. Duncan was right, or was at least on the proper path. "Does everyone have a chip?"

"No, not everyone." Egan shook his head. "But most of us, yes. The delivery mechanism for Version 1 was crude, but Version 2 made things much better. If you've had a vaccination in the past decade, you've probably been implanted with the nanochips without knowing. You know of anyone who hasn't had a vaccination in the last decade?"

Vaccinations were required by all citizens under penalty of banishment.

"Do you have one?" Jonah asked.

"No, I destroyed mine. I'm sure that's why I was arrested, at least in part."

"Why did you destroy the chip?" Jonah asked.

"I didn't like the things it was making me do, or the thoughts I was having."

"What sort of thoughts?"

"Dark thoughts," Egan said. "Once I got rid of it, I started seeing the light. You will too."

"What do you mean?" What in the hell was Egan planning to do?

"While you've been more forthcoming, I still have the feeling you know more about my arrest than you're saying."

"I don't know anything other than what I've told you. As far as I know, they thought you were working with the Underground."

"Yeah, I know; you *said that*." Egan finally sat back in his seat. "And I believe *you* believe it. But I also think you know something more. Since you probably have no idea what you don't know, I'm going to have Father Truth get rid of your chips. We've got something that will seek out and destroy both chips inside you — your ID and the control one."

"Why the hell didn't you use it before now?"

"There can be ... side effects."

"What kind of side effects?" Jonah asked, trying to mask his nerves.

"Don't you worry about that. If you have any, you'll be too far gone to care."

Jonah held his eyes without flinching. "Then what? What if you find something? What does that mean for me and my trial?"

"You'll still face the council. But perhaps, if you're helpful, we can grant leniency."

"And if not?" Jonah said.

"Well," Egan shrugged. "Then you die."

TWENTY-FIVE

Adam Lovecraft

Adam woke up sometime in the middle of the night, terrified before he opened his eyes. A hand, not a grown-up's, was pressed hard on his lips.

"Say a word and you fucking die," Morgan whispered, once Adam finally had the courage to see who was there.

Tommy and Daniel stood behind him, both glaring down at Adam even though he could barely see them in the sleeping hall's scant light.

He tried to stay silent, knowing Morgan meant what he said, but as he squirmed against the mattress, an involuntary whimper fell from his mouth. Morgan's hand pressed harder on his face, pinching his cheeks tight.

Tommy leaned in, slipping the tip of a knife just under Adam's chin.

"We're going for a little walk," Daniel said.

Adam managed to hold his second whimper inside as Daniel pulled him from the bed and roughly whispered, "We're going to the bathroom. You make a sound or try to run away, then Tommy will cut your throat. We'll leave your body in the hallway and put the knife in Johnny Ross Wells's locker. Nod if you understand."

Adam nodded, trying to hold back the tears.

They cut through the sleeping hall as he wondered how many kids were awake, pretending to sleep so the same thing wouldn't happen to them.

They stepped into the hallway, then crept to the bathroom. Once inside, Daniel slammed Adam into the cold tile. Pain screamed across the back of Adam's head as it hit, and likely cracked the wall.

Daniel's fist pulled back like a slingshot. He was prepared to take a punch in the gut, but the strike came lower, an explosion of ungodly pain in his balls.

Adam fell hard to the filthy bathroom floor, crying.

"How do the grapefruits feel now?" Daniel curled his fingers into Adam's hair and dragged him over to a stall.

Adam wanted to cry out, scream, something, but kept his cries stifled, hostage to whatever ride they planned.

Daniel shoved him through the stall, then hard onto his knees. The stench of caked urine stung Adam's nostrils.

Tommy was on top of him again, pushing the cold knife against his neck, so close that he had to be cutting it. "Better stop your crying, or we'll leave you for dead. No one will doubt it was Johnny that done it."

Johnny had always been nice to Adam, but he was prone to violence and would be an easy kid to set up for a stabbing.

Morgan crammed into the stall between Tommy and Daniel, though Adam couldn't see anything with his face near the toilet. "Why'd you rat on us?"

Adam could barely think through his terror. He could swear innocence, insist he had no choice, but would that be enough? He never wanted to hurt anyone, especially his only friends — choosing between his friends and Keller had seemed like an obvious choice, until now.

"I'm so, so sorry," Adam whimpered, hating himself for not being able to hold his tears inside, worried that Tommy would slit his throat anyway. "I never meant to do anything wrong; they took me to the schoolmaster's office!"

Tommy pulled the knife away, turned Adam around, lifted him to face them all in the tiny stall, then reeled back and punched him hard below the throat.

Adam gasped, clutching at his neck, swallowing to keep from vomiting.

"I can kill you right now, and no one will know it was us."

"No one would even care," Daniel added his taunt to Tommy's threat. "*Freak!*"

Adam swallowed his tears. "I *had* to tell on you guys! Mr. Keller already knew, and if I didn't admit the truth, they would've done something worse. I was *protecting* you! Besides, he said that you guys had already told on me! He already knew and was just testing me to see if I'd lie."

"Yeah, right!" Daniel punched him hard in his left ribcage.

Adam ignored the pain, insisting, "I swear, why would I ever want anything bad to happen to you? You're my only friends."

All three laughed out loud.

Morgan said, "You think we're friends? We're not friends, Freakshow. We only talked to you because your daddy was in the Games, and then your sister. Without your fucked-up family, you're just another freak destined to die one day in the Quarter!"

Tommy's knife was back under his throat. "Give us one reason not to kill you now."

Adam had at least a hundred, but he couldn't get a single one out.

Morgan turned to Tommy. "What do you think?"

"That he's dumb enough to believe everything he said." Tommy dragged the knife from Adam's neck to his chin, then around his lips as Adam shuddered and tried not to bawl. "But if we let his deed go unpunished, people will talk. Then maybe *they'll* start disrespecting us, too. That can't happen inside the Rock." He turned to the others. "So, should we punish him, or just go ahead and kill the freak?"

"Finish this," Morgan said.

"Yeah, I can't think of a reason to keep this asshole alive." Daniel laughed and punched Adam in his side again, pulling him into a headlock.

Tommy brought his knife to Adam's face.

He sobbed and whimpered, squirmed and squealed, certain he was seconds from dying. Hot piss poured down his pajama bottoms. The smell, along with the fear churning in his guts, made him want to vomit.

Then he did. Daniel's fist landed on his guts, launching a violent spatter of liquid chunks from Adam's mouth.

Daniel threw him down, the toilet seat smacking hard into his jaw.

Adam's world was pure pain as they laughed, taking turns kicking and punching him.

Every time he tried to move, another hand shoved him back down, his face against the filthy toilet seat. Adam wondered how long the abuse could continue, and wished to God that he would die right there on the spot.

End it now.
Please.
I've got nothing.

Z2134

My family is gone. My mother is dead. Please, God, just kill me before they do.

The laughter was followed by spitting, then the unmistakable warm stream and reek of urine. One, or maybe all of the boys — Adam couldn't tell — were pissing on him.

He struggled to stand but was kicked hard again, this time in the back. He screamed out, this time loud enough to bring a counselor. He didn't even care if a knife followed.

"Let's go!" Morgan said to the others, and they left the stall.

Adam stayed perfectly still, afraid of moving until they were all gone.

He heard them leave the bathroom and was about to sit up and turn around when he felt Tommy's blade back at his throat and his other hand on Adam's shoulder. Then, a whisper: "You even *think* about ratting us out *ever* again, we'll fucking *end* you. Got it, freak?"

Adam whimpered yes, and then Tommy retreated.

He waited until he heard the bathroom door shut and then turned around, stood up, and shuffled slowly to the sink, hoping both that someone would come and that nobody would. He turned on a sink and washed the blood and piss from himself, one eye on the mirror in shame.

Suddenly the bathroom door opened.

Adam gulped as Brian Bob, the heavyset counselor with the goatee, who was sometimes nice and often not, met his gaze in the mirror. "What the hell? Is that you, Lovecraft?"

"Yes, Mr. Bob."

"What happened?" Mr. Bob looked around the bathroom. His eyes caught the piss and vomit on the floor before finding Adam's many bruises and cuts. "Who did this?"

"I can't say. They'll kill me."
"Come on, we're going to the nurse's office."

ADAM WAS ALLOWED to shower and sleep in the nurse's office after she put ointments on his wounds and offered him some pills to ease the pain.

Mr. Bob, who had been extra kind to Adam following the ordeal, kept asking questions. Adam felt bad that he couldn't say anything. But if his "friends" had nearly killed him over something as small as ratting them out for stealing food, what would they do if he snitched on them for this?

This was serious.

But Adam didn't know if it rose to the occasion of being serious enough to get the kids put in prison, and that was the only way he could ensure his safety. Without knowing that, he didn't dare utter a word.

After a breakfast of a hot roll and meat links brought to Adam by Mr. Bob, he returned and requested that Adam accompany him to the schoolmaster's office.

He walked gingerly down the hall, his every movement etched in pain, telling himself repeatedly that no matter what, he'd have to stay strong and keep quiet. *Tell no one.*

But when the door opened to the schoolmaster's office, Chief Keller was sitting behind the desk instead of Bertram. "Good morning, young Lovecraft. I hear you've been having some trouble."

TWENTY-SIX

Anastasia Lovecraft

ANA WOKE up confused as Kirkman's voice was piped into the box surrounding her.

In a monitor above her, she saw Liam and the child in their own separate boxes. When Kirkman announced that they were in a new mini-game, Ana knew only one thing: *someone was about to die.*

The barn doors opened, and she was momentarily blinded by beams of brilliant light interrupted by shuffling shadows which gave way to the influx of zombies.

Liam's screams over the monitor in the roof of her plastic cell pulled her attention up to it rather than over to his box. Kirkman smiled from ear to ear on the center screen. The other two showed Liam and the child. Liam was still screaming, now mostly obscenities. The girl was screaming too, even though she couldn't form words, backing from one corner into another as zombies surrounded her box.

Zombies spilled into the barn, splintering into three clusters, each headed straight for the boxes. Ana lost herself to the first scream as a pair of the monsters slammed her plastic cell, jostling it. Surprised by the sudden sway, she made a small, involuntarily jump into the air, like a cat on coals, screaming without wanting to.

Zombies were everywhere, so thick Ana no longer saw the barn door. They clawed at all three boxes. The girl's screams crackled in the speakers.

Liam stopped screaming and was instead silently glaring at the swarm of undead outside his plastic wall, likely thinking he was momentarily safe — though Ana had to assume Liam was smart enough to know the mini-game was only beginning.

Kirkman's voice blared through the speaker in her box, as if to answer her immediate fear. "Are you all ready to play The Killing Choice? I hope SO, because the members in our studio audience are hanging by the edges of their seats! Let's go over the rules, both for you and the fine folks watching at home. First, the good news, Anastasia. You're gonna live through this game. Isn't that GREAT?"

Kirkman laughed as if the planet spun on an axis made of his ego. Ana stared at the monitor, narrowing her eyes and letting Kirkman know how much she hated him, as she waited for the other shoe to drop.

"But," Kirkman said, about to drop said shoe, "and you just KNEW there'd be a BIG BUT, now didn't ya, Ana? BUT … one of your friends will NEVER make it out of the barn — at least not alive."

Kirkman cackled again.

Liam screamed, "You fuck—"

"Such filthy, filthy language," Kirkman tutted, cutting the audio before Liam could finish his tirade. "Good LORD, young man, don't you know there are children watching back in the City? Now …" he said, as the Darwin Game's sweeping score swelled behind him. "On with the rules! Ana, you're responsible for choosing who lives and who dies. In a few minutes you'll be asked to push the corresponding square on the monitor above you — either Liam's or Charlotte's."

So, that's her name.

"The choice is yours, but the killing is theirs!" Kirkman laughed, and Ana wondered if he actually thought that was funny. "The box you choose will be opened and exposed to the zombies! That unlucky 'winner' isn't likely to make it, though we suppose anything is possible. However, you and whoever you spare will then be escorted safely under the barn to an escape tunnel leading straight to safety!"

The score crescendoed, and Ana stared at the screen. Charlotte's eyes welled with tears, knowing her odds were slim. Charlotte wasn't only new to their group, but she was young and couldn't protect her like Liam, even if she'd already saved her life once.

"This isn't fair!" Ana screamed. "She's only a child."

"Awwww, such compassion from a murderer's little girl. Well, let's see how compassionate you truly are, Anastasia Lovecraft. Because there IS a third option."

Ana knew a tease when she heard it, especially from Kirkman. And still she dared to hope.

"Not picking either box within sixty seconds means automatically selecting your own box. This will instantly spare your opponents, taking them down to the tunnel below the barn while you stay topside and earn your survival from more than two dozen zombies!"

Ana didn't want Kirkman to have the joy of breaking her, or for the audience to see it. She tried everything to keep from crying, screaming, or showing any expression, but another zombie ran at her box, forgetting about the translucent wall between her and the world. The zombie slammed hard enough against the plastic to spatter it with a bloody smear.

She swallowed her rising bile as the box swayed, making her wonder how much longer she had before it fell, or worse, broke apart. She wondered if her cell would even sustain sixty seconds of zombies smashing into it.

"Now," Kirkman said, "I'm going to give each player a chance to beg for their life. First, your City 6 mate and secret Underground lover boy, Liam!"

Ana was already crying out as his monitor went live. "I don't know what to do, Liam."

His face was serious, eyes meeting hers. "I know it's a tough call, Ana, but you've gotta open the girl's box. I'm not saying this to spare my life; believe me, I don't give a fuck. I'm dead anyway. Until that happens, I'm the best chance you have at staying alive. Choose the girl and you're both dead."

Kirkman interrupted. "And they say chivalry is dead, ladies and gentleman. 'Kill the child, spare me instead.' Ah, Liam Harrow is a veritable knight in shining armor!" Kirkman cackled. "Do you kiss the ladies with those slippery lips? I tell ya, folks, these Underground scum have NO decency!"

The audience, being the eager sheep they were, booed. The camera panned across the crowd, and Ana saw the rage etched in their faces. She wondered how people could feel so much hate and rage toward strangers.

"Fu—" Liam started to say before his audio went dead.

"Charlotte Gray," Kirkman commanded, "plead your case!"

The girl looked up to her monitor, staring into the tiny green dot at the top that would capture her voice and broadcast her words, if only she could make them. Between her river of tears, her missing tongue, and the shrill, sudden scream as another zombie slammed into the side of her box, every one of her sounds was further proof that the girl wasn't fit for the Games.

"Oh yeah," Kirkman cackled, "I'm afraid the kitty's been playing with Charlotte's tongue for far too long! Let's all imagine together: If she *could* speak, surely she would say something like, *Please, please, not me. Anyone but me! I'm just a poor little tongueless child.*"

The audience laughed, fueling Ana toward an uncontrollable rage. She had to stay measured. Her father had told Kirkman to fuck himself, but with the network pulling strings and three lives in the balance, the bastards wouldn't need much of an excuse to end the mini-game with all of them dead.

She glared at the monitor, biting her tongue.

"Have you made your decision?" Kirkman asked. "Will it be your boyfriend or the poor, innocent child?"

Ana continued to stare at the monitors. Liam was speaking, likely with no clue that she couldn't hear a word. The girl stared at Ana from her monitor, hands cupped as if in prayer, pleading with her eyes.

Guilt rose into full bloom as Ana remembered scaring the girl away when she first encountered her in the woods. She'd only meant to scare her away, to protect her. The girl saved her and Liam's lives, now hers was on the line. In a just world, Ana would save the girl and leave Liam — the man who got her into this mess — to fend for himself.

But nobody ever claimed this was a just world. And if Ana died, who would be there for Adam? Still, she couldn't imagine opening the child's door. The girl could never survive a zombie attack. Liam might at least make it out of the barn alive.

Kirkman's voice cut through her thoughts. "One more thing, Little Miss Lovecraft. In order to make such an important decision, you need all the available information." His bright tone went even brighter. "Which is why I think you need to see *this*!"

The screen broadcasting Liam in his box went black, then brightened again as it played a recording of him marching into a City Watch office. He was refusing to spy on the Underground any longer.

He was a traitor!

To the Underground and — to her father?

She stared at the screen in openmouthed shock. It cut back to Liam in the box, silence screaming from his mouth as he protested.

"Seems your sexy lover Liam was really a spy working *against* the Underground. How's that for a WOW moment, ladies and gentleman?"

The audience *oohed*.

"How could you?" Ana said, not that Liam could hear her. She didn't finish with *betray my father?* since the Games had never announced Jonah as an Underground rebel, and she didn't want to risk anything happening to him in City 7 if word got out.

If Liam was a spy for City Watch, maybe *he* was responsible for her father's framing. Perhaps it was he, not she, who was to blame for those deaths at Duncan's church. Perhaps — Ana shuddered at the thought — he was responsible for her mother's death.

She swallowed, blinking back tears as she continued to glare at Liam: *You did this!*

Liam kept screaming, punching the plastic, his face red and raging.

"So, Anastasia, are you READY to decide? Remember, you've only got sixty seconds, which we'll be counting down on the center monitor. You can open Charlotte's box at any time by simply pressing her screen and sending the itty-bitty girl from City 2 into the zombies' mauling arms, or ... you can punish your lover for his shocking betrayal by feeding the Underground scum to the starving zombies! The choice is yours, Lovely Lovecraft."

Large white numbers appeared against a black screen on the center screen.

"The time is on the clock, and we're starting ... NOW!"

The monitor ticked life away for either Liam or Charlotte, demanding that a decision be made. 60 ... 59 ... 58 ...

She went back and forth in her mind, waffling between Charlotte and Liam. No straight line; no right, wrong, or easy decision. She had to decide.

Who to kill? Man or child? Friend or stranger?

New friend or traitor?

45 ... 44 ... 43 ...

A broth of rage bubbled inside as Ana turned her head from one screen to the other, hating Kirkman, the Games, and the universe for thrusting the awful choice upon her.

Liam had betrayed her father. But he had also saved her. It seemed that he had purposely surrendered his freedom at the moment when she was losing hers, thereby hurling himself into the Games.

Why would he do that?

Did Liam do it for me?

34 ... 33 ... 32 ...

Is that something a traitor would really do?

29 ... 28 ... 27 ...

She stared at Charlotte's monitor and the girl's sad eyes. She'd been through so much in her short life. Even if Ana spared her now, wouldn't she have to kill her in the end anyway?

How can I do this to her? She's so young. So innocent. And Liam is so guilty.

17 ... 16 ... 15 ...

There must be more to the story than what Kirkman is showing?

10 ... 9 ... 8 ...

There must be some logical explanation. Maybe it's what Liam is trying to scream, and that's why they're silencing his monitor.

5 ... 4 ... 3 ... 2 ...

Ana swallowed hard as she slammed her hand onto Charlotte's monitor, collapsing to her knees in a flood of tears and staring up at the screen instead of at the little girl's box, unable to look directly into her decision, but unwilling to grant herself a pardon from the horror.

Her speaker crackled as Charlotte's bloodcurdling screams filled Ana's box. The child's cell door opened, and the wave of monsters spilled in on her, tearing her to pieces.

Most of the visual carnage was buried beneath a sea of undead bodies, swarming in front of the lens as Charlotte drowned in their waves. But Ana heard every sound and imagined what was happening under the ripping flesh as it echoed against the plastic walls, one zombie after another reaching into her twitching body — as evidenced by her visible and still-shaking feet — and pulling handfuls of gore from her tiny body before shoving pieces into their mouths, groaning and growling and moaning from their bloody maws as blood spattered her box.

Ana lost it. She turned, spraying her own box with green-and-yellow vomit as she held her side and retched again.

Charlotte's box disappeared on the monitor above, along with Liam's and the expired countdown, then Kirkman's face filled every screen, along with his cackling voice.

"Ah, folks, we've got a coldhearted killer here — no

mercy from this one! Look out, players, the apple does NOT fall far from the murdering tree! Anastasia Lovecraft will kill anyone in her way, including teeny tiny little girls, and even after they saved her miserable life! I'd boo if this Game wasn't SO MUCH FUN!"

The audience laughed, then Kirkman grew mock serious: "Can Ana kill her lover when she must? Will she be able to forgive him before one of them dies, or has his betrayal changed everything? Stay tuned!"

Ana looked over to Liam's box. He was staring down at the ground, away from the camera.

Good, hide your face in shame. Asshole.

Both boxes began to descend into the tunnels below. Ana forced herself to look back at the carnage that had been a child sixty seconds before.

Oh God, what have I done?

TWENTY-SEVEN

Jonah Lovecraft

JONAH HAD no idea how long he was alone before Calla finally came into his room with food and water. Like before, she shoved bites into his mouth, chasing each swallow with a roughly-poured stream of water, more of which got onto Jonah's coveralls than down his throat. He noticed almost immediately, however, that something was different.

Calla seemed gentler. More than that, there seemed to be a new and odd understanding in her eyes.

He said nothing as she fed him, but once finished, Jonah asked Calla if she had seen the Games. After two minutes of awkward small talk, he followed his first question with the one on his mind, almost painful as he pushed it out of his throat.

"Is Ana still alive?"

"Yes." Calla nodded. "For now. She was put into a barn with her lover, Liam, and a lil' girl, Charlotte."

"*Lover?* Liam Harrow? From City 6?"

"Yes, they're workin' together. They're lovers, both workin' for the City 6 Underground."

Nothing made sense. So many things must have happened since he was framed and cast out from his City. How was it possible that Ana and Liam, a man he thought of as a son, had wound up in the Games together?

Jonah chose to ignore the "lovers" remark almost entirely, save for the nagging buzz rattling at the back of his head. Everyone knew Liam was a ladies' man, and of course Jonah saw Ana being attracted to someone like that, especially since Jonah had been absent for large patches of her life — first working too many long hours for City Watch, then for the Underground — but it seemed more like a manufactured way of packaging the players than like the truth.

"You said she was put in the barn; what do you mean?"

"They fell 'sleep in a cave, and woke in a barn. The TV man said they'd start ta' mornin' with a brand new mini-game, but they weren't awake."

Sweat beaded his brow. Nothing about a new mini-game was good. Mini-games usually meant death for at least one player, and often pitted them against each other. Liam clearly held an advantage over two girls, and Jonah knew the network crafted games for only two reasons: to manipulate results and viewer reaction.

"Will you let me know what happens?" Jonah tried to keep his voice from cracking.

"Yes." Calla nodded. "What's it like in ta' City?"

Jonah again tried to place her accent, wondering where it was from and why he'd never heard anything like it. Was this what a life spent in the Barrens sounded like? That seemed like an obvious answer, but it didn't make sense. Her father, Egan, spoke like anyone else from City 6. And surely their community had to be filled with countless others who had once lived behind the Walls. Why would the girl's speech be corrupted if she wasn't living in isolation?

Jonah smiled, not wanting to scare her, deciding to start his story softly, playing up the better stuff and gauging her reaction, tailoring his description to what she probably wanted to hear.

"It's fun," he said. "At least most of the time. The City is centered around clusters of entertainment, with giant arcades, bars, libraries, theaters, and even live music. Of course, the Games are everywhere — on TVs in our homes, in public meeting places, and even in the break rooms in some jobs. There are smaller cafes and restaurants, with two types of food: rationed and wonderful. The wonderful tastes like heaven but costs far too many credits — those are funds issued by the State."

"I know what credits are. What is the food like?" Calla looked like she was about to drool thinking of the food, making Jonah wonder if the mush and water she pushed through his mouth was any worse than what she ate herself.

"It's okay." Jonah shrugged. "Depending on your ration level. For the higher flats, I hear it's wonderful, and the few times my tongue got a taste, I'd have to agree."

Jonah smiled for Calla's benefit, but also at the memory. She stared, wide-eyed and waiting for more. "There's little variety in the food, and the cafes are mostly the same. The Social is the City's biggest gathering spot, a bar with food, drinks — both alcohol and sugar water, card games, and monitors broadcasting the Games. There's several of these bars, with at least one every few blocks. It's where most adults and some of the older kids meet up and spend time together."

"That doesn't sound so bad," Calla said. Jonah noticed that she was taking her time, speaking her words slowly, as if trying to mimic a more proper English. "Daddy says it's awful behind the Wall. There's lots of crime, poor people, and disease. An' you always hafta work hard, at jobs you don't choose."

"Well," Jonah didn't want to disagree with whatever her father had said, "it can be hard. But I'm guessing you have to work hard here, too, right?"

The girl nodded.

"But yes, there's lots of bad stuff, too. And bad people. Though the Watchers try to keep peace and order ... the good ones, anyway. Your father's right that it's probably best to be outside the Wall, assuming you can keep clear of the zombies. You're lucky to have this place." He nodded, gesturing around him. "You're protected from the zombies, and you have a safe community of good people to look after you."

"People?" Calla repeated.

"Yeah, in your village here, or whatever you're calling it."

"There's not many people here." She shook her head. "Only us."

"What do you mean, *only us*?"

"Me, the two boys from when we saved you, Father, an' Verosh."

"Verosh?"

"She's my mom now. She's from far away. She saved my dad after he won the Games."

That might explain the accent, but something still felt wrong. "What about the others?"

"We're here alone. Dad doesn't trust the others in the villages or the City. He says we hafta live here ... It's lonely most of the time."

"You mean there's no council? No—"

Calla's eyes fell to the floor, then drifted to the wall. "Oh. Uh … I've gotta go."

"Wait. I won't say anything to get you in trouble. I swear."

She turned, looking Jonah over from eyebrow to toe, seeming to work out whether she could trust him.

"I'll tell you whatever you wanna know about the City. Anything at all."

"Anything?"

"Yes." Jonah nodded. "Anything. But please don't leave. You're the only one here who treats me like a person."

Calla looked back at the floor, as if kindness were insulting, or an open invite to guilt. Then she stared at the man responsible for her mother's death. "I don't wanna know about the City. I want to know 'bout somethin' else."

"What?" Jonah said, stupidly afraid she would ask him about the birds and the bees.

"I want to know about my real mom, and why Dad says you killed her."

The birds and the bees would be easier.

"What was she like?" Calla asked.

"I didn't really know her, but from pictures, and when I saw her in court, your mother was beautiful. She had long brown hair, like yours. Big blue eyes, and a gentle voice; soft-spoken, like you. You look a lot like her, actually."

Calla's lips split into the first smile Jonah had seen on her since coming down into the tunnel. Tears threatened his eyes.

"What else?" Calla said, almost demanding.

"She loved your father very much."

"How do you know?"

Jonah wished he hadn't stepped into that particular quicksand. "She begged for the judge to show him mercy, to keep him from jail, like many wives begging for their husbands. But hers wasn't the mindless whine of someone who didn't care. The way she spoke of your father," Jonah held her stare, "with tears in her eyes and honesty in her voice — she truly loved him. It was in every note as she pled with the judge, swearing he was a sweet, dedicated husband and father, a good man incapable of the crimes assigned to his good name."

"Then why did they put him in jail? Why did you lie?"

"What did your father tell you?"

"Not much, but I listened outside in the hall when you were talking a few times. I heard things. I want to know more." Her eyes were a fire on Jonah. "*Why did you lie?*"

"At the time, my bosses told me your father was a bad man. *Dangerous*. They asked me to say something untrue, but I didn't know it was false when I agreed. It's difficult to explain." He cleared his throat, feeling too much like a monster. "But the short answer is, I followed orders, and have regretted my lie every day since."

"So, what happened to my mom?" Calla asked, tears flooding down both cheeks as she wiped her nose with a dirty kerchief pulled from her pants pocket.

"You don't know?"

"Only that she died; Dad never said why or how."

"Maybe you should ask him again. I don't think it's my place to say."

"Please, mister," Calla begged. "Nobody tells me anything, and I deserve to know. She was *my* mother."

Jonah's words were trapped in his throat. Everything had changed. Five minutes ago, he had pictured the tunnels packed with people, but that was a lie like his trial. With no council or fair judgement, Egan would likely kill him without a thought.

So his survival depended on getting out of the room and on the run.

Z2134

Calla was his only chance. He had to persuade her to free him.

"Are you sure you want to know?"

Calla nodded, still crying.

"Tell you what," Jonah said, feeling like shit for manipulating a little girl whose mother he'd already taken. Yet, his daughter's life depended on him swallowing his self-loathing to help her. "Cut these ropes and I'll tell you whatever you want."

Calla stared at Jonah for several long seconds before falling a few steps back.

"Please ... I would never ask you for something like this or use your mother as bait, but I love my daughter as much as your mother loved you. I'm so sorry about what happened to your mom. I can't ever take it back, no matter how much I want to. But I can save Ana, or at least try. Unfortunately, I don't think your father plans to let me leave." He peered into her eyes until she flinched. "Do you?"

"No." She shook her head, her tears falling faster. "He's going to kill you."

"I don't blame him, and you shouldn't either. He's upset about what happened to his life, to you, your mom, and your brother. He blames me, and I understand why. I agree, I *should pay* for my crimes, and I promise to return after I save Ana, assuming I don't get killed outside while trying to find her. Your father can put me on trial, or shoot me while I kneel and wait for the bullet. I won't fight my punishment, you have my vow. But if I don't get out of here, my daughter will die. You understand, right?"

"Tell me something about my mother."

Jonah nodded. "After your father was cast outside the Wall, your mother fell apart. Eventually, she was forced to live in the Dark Quarter. Do you know what that means?"

She gestured *yes* and he continued. "The Dark Quarter is a miserable place, and the people who live there are often forced into doing horrible things."

"Is that what happened to my mom?"

"She was taken advantage of by some awful people. Eventually, someone killed her." Ana's chances were dimming by the minute, so Jonah cracked his voice for effect. "They never found her killer."

"Did you see her?" Calla asked, her voice surprisingly strong. "When she was dead?"

"Yes. I was called in, the second Watcher on the scene."

"Why didn't you find her killer?"

Jonah stared at the girl, not wanting to bullshit, nor cruel enough to tell her the truth — that her mother's life didn't matter enough to warrant an investigation. Like anyone else in the Quarter, she was a box in a column whose numbers meant nothing.

"There wasn't any evidence to narrow the suspects. Too much crime in the Dark Quarter to keep track of." That much was true. Calla's mother could have been murdered by any one of the thousands of dirtbags living in the Quarter. "I'm sorry. It's not much, and if I could go back in time and change things, I would never have done anything to help put your daddy in jail."

"Where was I?"

"Huh?" Jonah asked.

"When my mom died. Where was I?"

"You were crying in a crib in the corner." He didn't want to remember.

"Did I see what happened?"

"You were just a baby. The City took you to the orphanage afterward. That's the last I saw of you ... until I saw you here."

Calla kept staring, as though studying Jonah, perhaps unsure of what to say. He wondered if she was going to ask why he'd never checked up on her in the orphanage. He didn't know how to answer that question. Yet another guilty log on a fire of shame. He tried not to shift, even as uncomfortable as he was in his seat.

Finally, she said something he didn't see coming. "What does icy cream taste like?"

Jonah couldn't help but laugh out loud, until his mirth finally receded into a smile. "It's called *ice cream*, and it's wonderful." He licked his lips, tasting the memory. "Ice cream is like sweet, creamy, frozen milk, but soft instead of hard. Like snow, if snow tasted good, and was creamy and thick. And as the cream fills your mouth, it turns your teeth as cold as your cheeks. There are a ton of flavors, at least in the Arcade, but in regular cafes it usually comes in mint or chocolate chip. The chips melt on your tongue, and the mint is like spicy if spicy was cold. Regular rations are vanilla, but even that's good."

"How do you eat it?"

"Like anything else, I suppose." He laughed again. "You can't eat it fast. When you set the spoon in your mouth, the cream melts on your tongue, all over your taste buds, almost like it's kissing them. The world looks different with ice cream in your mouth."

Something inside Calla softened enough to draw a smile on her face for the second time. It turned into a laugh. She pulled the knife from its sheath, then went to Jonah.

He flinched, thinking for a second's thin slice that the girl might have changed her mind and was on her way to slit his throat like he deserved.

But Calla cut the ropes from his wrists, then his feet, and his restraints fell to the floor. His body felt on fire as he stood, stretching his muscles, preparing for whatever lay beyond the door, wondering if Calla could forgive him. And if so, if Egan could do the same. Most importantly, Jonah wondered if he would he ever be able to forgive himself.

"Thank you, Calla. I promise you won't regret it. Now, can you tell me the best way to get out of here?"

"Everyone is eating lunch right now. Except for me. I've been gone too long, and I need to get back." She pointed at the door. "As long as you stay on the tunnel path, you should be fine. Take your first left, then head down the stairs. When you reach the bottom, you'll see the old tracks. Take those until you find the branch. Go right, then walk until you reach the ladder. Take that above ground."

"Are you going to be okay? What will you tell your father?"

"Don't worry about me. I'll be fine." Then she said, "Thank you."

"For what?"

"Treating me like a grownup and telling me the truth."

Jonah wiped his other eye. "You're welcome. And thank *you*."

She turned without another word and ran out the door and down the hall. He waited for her footsteps to fall silent, then opened the door and turned left as instructed.

The hallway was dark and narrow, lit by sporadic blinking light tubes not unlike those in the room where he was being held. The tunnel was cold, eerily silent, and felt like an ever-present weight surrounding him on all sides, waiting to come crashing down.

He followed her directions, listening intently for any sound that his escape had been detected. Farther from his cell, he moved faster, ignoring the echoes of his footsteps.

Z2134

He reached the ladder and noticed a small pile of debris to his left — broken crates, old books, empty tin cans, and a metal pipe that was thin and light enough to wield but long and strong enough to swing at an enemy.

Not a gun, but it was better than nothing.

He grabbed the pipe and put the end of it in his boot temporarily as he climbed the ladder, lifted the hatch, then crawled into the impossibly bright light of a brand new day.

I'm here, Ana! I'm coming!

The hatch opened into a snowy clearing surrounded by woods on all sides.

There was no other sign of the train station, its entrance, or underground tunnels within sight. But if Jonah could find his way to the station while avoiding being seen, he could then locate where the underground tracks surfaced aboveground.

Then he could follow those back to where the Games were being held.

But first he had to get out of sight.

Jonah ran toward a tree-lined ridge in the distance. Once out of sight he could double back and find the tracks. He'd made it maybe forty yards when a gunshot cracked like thunder on the dry, cold air.

Jonah turned and saw Egan behind him, running in angry pursuit.

TWENTY-EIGHT

Adam Lovecraft

Adam sat before Keller, terrified.

"Why so worried?" asked the chief, sitting on the other side of the schoolmaster's massive desk. "You're not in trouble, son. You're here because you need my help." He smiled again, but Adam had trouble meeting the man's eyes.

"Please, I can't help you unless you help me first. I need you to tell me what happened. You've nothing to be ashamed of. Remember our talk and what I told you about fear, Adam. Courage isn't the lack of fear, but rather, action in the face of it. Are you ready to take action?"

Adam didn't nod, shake his head, or say a single word.

"The only way to solve our little problem, and it is *our* problem, Adam, since your problems are now mine as well. That's what it means to have true friends. Our problems aren't solved until you earn respect, and you'll only earn respect if you target the strongest bully in the bunch then bring him to his knees. Are you ready to do that?"

"I can't fight them. Especially Morgan. Plus, my dad

said you should always turn the other cheek, and use what's in your head to avoid using your fists."

The smile faded from Keller's face for a flicker before returning. "Your father was only trying to protect you, and while his intentions were good, he coddled you, turning you into a victim who is too afraid to fight back. And you do know what happens to victims who don't fight back, don't you, Adam?"

"No, sir." He shook his head.

Keller slammed his open palms hard on the desk. "They keep being victimized!"

"What am I supposed to do? The counselors all say no fighting. I'll get in trouble."

"I promise, son, good things are happening to you now. You're my friend, so you won't be getting into trouble again." Keller leaned across the desk. "Just walk right up to the biggest bastard — I'm guessing it's Morgan — and punch him in the mouth as hard as you can. Then jump on top of him and keep hitting him until he's crying and begging you to get off."

"Really?" Excitement bloomed in his chest. "Just like that?"

Keller smiled, his widest one yet. "Just like that."

"But what if he pulls a knife?"

"Then you pull this." Keller reached into his jacket pocket and pulled a black cylinder from the interior. It looked like two fat pens stuck together, with one tip.

"What's that?" Adam asked, leaning across the desk.

Keller slipped the cylinder into his hand.

Adam stared, his eyes widening as he moved it from one curled palm to the other, feeling the weight; slightly heavy, though still lighter than it looked — no reason he couldn't carry it in his pocket and use it when needed.

"It's a mini-stunner. They're highly illegal; simply

carrying one on your person can get you into a world of trouble. Then again," Keller smiled, still wide but decidedly darker, "your friends aren't supposed to be carrying knives in the orphanage, either, right?"

Adam nodded.

"The trick is to keep the stunner hidden in your hand and not let anyone see it until it's too late for them to do anything about it. My best advice, young Lovecraft, is to sneak up on Morgan and punch him with all your might. If he manages to get up from the ground, even after you've given him your best knuckle sandwich, squeeze the buttons on either side of this little beauty and hit him with the tip. This special weapon delivers a powerful shock that will knock him out for a few minutes. I suggest you spend that time beating your enemy to within an inch of his life."

Adam was breathing so heavily in nervous excitement that he thought he might hyperventilate.

"You got that?" Keller asked.

Adam nodded. "Are you sure? Maybe I should just let things go and hope Morgan, Tommy, and Daniel forget about it."

"They won't forget. The only way to deal with a bully like Morgan, or his minions, is to teach them a lesson — one they'll *never* forget."

"When should I try?"

"Don't try. Do. I suggest waiting until lunch, dinner, or TV hall later tonight. Do it soon, and I'll discuss the situation with your counselors to make sure everything runs smoothly and nothing stands in your way."

Adam stared at Keller, without any idea what to say. "Why are you doing this? You put my dad and sister in jail. Why are you being so nice to me?"

"I don't hold the sins of your father or sister against you. Plus, you remind me of my own son."

Adam's next words fell out in a whisper. "You have a son?"

"I did, but he died in a bombing by the Underground several years ago. I see much of him in you — a quiet intelligence and kindness that idiots mistake for weakness. The City should look up to boys like you, helping them grow into tomorrow's leaders, rather than turning them into tomorrow's troubled prisoners and Quarter scum. Now," Keller offered Adam a final smile, "go out make me proud. We'll talk soon."

"Thank you," Adam said, then left the office feeling a foot and a half taller.

ADAM HELD the mini-stunner in his pocket. Like Keller's warm smile and promises, the tiny weapon filled him with confidence. He waited all day for one of the trio to mess with him, almost eager, though he'd never sought confrontation before.

After a late afternoon snack, with his tray cleared and the Chimney Rock gruel swirling in the pit of his stomach, he nearly bumped into Jayla. She smiled, but only for a second, hanging on the top of another look Adam couldn't place — sort of afraid, but mostly confused.

Her friend — a girl Adam had never seen before, and not one of the original three who had been with them in the kitchen — kept walking and called back for Jayla as they headed to the classrooms. The half-smile fell from her face, and she ran after her friend without a word to Adam.

He felt an odd sort of empty inside, all shell and no meat.

The day's remainder passed without incident. Adam ate his rations at dinner, as alone as he'd eaten his breakfast and lunch, feeling a fresh and horrible breed of invisible. He barely picked at his rations, chewing without tasting, and swallowing without chewing. He dumped his half-full tray into the trashcan. Then he set his empty tray on the stack, then headed for the bathroom.

Adam opened the stall, then sat to pee like always, feeling the usual flutter of guilt for not standing like his father taught him. His heart fell to his belly as he heard the door swing open and bang into the wall, followed by the unmistakable voice of Morgan.

"So, Freak, I heard you were called to the office today. What was that all about?"

"Nothing," Adam said, his voice quivering. He still had the mini-stunner in his pocket but was suddenly afraid to use it, especially once he heard Tommy and Daniel were outside the stall beside him.

"I can smell your shit," Tommy said, even though Adam was only going number one.

"Hurry the fuck up," Morgan said. "We'd like to kill you before it's time for pudding."

He couldn't use his mini-stunner if all three attacked him at once. Adam thought of a hundred questions he wished he'd thought to ask Keller, starting with how many charges the stunner was good for.

Morgan's fist was on the stall door as his voice echoed off the bathroom walls.

Adam prayed for someone to come in.

"Bullshit," Morgan said. "You ratted us out again, didn't you?"

Adam said nothing until Morgan's fist beat on the stall hard enough to scare him into an answer. "No," he squeaked, hating himself for feeling so small, especially with the stunner still in his pocket. "They took me to his office, but I didn't say a word!"

"Bullshit!" Morgan yelled.

The stall door burst open, breaking the latch, metal flying at Adam's chest before clattering on the floor.

Adam jumped, yanking his pants up as the three boys laughed and rushed at him, dragging him out of the stall and throwing him to the floor.

Morgan's hand was deep in his hair, fingers curling into a clump and dragging him back to the toilet by the root. "Admit you ratted us out, freaktard!"

Adam said nothing as Morgan shoved his head into the toilet. His nose and lips dipped into the urine-filled bowl, drenching his face in piss, into his mouth and up his nose. He choked, spitting and gripping either side of the bowl with both hands, trying to push himself back up as it felt like a hundred hands were forcing his head into the water.

Adam was going to die. But then he was yanked back, choking, gagging, eyes stinging as Tommy yelled, "Admit it!"

But then they shoved him back down, laughing hysterically as he grew certain that he was going to die before ever getting a chance to use Keller's special weapon.

"Admit it!" Tommy screamed again.

The bullies kept lifting him up, ordering Adam to "admit it" before shoving him back down. But they didn't care whether he admitted a thing, they wanted to drown him in his own piss.

Tommy kicked him hard in the back. "Fucking freak!"

The three of them backed away, laughing as Adam sobbed, crumpled over the toilet in pain, humiliated, wet, and reeking. Maybe it was the bray of their laughter. Or the way they left him helpless, hurt, and humiliated. Or maybe it was because he had been stupid enough to believe that they'd really wanted to be friends.

Whatever it was, he'd had enough.

Z2134

Adam found his power and got to his feet.

As the three boys were filing out the door, he yelled, "Hey, fucker!"

Morgan was the last one through the door. He turned back, face twisted in anger and surprise. Adam raced at him, mini-stunner concealed until the last possible second.

He squeezed the buttons on either side and thrust it into Morgan's chest.

His eyes shot open, with his mouth, a scream trapped as Morgan clutched at his chest and fell to the floor.

"What the fuck did you do?" Tommy called out, staring down at his buddy's body as it violently spasmed.

Tommy and Daniel looked up at Adam like they were going to kill him.

He thrust the mini-stunner forward, not even sure if it had another charge, and screamed, "You wanna die?"

The boys took a step back, then their attention was pulled to Morgan, who was shaking even worse, his eyes rolling back into his skull as pink foam bubbled past his lips in a river of phlegmy blood.

It was a half-minute before anyone spoke.

Then Tommy finally whispered. "*He's dead.*"

Daniel dropped to his knees and felt for a pulse. He looked up at Adam, and his face went from menacing to frightened. "You killed him!"

Then both kids ran from the bathroom.

Adam waited another minute, then slipped from the bathroom, making it a few feet before he heard Brian Bob behind him.

"Stop right there, Lovecraft!" Brian Bob grabbed him by the scruff of his neck and led him back into the bathroom, where he fell back against the wall in surprise. His giant hand tightened around Adam's neck as he barked into the comm on his collar. "We've got a situation here — I need City Watch ASAP!"

Adam pled through the four minutes it took for the Watchers to arrive, then through the two it took for them to roughly bind his hands and fix him with restraints.

"Keller said it was okay," he pled, over and over, more than a dozen times before they reached the ground floor of Chimney Rock, each time followed by, "He gave me the stunner to protect myself! Please, you have to call him. He'll tell you it's true!"

The Watchers ignored Adam, dragging him through Chimney Rock, kicking and screaming, out the front doors of the orphanage, down the steps, then into the back of the open City Watch van.

TWENTY-NINE

Anastasia Lovecraft

For several minutes following their escape from the barn, the only sound was the clomping of snow as Liam and Ana trudged numbly through the melting slush beneath the midday sun.

Neither of them said anything for what felt like forever, walking under the weight of their collective guilt and shared grief.

A cool breeze shook the pines above them, the sound soothing, calming Ana more with every step. Once confident that her anger was contained, she opened her mouth and asked the questions she'd been holding inside.

"Why did you do it?" She ignored the network orb hovering above — if they didn't want citizens to know about her father being a part of the Underground, they'd either sever the audio or switch the broadcast feed. "Why did you betray my dad?"

"Jonah was one of the finest people I've ever known," Liam said instantly, as if he'd been waiting for the question. "That's why I was angry when you assumed he was guilty."

Ana expected more, but Liam fell silent as they sloshed through the snow. Another minute's worth of tension-tainted silence until she finally turned to face him. "No, you don't get off that easy. You betrayed my father, Liam, and I'm on the wrong side of the Walls because of you. *You owe me an explanation!*"

"I owe you and Jonah my life, and you have it. That's fair, but that's *all* you get."

He kept walking, trying to avoid more conversation.

"Fuck you, Liam. If you can't be straight with me, I'll take my chances without you." She took a step toward him. "And I mean it. You know how stubborn my father is. Well, I'm no different. So what's it gonna be?"

Liam said nothing, and for nearly a minute Ana almost believed he would call her bluff, turn around and head in the opposite direction. But then he finally spoke without looking at her. "City Watch targeted my girlfriend."

Ana could tell he wanted to cry, even though she knew there wasn't a chance in hell that he would. "They would've killed her if I didn't play ball. I had no choice."

"*You* had a girlfriend?" She couldn't stop the sound of her surprise. "You settled on *just one* girl?"

"Yes." Liam looked away.

"What was her name?"

"Chelle, and she was sweet, Ana, the nicest girl I ever met. You would've loved her. Anyway, she got pregnant. The pills didn't work, and we didn't have a voucher. The baby was scheduled for termination, but we applied for an adoption waiver. Chelle wanted to keep it, more than anything."

"Why?" Ana wondered out loud.

There were plenty of citizens unable to have kids, who were eager to adopt a child, so long as it wasn't a Quarter kid. It didn't make sense to risk prison, Watchers, or ejection from the City, when you could get pregnant again with a voucher.

"Why not give the child a safe home through adoption?"

Liam shrugged. "I'm not exactly sure, she gave me 150 different answers, depending on the day. She was insistent, and even more stubborn than you, if you can believe it." His voice made another tiny crack, letting Ana know the worst was still inside.

"We didn't know what to do, but that was the first time I'd ever seriously considered leaving the City. There's a secret village in the Barrens where I thought we could go." He dipped his voice to a whisper, protecting their discussion from the orbs.

"I tried to set everything up, but passage doesn't exactly happen overnight. Someone reported Chelle, and City Watch came to get me. They knew I was Underground, and said if I wasn't willing to supply them with information, then they weren't willing to let Chelle go. They'd already arrested her, and assured me they'd dispose of our baby, and in case that didn't do it, they made it perfectly clear how easy it was to eliminate Chelle."

"Oh God!" Ana gasped.

"So I started helping — barely, but enough to keep our baby alive; a few things here and there while Chelle was in custody, which ended up being a lot longer than they promised. I reported a few citizens whose arrest wouldn't affect the cause, and a couple of people who deserved it for one reason or another."

Ana didn't like Liam playing junior Watcher, judging who was deserving of punishment. She let it go, knowing it was more important to hear the rest of his story while they had a moment's respite from the dangers of the Games.

"No matter how much I gave, the Watchers wanted

more, and then more after that. Then they wanted something big ... or else ..." He paused, clearly not wanting to finish the sentence.

"So you gave them my father?"

"I never thought any of ... any of *this* would happen." He gestured around him, as if piles of snow and naked trees were murdered mothers and guilty fathers. "I didn't think I gave them enough to go on, especially since Jonah covered his tracks well. I'm sorry."

Ana could feel her face flushing red with anger. She said nothing for fear of a scream.

"They didn't even act on the information for a while. So I kept my mouth shut, figuring he'd avoided capture. I thought we'd gotten lucky. But I guess now that they decided they'd take a different angle in bringing him down — murdering your mom and setting him up for the crime."

Ana closed her eyes to keep the tears inside. Liam was responsible for everything that had happened to her family. She wanted to scream, hit him, puke, something.

But instead, she listened as he continued his story.

"After they locked your dad up, I thought it was over. But no, they came back. They wanted more. But after what they did, I wasn't willing. I ran roadblocks, working both sides while trying to keep everyone safe. I did my best. But it wasn't good enough. City Watch terminated our baby, but by then Chelle was in her third trimester, less than two months from delivery. It ruined her. Maybe they did something else too, I don't know, but Chelle wasn't the same. She left me that day and never came back."

Ana stared at him, trying to reconcile her anger against his situation. He had acted to protect his family, never knowing he'd be responsible for the destruction of hers.

Liam wiped the back of his hand under his right eye.

"Can we keep walking? I'm freezing my dick off standing here."

"Of course," Ana said.

"After that, City Watch made me their bitch. Even though Chelle was no longer in custody, they threatened to arrest her and stack the charges, make her an accessory to my Underground involvement. Publicly humiliate her and put her in the Games. I had to go back, giving them just enough to satisfy but not enough to blow the Underground apart. There's thousands of people we've helped escape City 6. Thousands whose lives depend on the Underground and the hidden village."

Liam stopped mid-step, rubbing his hands across his folded arms. "So I kept giving them bits and bits ... until you were arrested. That was too much. I couldn't allow *you* to pay for my sins, not after what happened with Jonah. So I got myself thrown into the Games to protect you. I planned to help you reach the end, then get myself killed so you can go to City 7 and be with your father."

Ana stared at him, torn between guilt, anger, and gratitude until she was no longer sure what to feel. But she couldn't keep hating him. He did what he did and had his reasons. Now he was trying to make things right.

Even her father could appreciate that.

Liam gasped, startled as the trio of orbs descended in unison, swirling around them with a speed and pattern of blinking lights she'd never seen before. Liam's arm made a fence of protection around her.

"What's happening?" Ana didn't mean to whimper.

The three orbs hovered in place, and then, in an instant, all fell to the ground at once, their screens and lights going dark.

"What the hell?" Liam inched toward the closest one. "They're dead!"

Another orb appeared, black, racing from the woods and flying right at them.

"Is that a hunter orb?" Ana saw the weapon beneath its screen before she finished her question.

"Down!" Liam said, falling on top of her.

She braced for the impact of an energy blast, certain that they, or at least Liam, was about to be evaporated into ashes.

But no blast came. Instead, she heard a humming, then a man's voice. "Follow me!"

They looked up to see the orb's monitor showing a familiar face on its screen: *Duncan!*

Liam was running before Ana realized what was happening, grabbing her hand and pulling her behind him as he chased the orb into the forest. Behind them, they heard one of the "dead" orbs returning to life.

"Oh shit!" Liam turned back as a blue beam of heat fired over their heads and smashed into a large tree ahead, evaporating instantly.

"Fuck!" Liam screamed, then ducked, running in a zigzag, following the black orb deeper into the trees.

"You okay?" he called back to Ana, who was racing as fast as she could to keep pace, her hand still somehow in his.

"Barely," she said as Liam's fingers circled tighter around her hand.

Another blast hit the ground behind them, closer, sending up a chunk of earth.

"Help!" Liam screamed, then dropped to the ground, pulling Ana down with him.

He shoved her head into the snow and peeked past her. Ana looked up and followed his gaze and saw the orb they'd been following make a 180, spin through the air, then throw crackling blue light through the forest.

There was a deafening explosion, surprisingly loud considering the size of the orbs. Then Duncan's orb hovered back to a few feet above them. "It's okay," he reassured from the monitor. "Hang tight, we're almost there."

To punctuate the promise, the ground started moving about a hundred yards ahead. They felt the rumble before they saw the spot — a large, circular metal plate, camouflaged beneath the snow, spinning as it surfaced.

"Let's get going. We're getting you two out of here," Duncan called from the platform's middle. "And we don't have long."

THIRTY

Jonah Lovecraft

Jonah hid behind the tree, panting, trying to decide if he should take a peek back.

He might have outrun Egan, but probably not. Even if he had, the crazy fuck wasn't likely to surrender so easily. Something was wrong with the asshole, keeping his daughter and the others locked away, prisoners from society. Jonah could understand why he was hiding from City 6, but why hide from the Village? Those people helped one another and would certainly have considered him a hero. They could live normal lives.

But no, Egan had created a little enclave with nothing but himself, his wife (if they were actually married), a dwarf, and three 10-year-old soldiers.

How long does he hope to go on like this?

He wondered if Egan was being overly paranoid or had just gone fucking nuts.

Whatever the case, Jonah needed to put as much distance between himself and them as possible, and fast. But he had to lose Egan first.

Or kill the man.

His back against the bark, Jonah peered around the tree, watching Egan as he ran off in the opposite direction. That would've been great if he weren't screaming like an idiot. He may as well have tied a string of raw meat to his neck, saying, "Here, zombies, come and get me!"

"Jonah!" Egan's voice raged through the Barrens. "Come back here and face your crimes, you coward!"

Jonah's heart pounded as Egan's voice thundered. He dared another glance, casting his eyes eighty yards away or so, spying a path, winding up the ridge and away from the underground station. He could lose Egan and then double back the long way and catch the train tracks, find his way to Ana, assuming she was still alive or that he could find her in the Games.

His headache pounded in rhythm with his heart.

"Jonah!" Egan screamed again, moving mercifully farther away.

After another minute, Egan moved far enough that Jonah figured it was safe to race toward the path. He lowered himself to a launching position, ready to bolt, but stopped short when he saw one of the boys who had saved him from the shack — the one who had watched over Calla when she fed him for the first time — storming through the woods, rifle in hand, kicking up snow as Calla followed with a matching weapon.

Had Calla's treachery been discovered? Did she regret her decision to help him? Would she try atoning for her lapse in judgment by shooting him if given the chance?

Or was Calla still his only hope?

He had few options. Save for a pipe, Jonah was defenseless, and he couldn't count on anyone's help. He had minutes, if not seconds, to make a choice, then turn that decision to action. His enemies were armed, with their circle closing quickly around him.

Z2134

Inertia equaled death.

"Jonah!" Egan's scream was loud enough to knock trees down. Not just louder, *closer*. He was doubling back.

Shit. Shit. Shit.

The two kids were coming up through the woods behind Jonah, close enough that he didn't dare sneak another peek around the tree. He pressed his body as much into the trunk as he could and kept quiet as possible.

He looked up to the path again. He *might* be able to make it if he ran, but not quietly. Staying safe meant sitting tight and waiting for the group to either pass or head in a different direction.

Every step drew Egan closer to Jonah's hiding place in one direction, and the kids closer from the other. In seconds, all three would arc in a circle around him. He'd been reasonably lucky since leaving City 6, but fortune wasn't fat enough for him to believe he could escape detection from all three.

"Jonah!" Egan called, from what sounded like the other side of the tree.

He gulped, wondering how loud the swallow sounded outside his ears.

"Face your crimes, Jonah!"

"Coward!" the boy called, his voice and bootlicking message both aimed at Egan. Jonah wondered how many things Egan had said to fill the children with hate for their "enemy." Sadly, Egan wouldn't have to tell a single lie.

"Jonah! I know you're near." His voice fell to a hum, as if to prove his proximity. "Come out now and make it easier on yourself."

Jonah nudged his back harder against the tree as he heard one, or maybe even both kids, rush him, sending him deeper into panic. He'd rather die than murder children.

Run!
Run now, and damn it all.
If you don't, then you're dead.

Jonah ignored his instincts as bark bit into his flesh, knowing that running would earn a bullet in his back. He had to wait, bide his time, and hope they'd pass.

Even small, it *was* a possibility, and if there was one thing Jonah had learned while playing the Games — the one thing that kept him alive above all else — was that fortune rewarded the patient. Outwitting his opponents often meant out-waiting them, staying hidden even when it made more sense to run.

When fear forced your hand, you were most likely making the wrong move: the simple secret to his survival that Kirkman never mentioned.

The footsteps drew closer.

Calla appeared in front of Jonah, forty feet to his right, gun in hands, creeping through the snow and staring forward.

His stomach turned, tumbled, and went still. His entire body was half concealed by a shrub's worth of brush between him and Calla. If she failed to look, she might miss him entirely.

Jonah waited to see if the boy would follow but saw nothing, and he was too afraid to crane his neck for another look. It was possible that the boy was on the other side at a safe distance, but if Calla saw him and made any sound, no matter how small, the boy was probably close enough to usher Jonah's death into a certainty.

Egan's voice grew even more heated, now hot enough to melt snow. "Jonah! I *will* find you. And I'm going to fucking kill you when I do!"

Calla inched closer, twenty feet away, heading toward Egan, rifle held in front.

Z2134

Don't turn your head, don't look. Keep walking.

Calla turned.

Their eyes met.

Jonah's breath was buried in his throat as his mouth dropped open. He slowly shook his head, eyes wide and begging like a dog: *Please, no, please.*

Calla blinked twice, then kept moving, silent.

A gunshot split the calm, followed by a series of shrieks.

Calla spun around, looking briefly at Jonah, then past him toward the sounds. She raised her rifle, took aim, and fired.

The boy's scream tore through the air, shrieking as though he'd fallen through hell into an orgy of demons ripping his flesh. Calla screamed, racing toward Egan.

He might have heard Egan, but between muffled cries from the dying boy and Calla's shrieks, rising above the moaning, groaning, and slurping zombies, he couldn't be sure.

Jonah strained to hear as the zombies grew louder, both before and after the gunfire. He turned to Calla, who fired another several shots, then vanished from his sight as she hurled herself into battle. The boy made a few final gurgles, slipping into certain death.

Four shots tore through the forest, Jonah figured a couple from Calla and a pair from her dad.

"Oh God, no!" Egan screamed.

Before Jonah could launch himself toward the path, his curiosity got the better of him. He risked a glimpse and saw Calla and her father standing near the dead boy. The six zombies who weren't feasting on the child turned their attention on the living.

Egan and Calla fired into the approaching monsters, missing more than hitting.

The zombies kept coming.

Jonah gripped his pipe, wondering how many zombies he'd be able to beat to death and whether his efforts would do any good. Would he be able to help Calla and her father, or would he be risking his life only to add a few minutes to their collective death?

He turned to the path, bristling through instincts that screamed for him to run away. Jonah was frozen, his brain in a war with his guts until Calla's scream demanded his attention. He peered back and saw her backing away from a zombie, arms out as it gave chase. They were coming straight toward Jonah's hiding spot.

"Help!" she screamed.

Egan was wrestling with five zombies that had cornered him, helpless to save his daughter. Either out of ammo or unable to reload, he swung his rifle madly at the herd, holding them back as they crowded around him.

Calla's footsteps and cries grew louder as she raced toward the tree where Jonah waited, clutching the pipe in his hands. She shot past Jonah's tree, a zombie in close pursuit.

He waited for the zombie to pass, then leaped from his hiding spot and swung the pipe with a Watcher's trained precision into the back of its skull.

The zombie fell, its broken gourd splitting on the ground and spilling a bucket of blood.

Another zombie appeared from behind, so silent that Jonah didn't know it was there until it was running right past him, after the girl.

It was inches away from Calla, reaching out.

"Hey!" Jonah screamed.

The zombie stopped, almost confused, turning around, its white eyes narrowed on Jonah. Its lips parted, showing Jonah two rows of broken, blackened teeth, chomping into the meat of a dangling, rotted tongue and shredded flesh where its lips had once been.

The zombie groaned something indecipherable, then lurched forward, its clawed and charred fingernails opening and closing, moaning as if already tasting the savory meal waiting inside Jonah's warm flesh.

He lifted the pipe, then held it, poised to strike, while waiting for the zombie's next move. The zombie was swerving erratically, slow at first, then deceptively fast, as if purposely disguising its abilities to better surprise its prey. Jonah had seen a few of the undead do this during the Darwins and had been fortunate enough, so far, to anticipate their patterns of attack.

The zombie lurched forward as Jonah stepped back, keeping an ear on the action some thirty yards behind as Egan continued to battle a quad of zombies. Fortunately, none of Egan's undead had yet taken notice of Jonah or Calla, wherever she'd run off to.

The creature grunted, swiping as he tried to grab Jonah.

Jonah stepped back again and swung his pipe, slamming the monster hard in its forearm. The zombie shook off the pain and continued to charge.

Jonah kept stepping back, baiting the zombie, drawing it toward him and farther from where he'd last seen Calla. The creature charged, and Jonah thrust his body sideways and fell to the ground at the last second, just as the zombie ambled past, lost its balance, then stumbled hard and fell into the snow.

Jonah acted immediately, jumping on top of the zombie and bringing the pipe down repeatedly into the back of its skull.

It died twitching, its dark blood flooding the snow in a wide lake of crimson.

Footsteps behind Jonah were thunder rolling into the Barrens. He spun to face his attackers, the pipe tight in his hand.

He swung hard but fell back as he stopped himself mid-thrust, realizing it was Calla behind him.

His muscles cramped with an electric spasm, sending Jonah to the snow.

Calla's eyes widened at his fall, then she nodded a silent *thank you*, turned to her father, and ran toward him without another word.

"Wait!" Jonah cried, wondering what the hell the girl was doing.

"Wha—?" Calla said. "He needs help!"

"You don't have a weapon!"

She looked at his pipe. "Gimme."

Jonah shook his head, pulled the pipe back, then met her eyes. The girl was determined, would surrender anything to help her father. Jonah sighed, growled, then stuffed his best judgment into the deepest parts of his body and ran toward Egan.

There were still four zombies surrounding her father. Egan hadn't managed to kill a single one since Jonah last looked, though he had managed to somehow stay alive.

Jonah brought the first one down just seconds after jumping into the fray, crashing the pipe into the first zombie's face, hard enough to tear through its brain.

It shrieked as though the skin was ripped from its body, then fell to its knees as Jonah's second swing landed hard in its neck. It wailed again, then tried standing as Jonah beat its head, smashing repeatedly, shocked that the zombie kept rising even though he'd seen the same thing kill these fuckers on City screens hundreds of times.

The zombie finally died, face-down in a pile of red-

and-white goo, flecks of frozen ice blending in with the syrupy blood.

Jonah looked up and caught Egan's eyes, confused, horrified, and still fighting for his life.

Egan swung the butt of his rifle into a zombie's open mouth, ripping its jaw clean off before smashing its skull in.

Jonah swung his pipe hard, poking, stabbing, and bashing as he and Egan fell into an insane rage together, until there was nothing left but them, breathing, panting, covered in blood, and staring at each other.

Calla approached, trembling. "Are they all dead?"

Egan looked down and nodded before glaring at Jonah.

Neither spoke. Jonah had no idea what would happen next.

Egan snarled, then threw his empty rifle into the snow and charged at Jonah, swinging his fist.

Jonah swerved, dodging the assault and throwing his body into Egan.

He didn't want to fight, especially in front of the man's daughter, but Egan was leaving little, if any, choice.

The two men wrestled in the snow, with Jonah fighting him off just enough, but mostly letting Egan punch him repeatedly, even though his entire body had already been bruised and battered by the man.

Every blow, to his chest, face, head, and ribs felt like Egan was tearing him apart, bit by bit. Jonah relaxed, allowing the man to do his worst. "Go ahead! Kill me! Get it over with!"

"Stop!" Calla screamed, earning her father's startled attention. "Stop it! You can't bring 'em back!"

Egan froze, left hand curled into Jonah's collar, and his right hovering a foot from Jonah's face.

But then without warning, Egan slid off of him, fell

into the snow, then broke into sobs, burying his head in his bloodied hand as he shuttered.

Jonah sat, rose to his knees, then wiped the blood from his broken face as Calla dropped to her knees beside her father.

"He saved me," Calla said, crying into her father's chest. "He could've escaped, but he came back for me. And — for you."

Egan's eyes met Jonah's, still brimming with anger, but softening with a gratitude he couldn't manage to stifle. After a long moment, longer in the wind's frozen whistle, he said, "Thank you."

Jonah nodded. "Can I go save my daughter now?"

Egan shook his head. After a horrible second, he finished with "No."

Jonah's gut twisted into a knot.

He was going to have to kill Egan — beat him to death in front of his daughter — then leave her alone in the snow so he could go and find his.

But just as Jonah was steeling himself to do what he didn't want to do, Egan surprised him. "Come back with us. I'll give you something to help you find her."

"Yeah?" What else could he say?

"Yeah." Egan nodded, pulling Calla closer to him. "But then I want you the hell out of my life forever."

Jonah nodded, knowing that *nothing* was ever that easy.

THIRTY-ONE

Anastasia Lovecraft

ANA COULDN'T STOP STARING into the back of Liam's head as he and Duncan walked side-by-side through the network of catacombs, accompanied by Duncan's liberated orb, hovering above and illuminating the path ahead.

When they first entered the catacombs, Duncan explained that they ran under the woods and would lead past the Darwin Games borders. The catacombs had been built before the plague and were filled with mostly empty spaces for coffins. They also connected to the train tunnels, which would eventually lead to their destination.

Duncan then fell quiet, and the trio walked in silence — thick like fog, but harder to see through.

Ana figured Duncan had seen Liam's confession, like everyone in City 6, and knew he was a traitor. He was short with Liam and clearly angry over something, but still helpful while navigating the winding tunnels toward their possible salvation. After a forever that was likely around an hour, Liam stopped in his tracks and turned to Duncan.

"I guess you saw," he said.

"I don't wanna discuss it." Duncan didn't bother to stop walking.

Liam followed a step behind, quiet for five minutes or so until he could no longer accept the sourness of everything unsaid. He stopped again, set his hand on Duncan's shoulder, then pulled the man back toward him. "They were threatening to kill Chelle's baby — *my baby*."

Duncan stared at Liam, barely able to meet his eyes, let alone hold them. "And then they did. You brought a sword to a gunfight, then made a deal with the devil when you found out your weapon wasn't a match. How did that work out for you, Liam? How did it work out for *all of us*?"

"What did you want me to do? Risk my child? The woman I loved?"

"You did the worst possible thing, Liam. You played God, burning the thin bridge between all of our lives." Duncan's voice was sharp enough to cut into the countless things he wasn't saying.

"I didn't know they'd murder his wife. Or that they'd raid the church and kill Rose and Iris."

"Your hands are bloody." Duncan shook his head. "You should have come to me, should've told me. I could have helped, no different from what I'd do for anyone else. I could've protected your baby, gotten Chelle and the baby out of the City." He leaned into Liam and lowered his voice. "I had to do it eventually anyway."

"What are you talking about?" Liam almost mumbled, every word falling out slower than the one before, each holding something awful inside it.

"I got Chelle out, right before I left."

Liam swallowed loud enough to hear, even if Ana couldn't see it in the shadows.

"I sent her to West Village," Duncan said.

"Why the hell did you do that?" Liam snarled. "The passage is dangerous!"

"So was her staying behind the Walls, at least once you said you were done spying for them and made your death march."

Liam fell silent, tasting Duncan's words on his tongue.

Ana was embarrassed to ask, but: "What's West Village?"

He turned from Liam to Ana. "It's a village populated by dissidents and refugees. We've got nearly two thousand people living there now, beyond the State's reach. That's where we're headed."

"It's the village I told you about," Liam said. "Where I wanted to take Chelle and our baby."

"How long has it been there? How has the State not discovered it yet?"

"It's been there for two decades, with a smart system of ever-growing independence. We've taken plenty of precautions, it's well hidden, and the Barrens are bigger than you realize. Lack of perspective keeps you from seeing the whole picture, Ana. Same as everyone else. The Old Nation had a song that said, 'from sea to shining sea,' and those seas sandwiched thousands of miles between them. It's impossible for the State to be everywhere at once. Sure, they've sent orbs out to find the Village, plenty, but we've always been able to stop and seize them, then reprogram those orbs to help us track and capture other ones. Eventually, they stopped trying."

"So, we're gonna live there now?" Ana asked.

"Yes," Duncan nodded.

"If the Underground has this secret place, why not bring more people over? Start a new proper city?"

"Limited resources." Duncan shrugged, as if the answer was obvious. "We can't allow everyone in if we expect the resistance to last. We're selective, and there's a long process to escape the City and settle inside the Village. New citizens are expected to contribute, and we must be certain they won't betray the Underground. Few people know its location, and the only way to access the village on ground level is through these old catacombs and train tunnels. Besides, most people are happy behind the Walls since they can't see through the wool over their eyes. Few even try."

Ana glanced at Liam. He was somewhere else, off in his own world, probably thinking about Chelle and what would happen once they reached the Village. She turned back to Duncan. "Can you get Adam out of the City? Can we bring him to the Village?"

"We'll see. It was tough enough getting Chelle out. Everyone in the Underground is scared right now, and nobody's sure who to trust. The Watchers have picked up a few of our people and are looking for whoever is in charge."

Ana wanted to ask who that was, but didn't want information the Watchers could torture her for. "What will happen to Liam when we get there? Do they know what he did? Will they let him in?"

"We're going to jail him. Then try him as a traitor."

A chill ran through her. "But he was protecting his girlfriend and baby!" Ana surprised herself by defending Liam.

Duncan turned abruptly, his eyes locked onto hers. "We *all* lost people. Every one of us. The Underground is more than a single person, or even one family. It's an entire society. Generations are dependent on our rebels committing to the cause. Betray the Underground, and you put *everyone* at risk."

Duncan turned and went back to walking the catacombs. Ana followed, with Liam assuming the rear, all three renewing their vows of silence.

Liam stepped forward and turned to Ana, his eyes soft. "I'm sorry."

His apology quivered, cutting through her anger like a hot knife.

"It's okay," Ana said, though she hadn't fully forgiven him and still had too many questions to make his *sorry* mean as much as he probably wanted.

But her questions could wait. She didn't want to ask them, especially not in front of Duncan. They walked for what felt like hours, navigating the old tunnels, turning from one darkened passageway into another until they finally arrived at a large metal gate. Through the thin bars, Ana saw steps leading up to the world above — the Village!

She slowly approached the steps, thinking of everything she'd been through recently — her mother's murder, her father's sudden arrest, her testimony, his ejection from the City, their home being stolen from them and the look on Adam's face as his books were taken by the Watchers, her father in the Games, the church massacre, and choosing to kill Charlotte instead of Liam.

It was all too much.

A new orb descended from the darkness, hovering in front of the gate, watching as they approached. Its energy cannon crackled with azure light. She stepped back, nervous, certain they'd been caught, though neither Liam nor Duncan seemed fazed in the least.

Duncan approached the orb, then stared into the monitor. "Harbor 1228."

The orb acknowledged him with a blip, then floated upward. Its blue cannon fizzled dark.

Ana sighed, relieved as Duncan drew a key from his

coat and unlocked the gate. "Welcome to West Village," he said, ushering them through the swinging metal fence, then locking it behind them.

Thick plumes of dark smoke spiraled into the sky.

Duncan and Liam traded expressions of horror, then raced ahead together, Duncan drawing a pistol from the depths of his coat.

Before them was a large wooden wall, its gates wide open. Beyond the gates, the Village streets were littered with burned and bloodied corpses. Buildings had been reduced to smoldering, charred remains, some still on fire.

It looked as if someone had opened the gates of hell and set forth murderous, flaming beasts that ended everything in their path, leaving only death and destruction behind.

Ana's mouth hung agape as she struggled to kill her tears. Drawing closer to the open gates, she saw the familiar *CW* logo of City Watch painted in what looked like blood on the right gate.

"Oh God, it's gone," Duncan whispered. "It's all gone."

"Chelle!" Liam cried out, racing through the gate and into the Village. "Chelle!"

Then he froze in his tracks, looking up as he screamed.

Jutting from the ground were two dozen wooden spikes, standing roughly twenty feet high. And on each of them a head. He stood in front of one, a woman with dark hair hanging over her bloodied, puffy face.

"CHELLE!"

Duncan and Ana rushed over to Liam as he fell screaming to the ground.

THIRTY-TWO

Jonah Lovecraft

JONAH CROSSED the Barrens and went back to the train station, following Egan and Calla. They ignored the ladder where Jonah had ascended, running through a thicket of trees, then a wide clearing and into what looked like the remains of a long-forgotten depot, with snow-covered crumbles of concrete and exposed piping.

Egan ducked beneath a fallen concrete pillar, then descended a set of stairs into the tunnel. Calla quietly followed her father, with Jonah right behind her.

Inside the station, Jonah was led to a large room just inside the entrance. Egan opened the door, Calla hovering at his side, then pointed to one of the several dozen chairs in what used to be some sort of waiting area.

"You can wait there. I'll go get Father Truth. I need to tell my wife of Dani's death." Egan looked at Calla, apology for the loss like a dim light in his eyes, then turned back to Jonah. "Father will come in a few minutes, with everything you need."

Jonah nodded.

Calla followed Egan from the room, leaving Jonah completely alone.

It was maybe a quarter hour before Father Truth stepped through the door. During every one of those minutes Jonah strongly considered leaving the station, hating the thought of Ana fending for herself in the Barrens. He finally stood and was halfway to the door when Father entered with a large bag and a tiny smile. He sat the bag on a chair in front of Jonah, unzipped it, and pulled out a miniature-sized metallic globe.

The small globe had a little screen a few inches wide. It looked like a mini-orb, though not quite like a network orb or any other orb Jonah had ever seen.

"Is this State-made?" Jonah asked, turning it in his hand.

"Not exactly." Father shook his head. "But I can't tell you anything more than that, so I suggest you not ask."

"Can I ask what it does?"

"Wouldn't give it to you if you couldn't," Father said. "It taps into the TV feed, so you'll be able to see the same thing folks behind the Walls are seeing in real time. That's your best bet at finding Ana. Besides this." Father held up the bag, bulging at the sides, and handed it over to Jonah.

He sat down and pulled the bag into his lap, and peeked inside, eyes widening at the contents. "This is for me? All of it?"

Father nodded. "It is. Don't make me regret it."

Inside the bag were two guns, four boxes of shells, dried fruit, four vials of something labeled *health*, five bottles of water, and a hand-drawn map of the Barrens, which seemed to offer a decent trail as to where Ana might be.

"So can I go now?"

"After we destroy your chips."

"I thought you said it was dangerous," Jonah said.

"It's far more dangerous if you get tracked by hunter orbs. There's an energy field surrounding the station that prevents the orbs from tracking you here. But you're fair game once outside the field. So you want to do this if you want to live."

Father unzipped a small pack at his waist and pulled out a long, thin box, about the length of his hand. He unfastened the latch at the top, lifted the lid, then shook a translucent blue pill into his hand and gave it to Jonah.

"A pill? You've gotta be kidding."

"The pill has nanotech scrubbers, to destroy the chips. In your bag, I've also included another pill to give your daughter once you find her."

Jonah liked that he said *once* instead of *if*.

"You will be disoriented. You've convinced yourself that you can't afford any time to rest, but I'd loudly argue that you can't afford *not* to rest if you expect to save your daughter. I suggest waiting at least two hours before leaving, though you and Egan will both likely argue for one."

"I don't have two hours." Jonah shook his head. "Every minute I'm down here instead of up there looking for Ana is another minute I put her at risk."

"If they set hunter orbs on you, you're dead. So is she. Have faith in the daughter you raised, Jonah. Clear the chips and clear your mind, then rescue Ana." Father handed him the pill. "Unleash yourself."

Jonah popped it into his mouth, swallowed without water, then squeezed his eyes at the pain, slapping his right palm to the side of his head as an angry intensity tore through it.

He stood, dizzy, then tried to sit, but was afraid he'd fall on his ass. It was only a beat before he did. Jonah twitched on the floor, certain there was poison inside him and that despite his promises, Egan had managed to exact his revenge, after all.

"It's okay," Father said from somewhere on a distant planet. "Everything will be fine. The pill is murdering your mind's intruders. You must make it through the pain and know you're stronger than it, and that no matter how much agony you're in now, it's only temporary."

The world went black, and Father Truth disappeared.

Jonah was trapped in his own head. The words *murdering intruders* tore through his brain repeatedly until he opened his eyes and found that he was no longer in the station. He was back at his house, deep inside an old memory that somehow felt new.

He looked around the room at the aged panels of his apartment wooden walls, and the grimy light made the place appear cruel. He tried to make sense of his memory.

Molly looked up, smiling as she saw him. "Hey, sweetie, you're home early! Did you come to check up on us?"

Jonah didn't answer.

Instead, he pulled the shock stick from his belt, marched over to Molly, grabbed her by the throat with his left hand, pressing his fingers hard into her flesh as the eyes bulged from their sockets, then bashed her skull in.

Molly never had a chance to scream. But her daughter did.

Jonah turned, surprised to see Ana standing behind him, curdling the air with her deafening scream.

Jonah flashed awake, back in the train station, his entire body shaking.

Father sat next to him, looking down with his kind face.

"What the hell?" Jonah screamed. "No, no, no. I didn't do it. I didn't do it. What *was* that?"

"That," Father said, "was the truth."

TO BE CONTINUED …

The story continues...

The Darwin Games are over. The battle for survival has just begun ...

Between the terrifying zombies roaming The Barrens—monsters created by the plague that destroyed the Old Nation—and the ruthless, manipulative government that controls everything and everyone within the City Walls, no one is safe.

Get Z2135 Today!

A Quick Favor

Thank you for reading *Z2134*.

If you enjoyed this book would you please consider writing a review of it on your favorite bookselling site so other readers might enjoy it too. Just a couple of sentences. That would mean a lot to me.

Thank you!
Sean and Dave

About the Authors

Sean Platt is an entrepreneur and founder of Sterling & Stone, where he makes stories with his partners, Johnny B. Truant, and David W. Wright, and a family of storytellers.

Sean is the bestselling author of over 10 million words' worth of books, including the Yesterday's Gone and Invasion series. Sean is also co-author of the indie publishing cornerstone, Write. Publish. Repeat. and co-host of the Story Studio Podcast.

Originally from Long Beach, California, Sean now lives in Austin, Texas with his wife and two children. He has more than his share of nose.

David W. Wright is the co-author of edge-of-your seat thrillers including the best-selling post-apocalyptic series *Yesterday's Gone*, the paranoid sci-fi *WhiteSpace* series, and the vigilante series, *No Justice*, as well as standalone thrillers *12*, and *Crash* which was recently optioned for a movie.

David is an accomplished, though intermittent, cartoonist who lives in [LOCATION REDACTED] with his wife and son [NAMES REDACTED.]

He is not at all paranoid.

He is "the grumpy one" on *The Story Studio Podcast* with fellow Sterling and Stone founders, Sean Platt and Johnny B. Truant.

David writes about books, TV shows, movies, and

video games he enjoys; his struggles with anxiety and OCD; writing; and posts the occasional drawing at his personal blog at davidwwright.com

You can email him at david@sterlingandstone.net

We swear, he almost never bites. Unless you feed him after midnight.

For a full list of his most recent books visit sterlingandstone.net.

Also By Sean Platt

Z2134

Z2134

Z2135

Z2136

The Dead World Series

Dead Zero

Dead City

Dead Nation

Dead Planet

Empty Nest

The Beam Series

The Beam Season One

The Beam Season Two

The Beam Season Three

The Beam Season Four

The Beam Season Five

Robot Proletariat Series

En3my

Robot Proletariat

The Infinite Loop

The Hard Reset

Cascade Failure

Reboot

The Tomorrow Gene Series

Null Identity

The Tomorrow Gene

The Tomorrow Clone

The Eden Experiment

Karma Police Series

Jumper

Karma Police

The Collectors

Deviant

The Fall

Homecoming

Yesterday's Gone

October's Gone

Yesterday's Gone Season One

Yesterday's Gone Season Two

Yesterday's Gone Season Three

Yesterday's Gone Season Four

Yesterday's Gone Season Five

Yesterday's Gone Season Six

Tomorrow's Gone

Tomorrow's Gone Season One

Tomorrow's Gone Season Two

Tomorrow's Gone Season Three

Available Darkness

Darkness Itself

Available Darkness Book One
Available Darkness Book Two
Available Darkness Book Three

WhiteSpace

WhiteSpace Season One
WhiteSpace Season Two
WhiteSpace Season Three

Stand Alone Novels

Burnout

The Island

Crash

Emily's List

Pattern Black

Devil May Care

The Secret Within

Also By David W. Wright

Z2134

Z2134

Z2135

Z2136

Cold Vengeance

Cold Vengeance

Cold Reckoning

Hidden Justice

Hidden Justice

Hidden Honor

Hidden Shame

Hidden Virtue

No Justice

No Justice

No Escape

No Hope

No Return

No Stopping

No Fear

Karma Police

Jumper

Karma Police

The Collectors

Deviant

The Fall

Homecoming

Yesterday's Gone

October's Gone

Yesterday's Gone Season One

Yesterday's Gone Season Two

Yesterday's Gone Season Three

Yesterday's Gone Season Four

Yesterday's Gone Season Five

Yesterday's Gone Season Six

Tomorrow's Gone

Tomorrow's Gone Season One

Tomorrow's Gone Season Two

Tomorrow's Gone Season Three

Available Darkness

Darkness Itself

Available Darkness Book One

Available Darkness Book Two

Available Darkness Book Three

WhiteSpace

WhiteSpace Season One

WhiteSpace Season Two

WhiteSpace Season Three

Forevermore

ForNevermore Season One

ForNevermore Season Two

ForNevermore Season Three

Stand Alone Novels

12

Crash

Emily's List

Threshold

The Secret Within

www.ingramcontent.com/pod-product-compliance
Lightning Source LLC
LaVergne TN
LVHW031536060526
838200LV00056B/4523